# FEARLESS
# FOURTEEN

## Also by Janet Evanovich

# FEARLESS
# FOURTEEN

Janet Evanovich

ST. MARTIN'S PRESS  ⪰  NEW YORK

This is a work of fiction. All of the characters, organizations, and events portrayed in this novel are either products of the author's imagination or are used fictitiously.

FEARLESS FOURTEEN. Copyright © 2008 by Evanovich, Inc. All rights reserved. Printed in the United States of America. For information, address St. Martin's Press, 175 Fifth Avenue, New York, N.Y. 10010.

www.stmartins.com

LIBRARY OF CONGRESS CATALOGING-IN-PUBLICATION DATA

Evanovich, Janet.
    Fearless fourteen : a Stephanie Plum novel / Janet Evanovich. — 1st ed.
        p.   cm.
    ISBN-13: 978-0-312-34951-6
    ISBN-10: 0-312-34951-3
    1. Plum, Stephanie (Fictitious character)—Fiction.   2. Women boun-
ty hunters—Fiction.   3. Bail bond agents—New Jersey—Trenton—
Fiction.   4. Bank robberies—Fiction.   5. Trenton (N.J.)—Fiction.
I. Title.
    PS3555.V2126F43  2008
    813'.54—dc22

                                                          2008017664

First Edition: June 2008

10  9  8  7  6  5  4  3  2  1

Woohoo!

To Team Evanovich:
Alex, Peter, and SuperJen

Thanks to Sandy Sherwood
for suggesting the title for this book

# FEARLESS
# FOURTEEN

# ONE

IN MY MIND, my kitchen is filled with crackers and cheese, roast chicken leftovers, farm fresh eggs, and coffee beans ready to grind. The reality is that I keep my Smith & Wesson in the cookie jar, my Oreos in the microwave, a jar of peanut butter and hamster food in the over-the-counter cupboard, and I have beer and olives in the refrigerator. I used to have a birthday cake in the freezer for emergencies, but I ate it.

Truth is, I would dearly love to be a domestic goddess, but the birthday cake keeps getting eaten. I mean, you buy it, and you eat it, right? And then where are you? No birthday cake. Ditto cheese and crackers and eggs and the roast chicken leftovers (which were from my mother). The coffee beans are light-years away. I don't own a grinder. I guess I could buy *two* birthday cakes, but I'm afraid I'd eat both.

My name is Stephanie Plum, and in my defense I'd like to say that I have bread and milk on my shopping list, and

I don't have any communicable diseases. I'm five feet, seven inches. My hair is brown and shoulder length and naturally curly. My eyes are blue. My teeth are mostly straight. My manicure was pretty good three days ago, and my shape is okay. I work as a bond enforcement agent for my cousin Vinnie, and today I was standing in Loretta Rizzi's kitchen, thinking not only was Loretta ahead of me in the kitchen-needs-a-makeover race, but she made me look like a piker in the Loose Cannon Club.

It was eight in the morning, and Loretta was wearing a long, pink flannel nightgown and holding a gun to her head.

"I'm gonna shoot myself," Loretta said. "Not that it would matter to you, because you get your money dead or alive, right?"

"Technically, that's true," I told her. "But dead is a pain in the tuchus. There's paperwork."

A lot of the people Vinnie bonds out are from my Chambersburg neighborhood in Trenton, New Jersey. Loretta Rizzi was one of those people. I went to school with Loretta. She's a year older than me, and she left high school early to have a baby. Now she was wanted for armed robbery, and she was about to blow her brains out.

Vinnie had posted Loretta's bond, and Loretta had failed to show for her court appearance, so I was dispatched to drag her back to jail. And as luck would have it, I walked in at a bad moment and interrupted her suicide.

"I just wanted a drink," Loretta said.

"Yeah, but you held up a liquor store. Most people would have gone to a bar."

"I didn't have any money, and it was hot, and I needed a Tom Collins." A tear rolled down Loretta's cheek. "I've been thirsty lately," she said.

Loretta is a half a head shorter than me. She has curly black hair and a body kept toned by hefting serving trays for catered affairs at the firehouse. She hasn't changed much since high school. A few crinkle lines around her eyes. A little harder set to her mouth. She's Italian-American and related to half the Burg, including my off-and-on boyfriend, Joe Morelli.

"This was your first offense. And you didn't shoot anyone. Probably you'll get off with a hand-slap," I told Loretta.

"I had my period," she said. "I wasn't thinking right."

Loretta lives in a rented row house on the edge of the Burg. She has two bedrooms, one bath, a scrubbed-clean, crackerbox kitchen, and a living room filled with second-hand furniture. Hard to make ends meet when you're a single mother without a high school diploma.

The back door swung open and my sidekick, Lula, stuck her head in. "What's going on in here? I'm tired of waiting in the car. I thought this was gonna be a quick pickup, and then we were going for breakfast."

Lula is a former 'ho, turned bonds office file clerk and wheelman. She's a plus-size black woman who likes to squash herself into too small clothes featuring animal print and spandex. Lula's cup runneth over from head to toe.

"Loretta is having a bad morning," I said.

Lula checked Loretta out. "I can see that. She's still in her nightie."

"Notice anything else?" I asked Lula.

"You mean like she's tryin' to style her hair with a Smith & Wesson?"

"I don't want to go to jail," Loretta said.

"It's not so bad," Lula told her. "If you can get them to send you to the workhouse, you'll get dental."

"I'm a disgrace," Loretta said.

Lula shifted her weight on her spike-heeled Manolo knock-offs. "You be more of a disgrace if you pull that trigger. You'll have a big hole in your head, and your mother won't be able to have an open-casket viewing. And who's going to clean up the mess it'll make in your kitchen?"

"I have an insurance policy," Loretta said. "If I kill myself, my son, Mario, will be able to manage until he can get a job. If I go to jail, he'll be on his own without any money."

"Insurance policies don't pay out on suicides," Lula said.

"Oh crap! Is that true?" Loretta asked me.

"Yeah. Anyway, I don't know why you're worried about that. You have a big family. Someone will take care of Mario."

"It's not that easy. My mother is in rehab from when she had the stroke. She can't take him. And my brother, Dom, can't take him. He just got out of jail three days ago. He's on probation."

"What about your sister?"

"My sister's got her hands full with her own kids. Her rat turd husband left her for some pre-puberty lap dancer."

"There must be someone who can baby-sit for you," Lula said to Loretta.

"Everyone's got their own thing going. And I don't want to leave Mario with just anybody. He's very sensitive . . . and artistic."

I counted back and placed her kid in his early teens. Loretta had never married, and so far as I know, she'd never fingered a father for him.

"Maybe you could take him," Loretta said to me.

"*What?* No. No, no, no, no."

"Just until I can make bail. And then I'll try to find someone more permanent."

"If I take you in now, Vinnie can bond you out right away."

"Yeah, but if something goes wrong, I need someone to pick Mario up after school."

"What can go wrong?"

"I don't know. A mother worries about these things. Promise you'll pick him up if I'm still in jail. He gets out at two-thirty."

"She'll do it," Lula said to Loretta. "Just put the gun down and go get dressed so we can get this over and done. I need coffee. I need one of those extra-greasy breakfast sandwiches. I gotta clog my arteries on account of otherwise the blood rushes around too fast and I might get a dizzy spell."

———————

LULA WAS SPRAWLED on the brown Naugahyde couch hugging the wall in the bonds office, and Vinnie's office manager, Connie Rosolli, was at her desk. Connie and the desk had been strategically placed in front of Vinnie's inner-office door with the hope it would discourage pissed-off pimps, bookies, and other assorted lowlifes from rushing in and strangling Vinnie.

"What do you mean she isn't bonded out?" I asked Connie, my voice rising to an octave normally only heard from Minnie Mouse.

"She has no money to secure the bond. And no assets."

"That's impossible. Everyone has assets. What about her mother? Her brother? She must have a hundred cousins living in a ten-mile radius."

"She's working on it, but right now she has nothing. Bupkus. Nada. So Vinnie's waiting on her."

"Yeah, and it's almost two-thirty," Lula said. "You better go get her kid like you promised."

Connie swiveled her head toward me and her eyebrows went up to her hairline. "You promised to take care of Mario?"

"I said I'd pick him up if Loretta wasn't bonded out in time. I didn't know there'd be an issue with her bond."

"Oh boy," Connie said. "Good luck with that one."

"Loretta said he was sensitive and artistic."

"I don't know about the sensitive part, but his art is limited to spray paint. He's probably defaced half of Trenton.

Loretta has to pick him up from school because they won't let him on a school bus."

I hiked my bag onto my shoulder. "I'm just driving him home. That was the deal."

"There might be some gray area in the deal," Lula said. "You might've said you'd take care of him. And anyways, you can't dump him in an empty house. You get child services after you for doin' that."

"Well, what the heck am I supposed to do with him?"

Lula and Connie did *I don't know* shoulder shrugs.

"Maybe I can sign for Loretta's bond," I said to Connie.

"I don't think that'll fly," Connie said. "You're the only person I know who has fewer assets than Loretta."

"Great." I huffed out of the office and rammed myself into my latest P.O.S. car. It was a Nissan Sentra that used to be silver but was now mostly rust. It had doughnut-size wheels, a Jaguar hood ornament, and a bobble-head Tony Stewart doll in the back window. I like Tony Stewart a lot, but seeing his head jiggling around in my rearview mirror doesn't do much for me. Unfortunately, he was stuck on with Crazy Glue and nothing short of dismantling the car was going to get him out of my life.

Loretta had given me a photo of Mario and a pickup location. I cruised to a spot where a group of kids were shuffling around, looking for their rides. Easy to spot Mario. He resembled Morelli when Morelli was his age. Wavy black hair and slim build. Some facial similarities, although Morelli has always been movie star handsome and Mario was a little short of movie star. Of course, I might have been distracted by the multiple silver rings piercing his eyebrows, ears, and nose. He was wearing black-and-white Converse sneakers, stovepipe jeans with a chain belt, a black T-shirt with Japanese characters, and a black denim jacket.

Morelli had been an early bloomer. He grew up fast and hard. His dad was a mean drunk, and Morelli got good with his hands as a kid. He could use them in a fight, and he could use them to coax girls out of their clothes. The first time Morelli and I played doctor, I was five years old, and he was seven. He's periodically repeated the performance, and lately we seem to be a couple. He's a cop now, and against all odds, he's mostly lost the anger he had growing up. He inherited a nice little house from his Aunt Rose and has become domestic enough to own a dog and a toaster. He hasn't as yet reached the crockpot, toilet seat down, live plant in the kitchen level of domesticity.

Mario looked like a *late* bloomer. He was short for his age and had "desperate geek" written all over him.

I got out of my car and walked to the group of kids. "Mario Rizzi?"

"Who wants to know?"

"I do," I said. "Your mother can't pick you up today. I promised her I'd bring you home."

This produced some moronic comments and snickers from Mario's idiot friends.

"The name is Zook," Mario said to me. "I don't answer to Mario."

I rolled my eyes, grabbed Zook by the strap on his backpack, and towed him to my car.

"This is a piece of shit," he said, hands dangling at his sides, taking the car in.

"And?"

He shrugged and wrenched the door open. "Just saying."

I drove the short distance to the bonds office and pulled to the curb.

"What's this?" he asked.

"Your mother's been returned to lockup because she failed to show for her court appearance. She can't make her bail, and I can't take you home to an empty house, so I'm parking you in the bonds office until I can find a better place for you."

"No."

"What do you mean *no*? *No* isn't an option."

"I'm not getting out of the car."

"I'm a bounty hunter. I could rough you up or shoot you or something if you don't get out of the car."

"I don't think so. I'm just a kid. Juvie would be all over your ass. And your eye is twitching."

I hauled my cell phone out of my bag and dialed Morelli. "Help," I said.

"Now what?"

"You remember your cousin Loretta's kid, Mario?"

"Vaguely."

"I've got him in my car, and he refuses to leave."

"Possession is nine-tenths of the law."

Zook was slouched down, watching me from the corner of his eye. Arms crossed over his chest. Sullen. I blew out a sigh and told Morelli the deal with Loretta.

9

"I'm off at four," Morelli said. "If Loretta isn't bonded out by then, I'll take the kid off your hands. In the meantime, he's all yours, Cupcake."

I disconnected and dialed Lula.

"Yeah?" Lula said.

"I'm outside, and I have Loretta's kid in the car."

Lula's face appeared in the front window to the bonds office. "I see you and the kid. What's going on?"

"He won't get out of the car," I said. "I thought you might help persuade him."

"Sure," Lula said. "I could persuade the hell out of him."

The bonds office door opened, and Lula swung her ass over to my car and yanked the door open.

"What's up?" Lula said to the kid.

Zook didn't answer. Still pouting.

"I'm here to escort you out of the car," Lula said, leaning in, filling the doorframe with her red hair extensions and acres of chocolate-colored boob barely contained in a low scoop neck zebra-stripe sweater.

Zook focused on Lula's gold tooth with the diamond chip, and below that what seemed like a quarter mile of cleavage, and his eyes almost fell out of his head. "Cripes," he said, kind of croaky-voiced, shrinking back into his seat, fumbling to get out of his seat belt.

"I got a way with men," Lula said to me.

"He's not a man," I told her. "He's just a kid."

"Am too a man," he said. "Want me to prove it?"

"*No,*" Lula and I said in unison.

"What's this?" Connie wanted to know when the three of us walked into the bonds office.

"I need to leave Mario someplace for an hour while I hop over to Rangeman."

"I *told* you my name is Zook! And what's Rangeman?"

"I work with a guy named Ranger, and Rangeman is the security company he owns."

"Are you the Zook that writes his name all over town?" Lula asked him. "And what kind of name is that anyway?"

"It's my Minionfire name."

"What's a Minionfire?"

"Are you kidding me? You don't know Minionfire? *Minionfire's* only the world's most popular, most powerful, totally awesome, badass difficult game. Don't tell me you've never heard of the Nation of Minionfire?"

"In my neighborhood, we only got the nation of Bloods, Crips, and Islam. Maybe a few Baptists, but they don't hardly count anymore," Lula said.

Zook took his laptop out of his backpack. "I can hook up here, right?"

"Don't you have homework?" Connie asked him.

"I did my homework in detention. I gotta check on Moondog. He's a griefer, and he's massing the wood elves."

That caught Lula's attention. "Are these wood elves the same as Santa's elves?"

"Wood elves are evil, and they can only be stopped by a third-level Blybold Wizard like Zook."

"You don't look like no Blybold Wizard," Lula said. "You

look like a kid that's drilled too many holes in hisself. You keep doing that, and stuff's gonna start leaking out."

Zook's hand unconsciously went to his ear with the six piercings. "Chicks dig it."

"Yeah," Lula said, "they probably all want to borrow your earrings."

"Getting back to the problem at hand," I said, "I need to park Mario, or Zook, or whoever the heck he is. Ranger wants to talk to me about working a job for him."

"Oh boy," Lula said.

"A *real* job," I told her.

"Sure," Lula said. "I knew that. What kind of job?"

"I don't know."

"Oh boy," Lula said.


CARLOS MANOSO IS my age, but his life experience is worlds away. He's of Cuban heritage and has family in Newark and Miami. He's dark-skinned, dark-eyed, and his hair is dark brown and currently cut too short for a ponytail but long enough to fall across his forehead when he's sleeping or otherwise occupied in bed. He's got a lot of muscle in all the right places and a killer smile that is rarely seen. His street name is Ranger, a leftover from his time in Special Forces.

When I started working for Vincent Plum Bail Bonds, Ranger was doing mostly bounty hunter work and was my mentor. He's now co-owner of a security company with branches in Boston, Atlanta, and Miami. He wears only black, he smells like Bulgari Green shower gel, he's extremely private, and he eats healthy food. I'd be tempted to say he isn't a lot of fun, but he has his moments. And on those rare occasions when we've been intimate . . . *WOW*.

Rangeman Security is on a side street in center city Trenton. It's housed in an inconspicuous seven-story brick building, the name visible only on a small plaque above the door buzzer. The seventh floor is Ranger's private apartment. Two more floors are dedicated to housing Rangeman employees, one floor is occupied by the property manager and his wife, Ella, the fifth floor is control central, and the remaining two floors are conference rooms, first-floor reception, and private offices. There are two levels below ground and I've never gotten the personal tour, but I imagine dungeons and armories and Ranger's personal tailor toiling away.

I key-fobbed my way into the underground garage and parked next to Ranger's black Porsche Turbo. I took the elevator to the fifth floor, waved hello to the guys at the monitoring stations, and walked across the room to Ranger's office. The door was open, and Ranger was at his desk, talking on a headset. His eyes went to me, he wrapped up his conversation and removed the headset.

"Babe," he said.

*Babe* covered a lot of ground with Ranger. It could be good, bad, amused, or filled with desire. Today it was hello.

I sat in the chair across from his desk. "What's up?"

"I need a date," Ranger said.

"Is date synonymous with sex?"

"No. It's synonymous with business, but I could throw some sex in as a bonus if you're interested."

This got a smile from me. I wasn't interested for a bunch of complicated reasons, not the least of which was Joe Morelli. Still, it was nice to know the offer was on the table. "What's the business?"

"I've been asked to provide security for Brenda."

"*The* Brenda? The singer?"

"Yes. She'll be in town for three days doing a concert, some media, and a charity fund-raiser. I'm supposed to keep her dry and drug-free and out of harm's way. If I assign one of my men to her, she'll eat him alive and spit him out in front of the press. So I'm taking the watch, and I need someone riding shotgun."

"What about Tank?"

Tank is Ranger's next in command, and he's the guy Ranger trusts to watch his back. Tank's called Tank because that's what he is. He's seven feet of muscle packed into a six-foot, four-inch, no-neck body. Tank is also Lula's current boyfriend.

"Brenda's management team has requested security be invisible at public functions, and it's hard to hide Tank," Ranger said. "Tank and Hal will work shifts standing guard at Brenda's hotel. When she's at large, we'll take over. She can pass us off as traveling companions, and you can go into the ladies' room with her and make sure she doesn't test-drive mushrooms."

"Doesn't she have her own bodyguard?"

"He slipped and broke his ankle getting off the plane last night. They've shipped him back to California."

"I'm surprised you're taking this on."

"I'm doing it as a favor for Lew Pepper, the concert promoter." Ranger passed a sheet of paper to me. "This is Brenda's public appearance schedule. We need to be at her hotel a half hour ahead. And we're on call. If she leaves her room, we're there."

I looked at the schedule and chewed on my lower lip. Morelli wasn't going to be happy to have me spending this much time with Ranger. And Brenda was a car crash. Like Cher and Madonna, she didn't use a last name. Just Brenda. She was sixty-one years old. She'd been married eight times. She could crack walnuts with her ass muscles. And she was rumored to be mean as a snake. I couldn't remember her last album, but I knew she had a cabaret act going. Baby-sitting Brenda had "nightmare" written all over it.

"Babe," Ranger said, reading my thoughts. "I don't ask a lot of favors."

I blew out a sigh, folded the paper, and put it in my jeans pocket. "Looks like the fund-raiser is tonight. Meet and greet at five-thirty. I'll meet you in her hotel lobby at five."


ZOOK WAS IN the land of Minionfire when I rolled into the bonds office. Connie was working on the computer at her desk, and Lula was packing up, getting ready to leave.

"I gotta get home and beautify," Lula said. "Tank's coming over tonight. This here's the third time this week I'll see him. I think this is getting serious. I wouldn't be surprised if he was gonna pop the question."

"What question are you thinking about?" Connie asked.

"The big question. The *M* question. He probably would already have asked the *M* question, except he's so shy. I been thinking I might help him along with it. Make it easy on him. Maybe I need to get him liquored up first, so he's nice and relaxed. And maybe I'll stop at the jewelry district on the way home and get an engagement ring, so he don't have to do a lot of shopping. You know how men hate shopping."

"How're we doing with Loretta's bond?" I asked Connie.

Connie slid a glance at Zook, bent over his laptop, and then looked back at me. The silent communication was *no luck so far*. Hard to get someone to post a couple thousand dollars in bond when the last person to post bond for Loretta ended up forfeiting their money.

Lula had her bag on her shoulder and her car keys in her hand. "What'd Ranger want with you?"

"He's running security for Brenda for the next three days, and he wants me to ride shotgun."

MORELLI LIVED HALFWAY between my apartment at the edge of Trenton proper and my parents' house in the Burg. It was a modest two-story row house on a quiet street in a stable blue-collar neighborhood. Living room, dining room, kitchen, and powder room on the first floor. Three small bedrooms and bath upstairs. So far as I know,

he'd never eaten in the dining room. Morelli ate breakfast
at the small table in the kitchen, lunch at the sink, and
dinner in front of the television in the living room. There
was a single-car garage at the back of the property, accessible by a rutted alley, but Morelli almost always parked
his SUV at the curb in front of the house. The backyard
was narrow and strictly utilitarian, only used by Morelli's
dog, Bob.

I parked and looked over at Zook. "You know Joe
Morelli, right?"

"Wrong."

"You're related."

"That's what I hear." Zook studied the house. "I thought it
would be bigger. It's all my uncle talks about since he got out
of prison. He said it was supposed to go to him, but Morelli
swindled him out of it."

"Hard to believe of Morelli," I said.

"I thought he was supposed to be the big, bad, tough
cop and lady-killer. What's he want with this dorkopolis?"

In the beginning, I struggled with that one, too. I saw
Morelli in a cool condo with a big-screen television and a
kick-ass sound system and maybe a pinball machine in his
living room. Turns out Morelli was tired of sailing that ship.
Morelli went into Rose's house with an open mind, and the
house and Morelli took stock of each other and adapted.
The house gave up some of its stuffiness, and Morelli
dialed down his wild side.

I pulled the key from the ignition, got out of the car, and
walked to the front door with Zook trailing after me.

"This is so lame," Zook said, dragging his feet. "I can't believe my mother tried to rob a stupid booze shack."

I didn't know what to say to him. I didn't want to make out like armed robbery was okay, but at the same time, I didn't want to be gloom and doom. "Sometimes good people do dumb things," I said. "If you hang in there with your mom, it'll all work out . . . eventually. Step back when I open the door, or Morelli's dog will knock you over."

I unlocked the door, and there was a *woof* and the sound of dog feet galloping toward us from the kitchen. Bob appeared, ears flapping, tongue out, slobber flying in all directions. He hurtled past us, leaped off the small porch, went straight to the nearest tree, and lifted his leg.

Zook went wide-eyed. "What kind of dog is he?"

"We're not sure, but we think he's mostly Golden Retriever. His name is Bob."

Bob peed for what seemed like half an hour and trotted back into the house. I closed the door after him and checked the time. Four o'clock. Morelli's shift ended at four. It would take him thirty minutes to drive home. I had to be dressed and at the hotel by five. The hotel was thirty minutes from my apartment at this time of night. It wasn't going to work.

Zook looked around Morelli's living room. "Can I go wireless here?"

"I don't know. Morelli's computer is upstairs in his office, but I've seen him work down here as well."

Zook pulled his laptop out of his backpack. "I'll figure it out."

"That's great, because I have to go. Morelli should be home any minute now. I'm going to trust you to stay here and wait for him and not get into trouble."

"Sure," Zook said.

I called Morelli on his cell. "Where are you?"

"I just turned onto Hamilton."

"We're at your house. Unfortunately, I have a job at five, and I have to go home first to change, so I'm going to leave Zook here alone for a few minutes."

"Who's Zook?"

"You'll see. And just a suggestion, but you might want to put the Kojak light on the top of your car and step on the gas."

# TWO

I LIVE IN a one-bedroom, one-bath unit on the second floor of a no-frills, three-story, redbrick apartment building. There's a small lobby with a small unreliable elevator. The front entrance looks out on a busy street filled with small businesses. The rear exit backs up to a tenant parking lot. My bedroom and living room windows look out at the parking lot. Lucky me, because this is the quiet side, except at five A.M. on Mondays and Thursdays, when the Dumpster gets emptied. I share my apartment with a hamster named Rex.

I rocked to a stop in the lot, bolted from the car, bypassed the elevator, and took the stairs two at a time. I ran down the hall and rammed my key into my front door. I yelled *hello* to Rex on my way to the bedroom. No time for extended pleasantries.

Ten minutes later, I was out the door in black heels and my little black suit with a white tank top under the jacket. I'd spruced up my makeup and fluffed out my hair, and I'd dropped my Smith & Wesson into my purse. The gun wasn't loaded, and I didn't have time to hunt for bullets, but if I had to whack someone in the head with my purse, it was nicely weighted.

I took a call from Morelli while I unlocked my car.

"I just walked into my house, and the kid is wearing a black satin cape, he only answers to the name Zook, and he seems obsessed with someone named Moondog."

"Order a pizza and go with it," I told him.

I WAS FIVE minutes late when I pulled into hotel parking. This wouldn't be an issue if I was meeting anyone other than Ranger. Ranger has many good qualities. Patience isn't one of them.

I ran through the parking garage, slid to a stop when I got to the hotel lobby, adjusted my skirt, and crossed to where Ranger was standing. He was wearing black slacks, black blazer, and a black dress shirt with a black tie. The black tie had a black stripe. If *GQ* ran an issue on contract killers, he'd make the cover.

"Nice," I said to him.

"Playing the role," Ranger said.

I followed him to the third floor and the only suite in the hotel. Tank was in front of the suite door, arms crossed, feet at parade rest. He was dressed in the usual Rangeman black T-shirt and cargo pants, with a gun at his hip.

"Any problems?" Ranger asked.

"No," Tank replied. "She's been inside since I came on duty."

"We'll take it from here," Ranger said.

I watched Tank walk to the elevator and thought about Lula out shopping for an engagement ring. I could sort of see Tank and Lula engaged, but the mental image of them settling into married life went right to the top of the bizarrometer.

Ranger rapped on Brenda's door and waited. He rapped a second time.

"Maybe she's in the bathroom," I said.

Ranger took a pass card from his pocket, inserted it in the lock, and opened the door. "See if you can find her."

I tiptoed into the entrance foyer and looked into the living room area. "Hello," I called.

A young woman popped out of the bedroom. She was slim, and her face was pinched and had the hungry, haunted look of someone who'd recently quit smoking. Her short dark hair was pushed behind her ears in a non-style. She was wearing a skirt and a cardigan and flat shoes. She didn't look happy. "Yes?" she asked.

"Security," I told her. "We're here to escort Brenda."

"She's getting dressed."

"Honestly," Brenda yelled from the bedroom. "I don't know *why* I have to do these *things*."

Brenda was Kentucky born and raised. Her voice was country, and her style was ballsy. From what I read in the tabloids, at sixty-one she was on a slippery slope as an aging star. And she wasn't going down gracefully.

"It's a charity event," the young woman said. "It's a good-will gesture. We're trying to erase the image of you running over that cameraman last month."

"It was an accident."

"You ran over his foot, and then you put your car in reverse and knocked him down!"

"I got confused. For crissake, get off my case. Who do you work for anyway? I want a glass of wine. Where's my wine? I specifically requested that the cooler be stocked with New Zealand sauvignon blanc. I *must* have my blanc!"

I looked at my watch. "Are you responsible for getting her there on time?" I asked Ranger.

"I'm responsible for getting her there alive."

"I'm responsible for getting her there on time," the dark-haired woman said. "I'm Nancy Kolen. I'm the press secretary assigned to this trip. I work for Brenda's record company."

"I have *nothing to wear*," Brenda said. "What am I supposed to wear? Honestly, why am I always surrounded by amateurs? Is it too much to ask to have a stylist here? Where's my stylist? First no blanc, and now no stylist. How am I supposed to work under these conditions?"

Nancy Kolen disappeared into the bedroom, and ten minutes later, Brenda swished out, followed by Nancy.

Brenda was slim and toned and spray-tanned to something resembling orange mud. She had big boobs, lots of curly auburn hair tipped with blond, and her lips looked like they'd been inflated with an air hose.

She was wearing a red knit strapless tube dress that could double for skin, four-inch spike-heeled shoes, and a white sheared mink jacket. She looked like Santa's senior off-season 'ho.

Ranger was standing pressed against my back, and I could feel him smile when Brenda entered the room. I gave him an elbow to the ribs, and he exhaled on a barely audible bark of laughter.

"Look at who we got here," Brenda said, eyeing Ranger. "I swear, you are so hot, I could just eat you up. Sugar, I gotta get me some of you."

Ranger's smile was still in place. Hard to tell if he was enjoying himself or being polite.

"Stephanie and I are providing security," he said.

"Do you have a name?"

"Ranger."

"Like the Long Ranger?" Brenda asked.

There was a moment's pause while I debated correcting Brenda, but truth is, we all knew exactly what she was asking. Finally, Ranger stepped forward and opened the suite door.

"Like an Army Ranger," he said.

Brenda slithered through the door, rubbing against Ranger in the process. "I hear Army guys have big guns."

Nancy and I did some eye-rolling, and Ranger remained pleasantly impassive.

I was the last to leave the room. "I've seen your gun," I whispered to Ranger. "Would you like me to tell her about it?"

25

"Not necessary, but we could discuss it over a glass of wine later."

Nancy took the lead and punched the elevator button. The doors opened, we stepped in, and Brenda moved close to Ranger. "So, Hot Cakes, are you with me for the night?"

"Stephanie and I will be with you until you return to your hotel room," Ranger said.

"Sometimes I need my bodyguards to spend the *entire* night with me," Brenda said to Ranger.

This produced more eye-rolling from Nancy and me and more passive pleasantness from Ranger. The doors opened, and we moved into the crush of people in the lobby. Nancy led the way, and I followed Nancy, with Brenda sandwiched between Ranger and me. We cut a swath through the crowd to the meet-and-greet room. Once we were inside the room and the door was closed behind us, the atmosphere became much more calm. These were patrons of the charity, and they'd paid a huge amount of money to have a private audience with Brenda. She accepted a champagne flute, drained it, and reached for a second.

"This isn't so bad," I said to Ranger. "It's not like someone is shooting at her. And so far, she hasn't totally exposed herself. You got groped in the elevator, but you're probably used to that."

"Yeah," Ranger said. "It happens a lot."

A forty-something woman approached Brenda.

"What is this?" the woman asked, pointing to Brenda's jacket.

"A jacket?"

"What *kind* of jacket?"

"What kind do you think it is?"

"I think it's mink."

"Bingo," Brenda said.

"You have a lot of nerve," the woman said. "Was this done as a deliberate insult?"

"Sweetheart," Brenda said, "when I insult someone they *know* they've been insulted."

Nancy's eyes went to the size of goose eggs, and she frantically thumbed through her event schedule. "Oh crap!" she said. "Oh *shit*."

I looked over her shoulder and read down the clipboard. THURSDAY'S EVENT WILL BENEFIT THE HUMANE TREATMENT OF ANIMALS.

The woman narrowed her eyes at Brenda. "Take that offensive jacket off immediately."

"Bite me," Brenda said. "And what's your problem, anyway?"

"Do you have any idea how many little minks it took to make that jacket?"

"Oh puhleeze," Brenda said. "Don't give me that tree-hugger crap. Look, if it's an issue for you, just think of it as Russian weasel."

The woman snatched a glass of red wine from a waiter, dumped it on Brenda's jacket, and Brenda tossed her champagne in the woman's face. Ranger reached for Brenda, but Brenda already had her hands around the woman's throat. There was a lot of kicking and shrieking of obscenities, and by the time Ranger got the women separated, Brenda's boobs had popped out of her dress and the skirt had ridden up to her waist. Ranger dispassionately yanked the dress up over Brenda's breasts and pulled the skirt down over her ass, apologized to the other woman, and dragged Brenda out of the room and into the lobby. Nancy and I rushed after Ranger and Brenda, and we all jumped into the elevator.

Nancy crossed *meet and greet* off her schedule. "One down," she said. "We have ten minutes before the dinner."

RANGER AND I elected not to sit at the head table with Brenda. We took a position on the wall toward the front of the room, so we could better see if anyone was rushing at Brenda with a glass of red wine.

Brenda had changed into a black satin bustier, tight jeans studded with rhinestones, and she had an animal-friendly black cashmere wrap draped over her shoulders.

My cell phone vibrated, and I looked at the screen. It was Morelli calling. "I need to take this," I said to Ranger. "I'm going to step outside for a moment."

I found a quiet corridor and dialed Morelli.

"How's it going?" I asked Morelli.

"I don't know. He hasn't stopped playing since I got home. He can play and eat at the same time. I think he took the computer into the bathroom with him. It's kind of creepy. You're coming back here tonight, right?"

"Um . . ."

"Let me rephrase that. *What time* are you coming back here?"

"Hard to say. I'm running security for Brenda."

"*The* Brenda?"

"Yeah. I'm working with Ranger."

There was a full sixty seconds of silence where I suspected Morelli was staring down at his shoe, getting a grip. Morelli thought Ranger was a dangerous guy from multiple points of view. And Morelli was right.

"Don't you want to hear about Brenda?" I asked him.

"No. I don't care about Brenda. I care about you. I don't like you working with Ranger."

"It's just for a couple days."

"I'm out of the house at six tomorrow morning. You need to be here to make sure Picasso doesn't spray paint the dog again."

"Zook painted Bob?"

"He did it before I got home. He said he had to protect Bob from the griefer. He pulls anything like that again, and I'm going to make the griefer look like the Tooth Fairy."

RANGER WAS LEANING against the wall, arms crossed over his chest, calmly watching the room when I returned.

"Did I miss anything fun?" I asked him.

He made a small side-to-side movement with his head. "No."

"Brenda is waving her glass around."

"I told the wait staff not to give her a refill, and she's feeling neglected."

"Hey!" Brenda called to a passing waiter. "Hell-*O*!"

The waiter scurried away, and Brenda waved the glass at another guy. Brenda lapped at the empty glass and waggled her tongue at the waiter. A red scald rose from his collar to the roots of his hair, and he ran for the kitchen.

A waiter carrying plates of food passed behind Brenda, and in the blink of an eye, Brenda had the guy by his nuts. The waiter stopped in mid-stride, tray aloft, mouth open. I couldn't hear Brenda from where I stood, but I could read her lips.

"I need a drinky-poo," Brenda said to the waiter. "Nod your head if you understand."

The waiter nodded his head, and Brenda released him.

"I have to give her credit," I said to Ranger. "She knows how to get a man's attention."

An hour later, we escorted Brenda to her room.

"I want to party," Brenda said in the elevator. "Isn't there a party somewhere?"

Ranger stayed stoic, saying nothing, and I followed his lead. If Brenda had been sober, she would have been hard to control. As it was, her eyes were unfocused, and her attention span was short. The elevator doors opened, Brenda lurched out, walked into a potted plant, and got knocked on her ass.

"Whoops," Brenda said. "Where'd that come from?"

Ranger scooped her up and pointed her in the right direction. She tried to grab him, and he jumped away.

"You need to take point on this," Ranger said to me. "If she grabs me one more time, I'm going to have to shoot her."

I linked arms with Brenda and walked her down the hall to her suite. I opened the door and maneuvered her inside. I herded her into the bedroom, and she crawled into bed fully clothed.

I turned the light off in the bedroom and joined Ranger in the living room. He locked the liquor cabinet, pocketed the key, and we left the suite.

"Tank has the night off, and Hal doesn't come on until midnight," Ranger said. "I'll stand guard until then."

"I'll stand with you," I said. "Just in case Brenda comes out and attacks you and you're tempted to shoot her."

# THREE

HAL WAS ONE of the younger guys on Ranger's team. He was big and blond and blushed when embarrassed. He was over-muscled and looked a little prehistoric. He showed up ten minutes early.

"Call me if there's a problem," Ranger said, giving Hal the room key. "Don't go into the suite alone. If you need to enter and can't wait for me, get hotel security to go in with you."

Hal nodded. "Yessir."

Ranger walked me to the parking garage, gave me a friendly kiss goodnight that sent a flutter of emotion through me that I'd rather not name, and watched me drive away.

I got back to Morelli's house a little after midnight. Morelli's porch light was on and a nightlight was burning in the hall leading to the stairs. The rest of the house was dark. I unlocked the front door and stepped inside. The house was quiet. Everyone was asleep, including Bob Dog.

I didn't need light to find my way around Morelli's house. I spent a decent amount of time there, and it was almost identical to the house where I grew up. I made my way into the kitchen and checked the fridge for leftovers, hitting the jackpot with pepperoni pizza.

I put the pizza box on the counter, and the cellar door crashed open next to me. A stocky guy jumped out, ran for the back door, and instantly was gone into the dark night. I was too startled to scream, too freaked to move. After a second or two, my heart resumed beating and brain function kicked in.

"What the—" I said to the empty kitchen.

I heard footsteps on the stairs, and Morelli sauntered into the kitchen. He was wearing a T-shirt and boxers, and his hair was tousled.

"I thought I heard you come in," he said. "How was Brenda? And why is the back door open?"

I was breathless. "Some guy . . . some guy charged out of your basement and ran out the back door."

"Yeah, right."

I had my hand over my heart in an effort to keep it from jumping out of my chest. "I'm serious!"

Morelli went to the door and looked outside. "I don't see anyone."

"He ran away!"

Morelli closed and locked the door. "Someone actually was in my cellar?"

"He scared the bejeezus out of me."

"Anyone we know?"

"It was dark. He was chunky. Dressed in dark clothes. I didn't see his face. It happened so fast, I didn't get a good look."

"Hair?"

"He was wearing a knit hat. I couldn't see his hair."

Morelli opened a kitchen drawer, removed a gun, and stepped to the cellar door.

"Wait," I said, "maybe we should call the police."

"Cupcake, I *am* the police."

"Yes, but you're *my* police, and I don't want you to get shot."

"I'm not going to get shot. Stay here in the kitchen."

No problem with that. I had no desire to follow Morelli into his spooky basement.

Morelli flipped the light switch and padded barefoot down the stairs. He stood for a moment, looking around, and returned to the kitchen.

"I can't imagine why anyone would be in my basement," he said. "There's nothing down there. Just the furnace and the water heater."

"Sometimes people have offices or playrooms down there," I said. "Maybe he was looking for something to steal."

"My laptop is on the table. He didn't take it. He left the Xbox and television in the living room."

I took a piece of pizza from the box and tried to get it to my mouth, but my hand was still shaking. "Maybe he didn't get to it. Maybe he started downstairs, and I scared him off."

Morelli dialed dispatch and reported the break-in. "Ask

someone to do a couple drive-bys and keep their eyes open," he said.

Bob trotted into the kitchen and stood looking at the pizza box. He couldn't hear a burglar break into the house, but wave a piece of pizza around and he was there. Pink and green fluorescent paint glowed in the dark on Bob's back.

"The label on the spray paint said it would wash off with water. I'll hose him down tomorrow," Morelli said.

I fed Bob my crust, and Bob smiled and wagged his tail.

Morelli draped an arm across my shoulders. "There's a way you could make me look that happy."

"Someone just broke into your house. How can you think about sex?"

"I always think about sex."

"Mario is in the guest room!"

"Yeah, you'd have to try to control yourself and not make a lot of noise."

"He's just a kid. You need to set a good example."

"Which means what?"

"The couch. Zook's in the guest room, and you wanted me to spend the night, so I assumed you'd sleep on the couch."

"You assumed wrong."

"We're not married."

"No, but we're old. There are different rules when you get old," Morelli said.

*"I'm not old."*

"Not to me, but to Zook anyone over twenty is old."

"Okay, that does it. I'm going home. I'll be back tomorrow morning at the crack of dawn."

"Oh for crissake," Morelli said. "I'll sleep on the friggin' couch. There's a sleeping bag in my office. Throw it down with a pillow."

I OPENED MY eyes and squinted at the clock. The room was dark, but the glowing blue digital readout told me it was five in the morning. And the sound of a drawer being opened and closed told me I wasn't alone. I reached for the bedside lamp, switched it on, and stared at Morelli. His hair was damp from the shower, he was freshly shaved, and he was naked.

"What's going on?" I asked him.

"I need clothes."

No kidding. "I would have gotten them for you. What if Mario sees you walking around naked in my room?"

"First, it's not *your* room. It's *my* room. Second, I doubt he'd be shocked. You have to stop worrying about Zook. Third, he's asleep."

"Did you sleep okay?"

"No. The couch sucks."

Morelli was dressing in his usual uniform of jeans and T-shirt while he was talking. If the occasion dictated, Morelli sometimes wore slacks and a dress shirt, but Morelli avoided suits. He looked like an Atlantic City pit boss in a suit. And no one could keep a straight face at

Morelli in khakis. Morelli was as far from preppy as a guy could get.

He sat on the bed, laced his shoes, leaned over me and nuzzled my neck. "I like when you're all warm and soft from sleep." He looked down at the shoes he'd just laced and thought for a moment. "These could come off."

"Tempting." *Really* tempting. "Will you be late for work if you take your shoes off?"

"Yeah. Don't care. If the choice was a promotion and raise or *doing* you and getting fired, there'd be no contest."

"The power of testosterone."

"I thought it was love, but you could be right . . . it could be testosterone," Morelli said. "Not that it matters, because bottom line is . . . *I want you bad.*"

I had the T-shirt halfway over his head. "Take your shoes off . . . *fast,*" I told him.

There were scuffling sounds in the hall and a timid knock on the bedroom door. "Anybody home?" Zook asked.

Morelli flopped spread-eagle onto the bed. "Crap."

"Uno momento," I called to Zook.

"I'm not sure what I'm supposed to do," Zook said from the other side of the door. "Should I go downstairs and look for cereal?"

"Yeah," Morelli said. "Just prowl through the cupboards. Stephanie will be down in a couple minutes."

I was already out of bed and searching for clothes. I went with one of Morelli's T-shirts and a pair of his sweats. I stayed over from time to time, but I didn't leave a lot of things at his house. Some underwear, socks, an extra pair of running shoes, some unmentionable personal products.

Zook had a box of Frosted Flakes in his hand when I walked into the kitchen. "My favorite," I said to him.

"Do you live here?"

"Sometimes."

"So you could be my, what . . . aunt-in-sin?"

"It's my understanding that Morelli's some sort of distant *cousin,* so technically . . . I wouldn't be an aunt of any sort."

I took a carton of milk from the refrigerator and set out a couple bowls. Morelli waltzed in and got coffee brewing.

"You're up early," Morelli said to Zook. "When do you have to be at school?"

"Not until eight, but I didn't know how long it would take to walk."

"You're not walking," Morelli said. "Stephanie's taking you to school, and she's going to watch you go through the door."

"Dude, that's so untrusting," Zook said.

"Yeah, deal with it."

Bob was sitting, tail wagging, looking at the cereal box. I knew Morelli had already walked and fed Bob, but that was meaningless in the world of Bob. Bob was the bottomless pit when it came to food. Bob was also the poster dog for canine graffiti art. I looked more closely and realized the pink and green swirls outlined in black on his back spelled out *Zook.*

"Pretty cool, hunh?" Zook said.

Morelli cut his eyes to Zook. "It's not cool. You painted my dog."

"Yeah, dude. He's awesome. And totally arcane."

"What's arcane mean?" I asked.

"Magical."

I thought I saw some steam starting to wisp out of Morelli's ears and off the top of his head.

"Why don't you grab a doughnut and some coffee on the way to work," I said to Morelli. "I'll take care of everything here."

Morelli blew out a sigh and felt his pockets for Rolaids. "I have to run anyway. Early morning meeting. See you tonight." He gave me a quick kiss and left the house.

When I heard the door close, I turned on Zook. "What the heck were you thinking? You don't go around painting a man's dog without his permission. You don't even do it *with* his permission. It's rude and insensitive and . . . wrong!"

I was yelling and waving my arms, and Zook was calmly pouring milk on his cereal.

I leaned palms on the table and got into his face. "Are you listening?"

Zook looked up at me. "What?"

"I'm yelling at you."

"I didn't notice. It sounded like dinner at my grandma's house."

Okay, I could relate to that. "Did you paint anything other than Bob?"

"I sort of painted the garage."

I went to the back door and stared out at the garage. It looked a lot like Bob. *Zook* in bright pink and green, outlined in black. Magical designs swirled around the name. It was glowing in the semi-dark.

"Has Morelli seen this?"

"I don't think so. He didn't say anything."

"You need to lose the paint before he gets home."

"But it represents the power of Zook! It's my portal."

"What do you mean it's your portal?"

"Okay, so it's not a portal, but it could be someday."

"You're not serious."

"That's the way it happens in the game."

"This isn't the game."

"Yeah, but Zook likes to keep in the zone."

I squelched a major mental head slap. It could be worse, I told myself. He could be spending his day surfing porn sites.

I was still at the back door, and it occurred to me that I wasn't seeing any sign of forced entry from last night. I went to the front door and checked out the lock and the doorjamb. No forced entry there, either. I went window to window. All locked and intact. Hard to believe Morelli hadn't locked the back door. That meant either someone let the intruder in, the intruder was good with locks, or he had a key.

"Did you let anyone into the house yesterday?" I asked Zook.

"The pizza delivery guy."

"He didn't go into the cellar and stay there, did he?"

"No. He left in his pizza car."

I sat at the little kitchen table with Zook and ate a bowl of cereal and drank my coffee. I had a bad feeling about the guy in the cellar. And I didn't know what to do about Zook. He was pushing his cereal around in his bowl, letting it get sogged up with milk. He was frowning and chewing on his lip.

"What?" I asked him.

"Nothing."

"It's something. What is it?"

"It's my stupid mother, sitting in that stupid jail."

"You're worried about her," I said.

"It's all her own stupid fault. She robbed a stupid liquor store. I mean, it wasn't even a bank. A bank, I could see. That could be lots of money. My uncle robbed a bank and they never found the money, and now he's out and he's gonna be on easy street. But my dumb mother robbed a liquor store, and all she took was a bottle of gin! And now my stupid relatives won't even bail her out."

"Connie's working on it. Hopefully, we'll find a way to get your mom out today. In the meantime, Morelli will look in on her and make sure she's okay."

"I don't ever want to grow up. Growing up sucks. People do stupid things."

"Growing up isn't so bad," I told him. "What do you want to do when you get out of school?"

He kept his eyes glued to his bloated cereal. "You'll think it's dopey."

"And?"

"I want to be an engineer and design roller coasters."

I was dumbstruck. "*Wow*. That's fantastic."

"Yeah, except I'll never get into college because my grades suck, and we have no money."

"So fix your grades and go to a state school. That's what I did. You could even try for a scholarship."

Morelli called on my cell phone.

"Tell Zook, or whoever the hell he is today, that his mom says *hello*. She isn't happy, but she's managing."

"Thanks. I'll pass it on. Any information on last night?"

"You mean the break-in? No. No other disturbances in the neighborhood."

# FOUR

CONNIE WAS AT her desk when I walked into the office. I dumped my shoulder bag on the couch and cut my eyes to Vinnie's inner sanctum. The door was closed.

"He's not here," Connie said. "He's at a bail bonds conference in Shreveport."

"What's happening with Loretta Rizzi?"

"Not a damn thing. It's pathetic," Connie said. "No one wants to take a chance on her."

"You could bond her out on her own recognizance."

"Vinnie would kill me."

"He wouldn't have to know."

"Vinnie knows everything. He has this office bugged."

"I thought you debugged it."

"He keeps hiding new ones."

"I have to get Loretta out. Morelli and I aren't ready for parenthood. If I was going to target one of her relatives, who would be my top choice?"

"Her brother. He's got a stash somewhere. He stole nine million dollars, and it was never recovered."

"Do you have an address?"

"He's staying at his mother's house on Conway Street."

"I know the house."

"You might want to take Lula. Word is he's unstable."

"Where *is* Lula?"

"Late. Like always."

I caught a flash of red in my peripheral vision and Lula swept through the front door. Her hair was still fire-engine red, and her sweater, skirt, and shoes matched her hair.

"Speak of the devil," Connie said.

"I ain't no devil," Lula said. "I'm respectable, mostly. I'm an engaged woman. I got a ring and everything. I told you I had a feeling."

She held her hand out, and we looked at her ring.

"Wow, that's a big diamond," Connie said. "Is it real?"

"Sure it's real," Lula said. "I got it in the diamond district on Eighth and Remington."

"That's the projects," Connie said.

"Yeah. Scootch Brown runs that corner. He said this was a real good ring. He gave me a good price on it."

"So it was okay with Tank that you bought the ring?"

"Tank got a real important job," Lula said. "He don't necessarily have time to go shopping for shit like this."

"Does he know he's engaged?"

"Of course he knows," Lula said. "It was real romantic, too. He came over, and we always get right to it, if you know what I mean. So anyway, we got that out of the way, and then Tank fell asleep and I put the ring on. And then when Tank woke up, I told him how happy I was, and how he was such a sweetie. And then I celebrated by making him feel real good, and after that he fell asleep again."

"Congratulations," I said to Lula. "When's the wedding?"

"I haven't decided that. June might be nice."

"That's next month."

"Yeah," Lula said. "You think it's too far away? I don't like long engagements."

"You can't go wrong with June," Connie said. "Everyone wants to get married in June."

"That's what I figure," Lula said. "I always wanted to be a June bride, but I don't want one of them schmaltzy weddings with the big white gown and all. I just want to get married real quiet." She looked at me. "What about you? Did you have a big schmaltzy wedding?"

"Yeah. And then I had an even bigger divorce."

"I remember the divorce," Connie said. "It was spectacular. It was a real accomplishment, since you'd only been married about fifteen minutes." She handed a file over to me. "This guy just came in. Failed to appear for his court appearance. Not a big bond, but it shouldn't be hard to find him. He lives with his brother in a row house on Vine Street."

"What's the charge?"

"Indecent exposure."

"That sounds like fun," Lula said. "I might have to help you with that one."

I read through the bond document. "He's eighty-one."

"Now that I think about it," Lula said, "I got a lot to do. I might not have time to round up some eighty-one-year-old naked guy."

"I'm sure he's not *always* naked," I said to Lula. "He probably just forgot to close the barn door."

"Okay, I'll go with you, but I don't want to get involved with no eighty-year-old doodles, you see what I'm saying?"

"Before I forget, Mary Ann Falattio is having a purse party tonight," Connie said. "Are you interested?"

Mary Ann Falattio's husband, Danny, hijacked trucks for the Trenton Mob, and from time to time, Mary Ann supplemented her household budget by tapping into the merchandise stored in her garage. "What's she got?" I asked Connie.

"She said Danny got a load of Louis Vuitton last night. Picked them up at Port Newark."

"I'm in," Lula said. "I could use a new bag. She just get bags or did she get shoes, too?"

"I don't know," Connie said. "It was a message on my machine."

I shoved the new file into my pocket. "I'm working tonight. Brenda's having dinner with the mayor. If she passes out early enough, I'll stop by."

There was still rush-hour traffic clogging Hamilton when Lula and I left the bonds office. The sky was as blue as it gets in Jersey, and the air was warm enough that I could unzip my sweatshirt.

Lula walked half a block to my parked car and stopped short, eyes bugged, mouth open. "Holy cow."

*Zook* was written over the entire car in black and scarlet and gold, surrounded by swirling flames edged in metallic green.

"He did it when I took a shower this morning. He said it would wash off," I told Lula.

"Too bad. It's a real improvement on this hunk of junk car."

"It's supposed to protect me from the griefer."

"You can never have too much protection," Lula said.

We buckled in and I drove the short distance to Conway Street.

"I'll just be a minute," I told Lula. "I need to talk to Dominic Rizzi."

"Holler if you need help. I hear he's a nut case."

Alma Rizzi's small front yard was bare of landscaping, with the exception of a plaster statue of the Virgin Mary. The Virgin and the weather-beaten gray clapboard house behind it were stoic. They'd seen it all. Good times and bad.

I knocked on the front door and Dom answered. He was about five-feet-nine, with a barrel chest and a head like a melon. He was a couple years older than Loretta, and a lot of pounds heavier. He looked like Friar Tuck with road rage.

"Stephanie Plum," he said. "You got a lot of nerve coming here. First you put my kid sister in jail, and then you kidnap my nephew. If I wasn't on probation, I'd shoot you."

"I didn't kidnap Mario. Loretta made me promise to

take him. And if you'd bail her out, he could go back home instead of living with Morelli and me."

Dom went goggle-eyed. "Mario is living with Joe Morelli? That bastard has my nephew?"

"Yeah."

"In his house?"

"Yeah."

Dom was just about vibrating in front of me, hands fisted, neck cords bulging, spit foaming at the corners of his mouth, face purple.

"Sonovabitch. Sonovabitch. I'm gonna kill that snake Morelli. I swear to God, I'm gonna kill him. I'm gonna cut off his head. That's what you do to a snake."

Yikes. "Yeah, but not when you're on probation, right?"

"Fuck probation. He deserves to die. First he got my kid sister pregnant. And then he took Rose's house. And now he's got Mario."

"Whoa, wait up a minute. What do you mean he got Loretta pregnant?"

"It's obvious," Dom said. "Take a look at the kid. Recognize anyone?"

"Loretta and Joe are vaguely related. It's not shocking that there'd be a family resemblance."

"It's more than a family resemblance. Besides, I caught them in the act. They were doing it in my old man's garage. Nine months later, Mario popped out of the oven. That piece of shit Morelli. I should have killed him then."

I was stunned. I'd seen the resemblance, but this had never crossed my mind. Morelli had been pretty wild in high school and his early twenties. He hadn't been my favorite person, and I was willing to believe a lot of bad things about him. This went beyond what I would have expected. Hard to believe he'd have a romantic relationship with Loretta and then walk away from her and the baby.

"I know Morelli had a Casanova reputation in high school, but this is out of character," I said to Dom. "Family and friends were always important to Morelli."

"He ruined my kid sister's life. She was smart. She always got the good grades. She could have been something, but she had to quit high school. And now she's in jail. This is *his* fault. He stole her future, just like he stole mine. You tell the sonovabitch to live in fear. You tell him to watch his back, because I'm gonna chop the head off the snake. And you tell him to stay far away from my nephew," Rizzi said, eyes narrowed.

"If you'd post the security for the bond on Loretta . . ."

"I'm living in my mother's house. Does that say something? Like maybe I haven't got a cent? No job. No money. No goddamn house."

"I thought you might have some cash laying around."

"What are you, fucking deaf? I have nothing."

"Okay then. Good talking to you. Let me know if you find some money. Just give me a ringy dingy."

I turned and practically ran back to the car. He was friggin' scary. And I couldn't believe I told him to give me a ringy dingy! Where did that come from?

Lula was eyebrows up when I slid behind the wheel. "Well, how'd that go?" she asked.

"Could have been better."

"He gonna bond Loretta out?"

"Nope."

"Sounded to me like he was yelling about something."

"Yep."

"You want to talk about it?"

"Nope." What on earth was I supposed to say? He saw Morelli boinking Loretta and getting her pregnant? I could barely *think* it, much less *repeat* it.

"Hunh," Lula said. "I was gonna make you my maid of honor, but I might have to rethink that if you're gonna go all secret on me."

"I thought you were going to have a quiet wedding."

"Yeah, but you gotta have a maid of honor. It's a rule."

Vine Street ran off Broad and was at the edge of the Burg. I cruised along, checking off the numbers of the row houses.

"What's this guy's name?" Lula wanted to know.

"Andy Gimp."

"That's a terrible name. That's a strike against you right from the start."

"He's eighty-one. I imagine he's used to it." I pulled to the curb and parked. "Showtime."

"I hope not," Lula said. "I finally got me some good stuff. I don't want to ruin my mental image. I don't want some old wrinkled wanger burned into my cornea when what I want to remember is Tank and the big boys."

I took a business card and a small can of pepper spray

out of my purse and rammed them into my jeans pocket. "Big boys?"

"Yeah, you know . . . the fuzzy lumpkins, the storm troopers, the beef balls."

I covered my ears with my hands. "I get it!" I stepped onto the small cement front porch and rang the bell. A little old man with wispy gray hair and skin like a Shar-Pei answered.

"Andy Gimp?" I asked.

"Nope. I'm Bernie. Andy's my older brother," the man said. "Come on in. Andy's watching television."

"I got a bad feeling about this," Lula said. "If this is the younger brother, what the heck does the older one look like?"

"Hey, Andy," Bernie called out. "You got company. You got a couple hot ones."

I followed Bernie into the living room and immediately spotted Andy. He was slouched into a broken-down over-stuffed chair facing the television. He was wearing a white dress shirt buttoned to the neck and black socks and black shoes, and that was it. No pants. He looked like a bag of bones with skin cancer. He was milk-white skin and red splotches everywhere. And I mean *everywhere*. There was a lot of nose and a lot of ears, and gonads hanging low between his knobby knees.

"Come on in," he said, gesturing with big boney hands. "What can I do you for?"

"I knew it," Lula said. "I knew it. I knew it. I knew it.

This here's gonna haunt me forever. This is what I got to look forward to after a hundred years of marriage. This here's what happens to outdoor plumbing when a man gets old. I don't know if I can go through with the wedding."

"Age don't got nothing to do with it," Bernie said. "He's always looked like that."

"You're not wearing any pants," I said to Andy Gimp.

"Don't like them. Never wear them."

"Fine by me," I said, "but you didn't show up for your court appearance."

"Are you sure?"

"Yep."

"I had it marked on my calendar," Andy said. "Bernie, where's the calendar?"

"Lost it," Bernie said.

"They say I didn't show up for my court appearance."

Bernie shrugged. "So what? They'll give you another one."

Andy was on his feet, looking for the calendar. He walked body bent, arms akimbo, feet planted wide for balance, his nuts practically dragging on the floor.

"I know it's here somewhere," he said, shuffling through magazines on the coffee table, rifling through a pile of newspapers on the floor.

"I'm feelin' faint," Lula said. "If he bends over one more time, I'm gonna pass out. I can't stop lookin'. It's a train wreck. It's like the end of the universe. You know, when you get sucked into that thing. What do you call it?"

"Black hole?"

"Yeah, that's it. It's like staring into the black hole."

Andy was distracted by the calendar hunt, so I gave my business card to Bernie and introduced myself.

"Lula and I need to take Andy to the courthouse so he can reinstate his bail bond," I told Bernie. "Can you get him to put some pants on?"

"He don't own none," Bernie said. "And I'm not loaning him any of mine. You don't know where he's been sitting."

"Hell, I'll buy him some pants if he'll stop bending over," Lula said.

"Won't do no good," Bernie said. "He won't wear them. He made up his mind."

Since I've had this job, I've hauled in a naked, greased-up fat guy, a half-naked homie, and a naked old pervert, and I've worked with a little naked guy who thought he was a leprechaun. A geriatric nudist wasn't going to slow me down.

"Get a jacket," I said to Andy. "We're going downtown."

"I'm not wearing pants," he said.

"Not my problem."

I walked him out of the house and settled him onto a newspaper on my backseat.

"The desk sergeant is gonna love this," Lula said.


AN HOUR LATER, Andy was in line at the courthouse, waiting to see the judge, and Lula and I were back on Hamilton Avenue, coming up to Tasty Pastry.

"Pull over!" Lula said. "I want to go into the bakery. I

gotta look at wedding cakes, and I wouldn't mind getting an éclair to settle my stomach. I think I got wedding jitters."

I thought that was a great idea. I didn't have wedding jitters, but I had guy-in-basement jitters, and Loretta jitters, and Joe Morelli fatherhood jitters. I might need *three* éclairs.

I parked the Sentra, and Lula and I marched into the bakery. Betty Kuharchek was behind the counter, setting out a cookie display. Betty is an apple dumpling woman who has worked at Tasty Pastry forever. If you pass her on the street, there's the lingering scent of powdered sugar icing.

"I'm gonna be a June bride and I need to consider some wedding cakes," Lula said to Betty. "I like the one in the window with the three tiers and the big white roses with the green leaves, but before I get down to business, I need an éclair."

"Me, too," I said to Betty. "I need three."

"*Three?*" Lula said. "I'm the one with the wedding jitters, and you're trumping me on éclairs. What's with that?"

"I have Zook and Loretta jitters."

"That don't seem like three-éclair jitters to me," Lula said. "That's barely a single éclair. That might be a half a éclair. Maybe I need more éclairs." She looked over at Betty. "You might want to put a couple more éclairs in that box."

Betty boxed up six éclairs and handed them over. "What kind of cake are you thinking about?" Betty asked. "Chocolate, vanilla, carrot cake, rum cake, chocolate chip, spice, banana? And then you get to choose the filling between the layers. Lemon pudding, chocolate mousse, whipped cream, coconut cream, tropical fruit filling?"

"I like all them cakes," Lula said. "The part I want to talk about is the bride and groom. The little people on top the cake have to be right. Tank and me are darker than the little people you got displayed. And we're more . . . full-bodied. You see what I'm saying?"

The door to the bakery opened and Morelli sauntered in, draped an arm around my shoulders, and gave me a friendly kiss just above my ear. "Saw your car parked at the curb," he said. "Nice paint job."

"Protects me from Moondog."

"One less thing for me to worry about," Morelli said.

I took the box of éclairs and went outside to talk. I opened the box and offered it to Morelli. "Hungry?"

Morelli's eyes went beyond the box to my T-shirt and traveled south. "Yeah," he said.

"Right now, I'm only offering éclairs."

Morelli blew out a sigh and took one. I did the same, and we stood in the sun with our backs to the building and ate our éclairs.

"I had a disturbing conversation with Dominic Rizzi," I said to Morelli. "His contention is that not only did you steal his Aunt Rose's house out from under him, but that you're Mario's father."

"That's ridiculous," Morelli said.

"Dom claims he caught you in the act with Loretta in her father's garage, and nine months later Mario was born."

Morelli chewed slowly and thought about it. "I went

through a lot of women back then. I don't remember all of them."

"Seems to me you'd remember having sex with your cousin."

"To begin with, Loretta's not exactly part of the family tree. It's more like she's in the forest."

"What the heck is that supposed to mean?"

"I don't know. It's like we're forty-third cousins or something." He finished eating and took a paper napkin from me. "I guess I have some vague recollection of a skirmish in the garage, but I don't recall doing it with Loretta."

"Then who was in the garage with you?"

"I don't know," Morelli said. "It was dark." He looked at the éclair box. "Can I have another one?"

"No."

"You're mad."

"Of course I'm mad. How could you have been so irresponsible? God, you were such a . . . *pig.*"

"That's not exactly a secret," Morelli said. "Everyone knew I was a pig. *You* knew I was a pig."

"There's more bad news," I told him.

"Terrific. What is it?"

"Dominic has decided you should die, and he's going to kill you."

"I need to have a talk with Loretta. And then I'll talk to Dom. See if I can get him interested in solving his mental health issues." He gave me a kiss on my forehead. "Gotta go. Are you working tonight?"

58

"Yes. Brenda has a press conference this afternoon and dinner with the mayor tonight."

"Will you be able to pick Zook up after school?"

"If I can't, I'll get someone else to do it. And I'm going to leave him with my parents this afternoon, if Loretta isn't bonded out. Dom is too irrational about you. I don't want to make things worse by putting his nephew in your house." And what went unsaid was that I was still spooked by the guy in the basement. Morelli's house didn't feel secure.

Morelli opened the driver's side door to his SUV and clumps of dog hair tumbled out and drifted off on a breeze. "Be careful tonight," he said.

"No problem. Brenda isn't dangerous."

Morelli angled himself behind the wheel. "I was thinking of Ranger."

Lula bustled out of the store, and we watched Morelli drive off. "That man is *fine*," Lula said, taking an éclair from the box. "I get a rush just looking at him."

I glanced over at her.

"Well, hell," she said. "I'm engaged. I'm not *dead*."

# FIVE

I WAS BACK in my black suit and black heels. In an effort to compete with Brenda, I'd added an extra swipe of mascara and I'd run a brush through my hair. If I'd had an extra hour and a half, I could have done a lot better.

I reached the hotel five minutes late, and Tank was still on duty in front of Brenda's door.

"Ranger's at a meeting with hotel security," Tank said. "I'll stay with you until he gets here."

Spending time with Tank was always excrutiating, because for the most part Tank didn't talk. Ranger didn't talk a lot, either, but he said a lot with his eyes and his touch. I'd reached a level of comfort with Ranger. Ranger looked at ease and in control when he was with me. Tank looked like he wanted to bolt and run.

"So," I said to Tank, doing some mental knuckle-cracking, searching for an icebreaker. "Congratulations."

"What?"

"On your engagement."

"Oh jeez," Tank said, his upper lip breaking out in a sweat. "You know about it?"

"Lula told me."

"What did she say? Did she say how it happened? You know, how I proposed?"

"She said it was very romantic."

Tank did a grimace. "Listen, can I talk to you real confidential? I mean, Ranger trusts you, and he doesn't trust *anyone*, so maybe I can trust you, too, right?"

"Sure."

"I don't remember proposing. I guess I was so nervous, I blanked out or something. I don't even remember buying the ring! All I remember is I fell asleep, and when I woke up, I was engaged. Lula was wearing the ring, and she was all excited."

Oh boy. "I guess the important thing is that you're happy about it," I told him. "You *are* happy, aren't you?"

"I don't know. I'm confused. You won't tell Ranger, will you? He'll laugh his ass off."

"Ranger laughs?"

"He laughs on the inside."

"You're going to have to tell Ranger sooner or later," I said to Tank.

"Why?"

"Because you'll get married and . . . ."

"Married! We just got engaged."

"That's usually followed by marriage."

Tank's eyes were blank and his face went gray under the

62

brown. He staggered back, went down to one knee, and crashed to the floor in a faint.

The elevator doors opened, and Ranger stepped out and spied Tank stretched out on the carpet.

"Fainted," I said.

Ranger walked to Tank and stood hands on hips, staring down at him. "Tank doesn't faint. I've been in firefights with him. He's a rock."

"Well, the rock fainted."

Ranger toed him, and Tank moaned a little and opened his eyes.

"Why did he faint?"

"I can't tell you."

Ranger cut his eyes to me. "Excuse me?"

"I promised."

Ranger gave Tank another nudge with his foot. Actually, it was almost a kick.

"I do," Tank said. "No, wait, I don't. I do. I don't." He shook his head, his vision cleared, and he looked up at Ranger. "Crap."

"You fainted," I told Tank.

"I did not," Tank said. "That's a lie."

Ranger grabbed Tank by the shirt and pulled him to his feet. No small task, since Tank had about fifty pounds on Ranger.

"Talk," Ranger said to Tank.

Tank looked at me.

"You might as well," I said to Tank. "He'll find out anyway. He always does."

"I'm engaged," Tank said. "I guess it's to get married."

Ranger didn't move for a beat. "Engaged," he finally said. "And you think it's to get married?"

Tank nodded his head.

"And your fiancée?"

"Lula," Tank said.

Ranger rocked back on his heels, grinning. "No wonder you fainted."

"You gotta help me," Tank said.

"No way I'm getting involved in this. You're on your own." Ranger glanced at the door to Brenda's suite. "Any word from the diva?"

"Haven't seen her all day," Tank said. "The PR person is in there."

Ranger checked his watch and rapped on the door. Nothing happened, so he rapped again, and Nancy answered. "Five minutes," Ranger said.

Ten minutes later, Ranger opened the door with his key card, and we walked in on Brenda. She was in a hotel bathrobe, and she was talking on the phone.

"I'm in the middle of something," she said to Ranger.

"We need to leave," Ranger said.

"Be a good boy or mommy will spank you," Brenda said to Ranger.

Ranger yanked the phone cord out of the wall, and the little plastic clip popped off and flew across the room.

Brenda looked Ranger over. "Very masterful," she said. "I like your style."

Hard to tell if it was sarcasm, or if Brenda was feeling like she wouldn't mind wearing Ranger's handcuffs. I was going with some of both.

Ranger looked at Nancy. "Does she have clothes?"

Nancy had a bunch of dresses draped over her arm. "We're working on it."

"Work on it faster," Ranger said.

I could hear muffled voices and scuffling sounds in the hall. There was a loud thud, someone shrieked, and that led to more voices all talking at once.

Ranger opened the door, and we looked out at Tank. He was surrounded by women carrying signs protesting Brenda and breast augmentation. Tank had one of the signs in one hand and a woman by the back of her jacket in the other. The woman's feet weren't touching the ground.

"What's going on?" Ranger asked Tank.

"They wanted to get in to see Brenda, but I wouldn't let them, and then this one hit me with her sign," Tank said.

"That's assault," Ranger said to the woman. "We could have you arrested."

The woman looked at Ranger and sucked in some air.

"Put her down," Ranger said to Tank, "and return her sign." He faced the rest of the women. "You can't protest here. You have to return to the lobby. You can have your demonstration down there. Brenda will be walking through in a couple minutes."

The women turned and got into the elevator and disappeared.

Ranger punched hotel security into his cell phone. "We have protestors in the elevator, heading for the lobby," he said. "I want them escorted out of the hotel."

"You're sneaky," I said to Ranger.

Ranger ushered me back into the suite. "Something to remember."

Brenda had crammed herself into a low-cut black sweater and tight black jeans. The sweater gave a first-rate display of her spectacularly augmented breasts. Truth is, for a moment I was just a teensy jealous. I was half her age, and I was worried that even on a good day, I didn't look as sexy as Brenda. She was wearing strappy heels and long, dangly diamond earrings that caught the light when she moved.

"What was that all about?" she asked.

"More animal cruelty protestors in the hall," I said. "They're gone." I thought this was easier than explaining about the breast augmentation issue.

"Honestly, I don't know what their problem is! It's not like I'm torturing puppies. It was a friggin' mink coat. Those minks were born to be coats. Has anyone ever explained that to them?" She turned and pointed her finger at Nancy. "I want *you* to talk to them. It's your job to make things run smoothly and effortlessly for me. This is all your fault."

"I'm getting a migraine," Nancy whispered to me. "I might have to skip the press conference."

"A migraine isn't going to get you out of this," I told her. "If you died, I'd drag your cold, dead body to that press conference. If I have to go . . . you have to go."

THE WOMEN AGAINST Augmentation were MIA when we walked into the lobby with Brenda. A few die-hard fans were milling around, clumped together behind the potted plants, but we swished through before they realized Brenda was in their space. Ranger was wasting no time moving her to the large conference room at the opposite end of the hotel. Nancy was practically running in an attempt to keep ahead of him as he towed Brenda, his hand wrapped around her wrist, partially to hurry her along, partially to keep her from grab-bing him. I was last in line, guarding the rear.

The conference room was filled with media when we arrived. A small, raised stage had been set in place. It held two chairs and a table with a vase of flowers and two hand-held microphones. Brenda took a chair and Lew Pepper, the concert promoter who had hired Ranger, took the other. Pepper looked over at Ranger, and Ranger deadpanned a cold-eyed stare, extended his index finger at Lew, thumb up to simulate a gun, and pulled the trigger. Lew laughed but looked nervous and pointed to the first reporter up.

A small man with gray hair tied back in a ponytail and wearing a lumpy sports coat of no specific color stood. "I'm from the Princeton paper, and I'd like to know if you feel the lyrics to your latest album are relevant in today's culture."

"They weren't even relevant when I *made* the album," she said. "I always try to avoid content in my songs."

A woman from a Hunterdon County weekly asked Brenda if she liked horses.

"Sure," Brenda said. "Doesn't everyone?"

That was followed by a guy who looked like he'd been kicked around the block a few times, recently. "I'm from the Newark paper, and I'd like to know what the gate is on this concert."

"Not as big as your booze bill," Brenda said.

Everyone laughed. These people all knew one another. This was a conference for local newsmen. Brenda was a big deal in Trenton, but New York wouldn't cross the river for her. But then, New York didn't cross the river for anyone.

Halfway through the interview, a guy from the Asbury Park paper stood and said he'd heard a rumor that Brenda was being harassed by a stalker who had unsuccessfully tried to kidnap her. Was that issue being addressed while she was in Trenton?

"Absolutely," Lew Pepper said. "No one's going to kidnap Brenda while she's in Trenton. All stalkers are going to have to be content with buying an album."

Everyone laughed but Ranger. Ranger was watching the room.

"Is it being addressed?" I asked him.

"He's in the third row. Pudgy guy. White hair. Black-rimmed glasses. In his forties."

"Why don't you have him ejected? Isn't there a restraining order against him?"

"Yes, but I'd rather have him where I can see him."

A reporter for one of the Trenton papers got the nod. He looked mid-twenties. Probably fresh out of college. He was slim and dressed in an oversize shirt and khaki slacks.

"Brenda," he said, "my grandfather has been a huge fan ever since he first heard you perform when he was in college. Do you expect to see much of that early fan base here at your concert in Trenton?"

"Cripes," Brenda said. "Your grandfather? How old *are* you? You look like the last guy I dated."

Nancy jumped out of her chair. "And that concludes our press conference. Thank you all for coming."

Ranger helped Brenda off the stage and handed her a can of soda and a cookie from the refreshment table set out for the press.

"Keeping her hands occupied?" I asked him.

"Trying."

He put his hand to Brenda's back and guided her through the crowd. I watched for the stalker guy and put myself between him and Brenda when he moved toward her.

"Are you her bodyguard?" the stalker asked.

"I'm part of the security team."

"I gotta talk to her."

"No can do," I said.

"You don't understand. It's critical. I had a new vision."

I moved closer to Ranger, closing the gap, and followed him into the elevator. The doors closed and Brenda's stalker was out of my life, stuck in the lobby with the rest of the crazies.

Brenda drank some soda and nibbled the cookie. "Where am I again?"

"Trenton."

She did an exaggerated eye roll. "I *hate* Trenton. It's dreary and provincial. Why can't I be in New York or Paris?"

"No one wanted you there," Nancy said. "We could only get you a gig in Trenton."

"That's ridiculous," Brenda said. "It's your incompetence that has me stuck here. Why do I always get the incompetent assistants?"

Tank was in the hall when we stepped out of the elevator. He was back to silent mode after spilling his guts about his engagement. I thought he probably wouldn't speak to me again for another four or five years. We lured Nancy and Brenda into the suite with the promise of room service and closed the door after them.

"Tank and I can take it for the rest of the afternoon," Ranger said. "I'd like you back here at six-thirty. The dinner is at seven. It's formal. Black tie."

"Formal! You never told me the dinner was formal. I haven't got anything to wear."

He gave me a credit card. "Take the corporate card. Get whatever you need."

My eyes went wide. "It's not that easy! Do you have any idea how hard it is to find the right gown? And then I have to accessorize. Shoes and a purse and jewelry."

"Babe," Ranger said.


ZOOK WAS WAITING when I rolled to a stop in front of his school. He was with the same odd assortment of friends, and they all applauded when they saw my car.

He slid onto the passenger seat, dropped his backpack between his legs, and buckled up. "I guess my mom's still in the slammer," he said on a sigh.

"I'm sorry."

"I feel sort of stupid that I can't help her."

"Yeah," I said. "Me, too."

My cell phone rang with a number I didn't recognize on the display.

"It's your new best friend, Dom," he said. "I'm watching you, but you'll never find me, so don't bother to look around. Just act like everything is normal. I don't want to freak the kid."

"Okay, what's up?"

"Just making sure you're not taking him back to Morelli's house. You take him back to Morelli's house, and I'm gonna have to kill you along with Morelli."

"Have you thought about getting help? Maybe seeing a doctor?"

"I don't need help. I know what I'm doing. You're the one who's gonna need help if you don't take good care of the kid."

And he disconnected.

This was a family beyond dysfunction. Dom's mother was probably the sanest of them all, and she was being fed pureed peas.

I pulled away from the school and hooked a left. Zook turned in his seat and looked out the back window.

"Who's the guy following you?" he asked.

I looked in my rearview mirror. White car right on my

bumper. Might be a Taurus. That probably meant it was a rental, since no one actually buys a white Taurus. My first thought was Dom. I stopped for a light and got a glimpse of the driver. White hair. Pasty complexion. Large, framed, black plastic Buddy Holly glasses. Definitely not Dom. It was the stalker. Must have followed me from the hotel garage. Just what I needed, one more nut to add to my collection.

"Hang on," I said to Zook. "I'm going to get rid of him."

I have a routine that I do in the Burg when I want to lose a tail. It involves a lot of cornering and rocketing down alleys, and it always works. It was especially easy this time, because the stalker was clearly an amateur. I lost him halfway through my drill.

"Cool," Zook said. "That was excellent. Do you know that guy?"

"He's a Brenda stalker. I don't know why he attached himself to me."

I rolled through the Burg and parked in front of my parents' house.

"I have to work tonight, so I'm leaving you with my parents," I told Zook.

"What about Morelli?"

"I thought we'd test-drive this arrangement. Variety can be good, right?"

My Grandma Mazur had the door open before we even got to the front porch. Grandma was dressed in her favorite lavender slacks, white tennis shoes, and flowered shirt. Her gray hair was freshly set in rows of curls, her nails were painted to match her slacks. She'd been a beauty in her time, but a lot of her had shrunk and sagged. This went unnoticed by Grandma, who seemed to get younger in spirit as her body aged.

"Who do we have here?" she wanted to know.

"This is Mario Rizzi, Loretta's son. Everyone calls him Zook."

"Zook," Grandma said. "That's a pip of a name. I wish I had a name like that." She took a closer look at him. "You got a awful lot of holes in you. How do you sleep with all those rings attached to your head? Don't it bother you when you roll over?"

"You get used to it," Zook said.

"You remind me of someone," Grandma said. "Stephanie, who does he look like?"

I gnawed on my lower lip. "Gee, I don't know."

Grandma snapped her fingers. "I know who it is. It's Morelli! He's the spitting image of Joseph when he was Zook's age."

"They're very, very distant cousins," I said.

Zook peeked into the living room. "This house has high speed Internet, right?"

"Sure, we got cable," Grandma said. "We're not in the Stone Age here. I blog and everything."

"I have to go," I said to Zook. "Don't paint anything. Moondog doesn't stand a chance against Grandma."

I left my parents' house and drove the short distance to Morelli's house to let Bob out to tinkle. I parked and let myself in through the front door. The house was quiet. No Bob feet galloping to greet me.

"Bob!" I yelled. "Yoohoo! Want to go out?"

Nothing. I walked through the dining room to the kitchen. Still no sign of Bob. I looked out the window over the sink and saw Bob sitting in the sun in Morelli's little backyard. Bob was wearing his collar but no leash. Morelli wasn't around. I opened the back door, and Bob rushed in, tail wagging, all smiley face.

I wasn't nearly so happy as Bob. I had creepy crawlies, plus the willies. I took Bob's leash off the kitchen counter, snapped it onto Bob's collar, and walked him straight through the house to the front door, out the door to my car.

I loaded Bob into the back of the Sentra and I called Morelli.

"I stopped by to let Bob out to tinkle, and he was sitting in your backyard," I said. "Did you let him out?"

"No. You were the last one out of the house."

"Bob was sleeping in your bed when I left. And I know your kitchen door was locked, because I remember checking it, but it was unlocked when I got here just now."

"Does it look like anything is missing? Any sign of forced entry?"

"I didn't hang around long enough to find out. I've got Bob in my car, and I'm dropping him at my mom's. You need to go home and walk through the house, and please don't do it alone, like a big, stupid, macho cop. Two break-ins in a row is too much of a coincidence. Something is going on here."

# SIX

IT HAD TAKEN me longer than I would have thought to get clothes for the dinner. I had Ranger's credit card, with a limit high enough to buy a house, but I couldn't spend beyond my own comfort zone. And then there were Ranger's rules, which he hadn't articulated but I knew existed. He'd want me in black, and he'd want me to wear something that would allow me to move about unnoticed.

I'd done a decent job, with the possible exception of the skirt. And lucky for Ranger, I'd run out of time before I got around to accessorizing at Tiffany's.

I hiked my skirt up over my knees so I wouldn't catch my heel in my hem, and I ran through the parking lot to the hotel. I was ten minutes late. I was wearing a white silk camisole under a short black satin jacket and a simple floor-length black skirt with a slit up the front that stopped a couple inches short of slut.

I barreled through the lobby and was sideswiped by the stalker. He reached out for me, and I slapped his hand away.

"I have to talk to you," he said.

"Go away," I told him, on the run for the elevator. "I'm late."

"It's important. It's about Brenda. I had another vision. There was a big pizza . . ."

I rushed into an open elevator, he tried to follow me, and I gave him a two-handed shove that sent him out of the elevator and onto his ass. The elevator doors closed and I checked my hair and makeup in the shiny gold door trim.

Ranger and Hal were in the hall when I stepped out. The shift had changed, and Tank was either getting ready to face Lula, or else he was at the airport, heading for South America and points unknown.

Ranger was wearing a perfectly fitted black tux, black shirt, black-on-black striped silk tie. I've seen him in SWAT black fatigues, black T-shirt and jeans, black slacks and jacket, and I've seen him naked. He always looks great, but Ranger in a tux was a heart-stopper. *Almost* as good as Ranger naked. Almost, because nothing was better than Ranger naked.

I returned the credit card, and he pocketed it with a smile. "Nice," he said, eyes fixed on the slit in the front of my skirt.

It was one of those moments that if Hal hadn't been present, we might have torn each other's clothes off right there in the hall.

Ranger knocked on the door, and Nancy answered.

"How long?" Ranger asked.

"Hard to say. She's undecided on gowns."

"I'm going to knock again in ten minutes, and she'll go to the dinner in whatever she's got on."

"Jeez," Nancy said. And she closed the door.

"Boy, you're tough," I told Ranger.

"It was a desperate, hollow threat."

Ten minutes to the second, the door opened, and Brenda flounced out in a very low-cut, skintight, iridescent white gown trimmed in long, fluffy white feathers. The feathers fluttered from her shoulders and the lower half of her skirt. I couldn't imagine what sort of bird had grown the fabulous feathers, but I suspected there were a lot of them running around bare-skinned.

"Wow," I said.

Brenda wiggled so the feathers would swirl around her. "It's from the Ginger Rogers collection."

No shit.

She sidled up to Ranger. "I'm not wearing panties. The dress is too tight. I thought you'd want to know."

"Eeuw," I said.

Brenda looked at me. "You have a problem with that?"

"Too much information."

Hal looked like he'd swallowed his tongue. Nancy took a large bottle of Advil from her purse, tapped out two pills, and popped them into her mouth. Ranger picked feathers off his black tux. The Ginger collection was molting.

We marched the bird-woman through the lobby to the

waiting motorcade. Downy feather remnants drifted like dust motes on air currents in our wake, and a blizzard of feathers whirled across the floor. A handful of fans and a few members of the press took pictures, and Brenda posed and smiled and flapped around.

I felt heavy breathing on the back of my neck and turned to see the stalker hovering in my personal space.

"You're breathing on me," I said to him.

"I thought if I got close enough I might be able to send you a mental message. It was an experiment."

"It failed. Go away."

"You don't understand. It's critical that I talk to you."

"No, *you* don't understand. It's critical that you go away, because if you keep bothering me, that Latino guy in the tux is going to throw you out a third-story window."

Ranger looked over at me, and the stalker backed up into a luggage cart.

Brenda moved toward the limo, and we all climbed in after her. Nancy and I sat in the seat facing backwards, and that left the seat next to Brenda for Ranger. He picked a feather out of his mouth and looked across at me and smiled. I pressed my knees together, but no matter what I did with my legs, from where he sat there was a direct line of sight up my skirt.


RANGER WALKED ME to my car in the parking lot. It was a little after midnight and Brenda was in her room, with Hal standing guard.

"That had to be the longest night in the history of the world," Ranger said. "I was captured by Colombian rebels and tortured for three days, and it was better than that dinner." He brushed feathers off his sleeve. "I don't know whether to have this cleaned or just throw it away."

"You look like you wrestled a big chicken."

He looked at my jacket and skirt. "Why aren't you covered with feathers?"

"I stayed away from Brenda."

"I didn't have that luxury," Ranger said.

"Yeah, I noticed. She was *all over you*."

He took his jacket off in an effort to distance himself from the feathers, but he had feathers stuck to his shirt. "I don't usually have that problem. Most women are afraid of me."

"Maybe she's not smart enough to be afraid of you."

"More likely, she knows I'm no match for her," Ranger said.


RANGER HAD OFFERED the use of his bed, but I didn't think that was a good idea. I'd checked on Zook, and he was with my parents, sleeping in my old bedroom. I had my own apartment, but that held little appeal tonight. Truth is, I missed Morelli. I cruised by his house and the porch light was on, so I parked and went to the door. Locked. I tried my key. Wouldn't work. He'd changed the locks. That was a relief. I rang the bell and waited. I heard the dog feet first, clattering down the wood stairs. Moments later, Morelli opened the door. He was in socks and jeans and a T-shirt. His eyes were soft and sleepy and his hair was more unruly than usual.

"I was hoping you'd come back tonight," he said. "I tried to wait up, but I fell asleep halfway through *Letterman.*"

He pulled me into the foyer and kissed me. "Did they feed you at the dinner? Do you need something to eat?"

"I'm starving."

"Me, too. I want French toast."

Morelli got the fry pan out and started it heating while I whipped eggs and soaked the bread. We sat at his kitchen table, and between the three of us, we went through almost a loaf of bread and a bottle of fake maple syrup.

I pushed back in my chair. "I see you've had your locks changed."

"Probably I should have done it sooner. I never bothered when I moved into the house. For all I know, Rose could have given keys out to half the Burg."

"So what was the deal with Bob in the backyard today?"

"I don't know," Morelli said, "but I'm not happy. I don't like people breaking into my house, and I especially don't like them messing with my dog. I went all through the house, and I couldn't see where anything was taken. It occurred to me that someone might have been dropping off rather than picking up, so I had a crew go through looking for bombs, drugs, and bugs. Nothing was found."

"I wish I could tell you more about the guy last night, but he caught me by surprise, and he was moving fast."

"Do you remember hearing a car take off?"

"No. My heart was beating so hard all I could hear was my own blood pressure. What's happening with Loretta and Zook?"

"I thought it was best to leave Zook with your parents. Loretta is still in jail."

"Have you had a chance to talk to her about the garage event?"

"No. Too many people listening. No privacy in jail. I'll wait until she's out."

Okay, I knew I shouldn't be concerned. To begin with, Morelli had way too much testosterone as a kid, but he wasn't really a bad person. And besides that, he's an amazing guy now. He's smart and responsible and honorable and loving. And it wouldn't matter if he had a son. It would feel weird, but it wouldn't matter. Having thought through all this, I was still a little freaked out.

"So what's your take on it?" I asked him, morbid curiosity winning out over trust and sensitivity. "Do you think it's possible that you're Zook's father?"

"I guess anything is possible, considering my hit-and-run lifestyle back then," Morelli said, "but I can't see me doing it with Loretta. And I think Loretta would have come to me for help by now. Besides, I always used condoms. Even in high school."

"You didn't with me."

Morelli grinned. "You were different."

"We were lucky I didn't get pregnant."

"Maybe," Morelli said. "Maybe not. If you'd gotten

81

pregnant, we'd be married now. It would all have been much more simple."

MORELLI WAS GONE when I woke up. Bob was in bed with me, and a note was attached to his collar.

> FEED BOB AND WALK HIM AND REMEMBER TO TAKE A BLUE PLASTIC BAG. MR. GORVICH (THE GROUCH NEXT DOOR) IS COMPLAINING. LOVE YOU, JOE.
>
> PS—MAKE SURE ZOOK GETS TO SCHOOL.
>
> PPS—THERE'S A NEW HOUSE KEY FOR YOU ON THE KITCHEN TABLE.

I stumbled into the bathroom, took a shower, and dressed for the day as a Rangeman employee. I dragged Bob out of bed, down to the kitchen, and fed him. Then I dragged him outside to go for a walk. I ignored Morelli's instructions and let Bob poop to his heart's content on everyone's lawns. I know it was irresponsible of me, but I wasn't up to bagging poop first thing in the morning.

I dropped my new house key into my purse and drove the short distance to my parents' house.

My mother's house always smells wonderful. Apple pie, roast turkey with stuffing, chocolate chip cookies, marinara sauce. Never air freshener. Air freshener was for sissies and slackards. My mother's house announced the day's menu. This morning, it was bacon and coffee and home fries with onion and green pepper.

Everyone was at the kitchen table when I walked in. My mother was manning the stove, frying the potatoes. My grandmother was at the table with Zook. Zook was dressed for school in his usual Gothic black getup. Grandma was a carbon copy, except for the piercings. Black jeans, black boots, black T-shirt with WARRIOR written in gold-and-red flames across her chest. Big chunky chain belt and a wooden cross on a chain around her neck. She looked like the Grandma from Hell.

"Nice outfit," I said to her. "What's the occasion?"

"I'm going online as soon as I'm done with breakfast," she said. "I'm gonna lay waste to the griefer."

I looked over at my mother and she made a gesture like she was going to hang herself.

"What's a griefer?" I asked. I'd heard Zook use the term, but I didn't actually know what it meant. I also knew Moondog was a griefer, but I didn't know what a Moondog was, either.

"A griefer's a snert," Grandma said. "A cheese player. A twink."

I nodded. "That makes it all clear."

"A cyberbully," Zook said. "I got your grandmother play-ing *Minionfire* last night, and Moondog terminated your grandma's PC. That's a player character. Had him take a dirt nap. Man, your grandma was really pissed."

My mother clanked the fry pan against the burner, and we all jumped.

"Excuse me," Zook said. "I meant she was . . . angry. Anyway, she was able to regen, and now she's rolling."

83

"Yeah," Grandma said. "I'm a newbie, so my PC runs at a pretty low level, but I've got some überelves camping for me. They're evil, but they're bitchin'.."

"Where'd you get the clothes?" I asked her.

"Harriet Gotler took me shopping after we paid our respects to Warren Kruzi. He had an early viewing. And I'm not Grandma no more," she said. "I'm Scorch."

"Scorch?"

"Yep, 'cause I'm hot. Get it? Scorch."

My mother was eyeing the cabinet alongside the stove where she kept the liquor.

"It's sort of early in the day," I told her.

She blew out a sigh and shook the potato pan. She brought it to the table and dumped the home fries into a bowl. She had eggs going in another fry pan, and she divided them up on everyone's plates.

MY STOMACH WAS filled with eggs and potatoes, Zook was at school, and I wasn't scheduled to meet with Ranger until eleven. I had a stack of skips to find, but nothing recent and nothing that interested me. For lack of something better to do, I stopped at the office.

Lula was on the couch, wading through a stack of bride magazines, marking pages with little red sticky tabs.

I looked over at Connie, and Connie did an eye roll.

"I saw that," Lula said. "Don't you do an eye roll about me. I gotta consider my options. I gotta keep an open mind. Tank could be real disappointed if he don't see me in a long white dress. And what about his mama? She could be expecting a wrist corsage. I gotta consider flowers. I don't want to get started on the wrong foot with his mama."

It was hard to imagine Tank having a mama. Much less one who would wear a wrist corsage.

"You said you didn't want a big wedding," I said to Lula.

"Yeah, but looking at the cake got the ball rolling."

"Have you talked to Tank about any of this?"

"No. I didn't see him last night. He called up and said he had one of them stomach viruses."

"Sometimes men don't like elaborate weddings," I said to Lula. Especially when they don't want to get married.

"That better not be Tank," Lula said, "on account of I'm starting to get into this wedding shit. And anyways, after all the things I do for him, the least he could do is marry me in a church and all."

"You do lots of things for Tank?"

"Well, I might in the future," Lula said.

My mother's ring tone went off on my cell phone.

"There's a strange man here, and he's looking for you," my mother said. "I told him you weren't here, but he won't go away."

"Does he have white hair and big black glasses?"

"Yes."

"I'll be right there."

"Me, too," Lula said. "Where we going? Who has white hair and glasses?"

# SEVEN

THERE WERE THREE cars lined up at the curb in front of my parents' house. The white Taurus was one of them.

"I never seen a real stalker before," Lula said. "I'm looking forward to this."

I parked in the driveway and slid from behind the wheel. "Let me do the talking. I don't want to make a big deal over this. And I especially don't want to freak my mother out."

"Sure," Lula said. "I understand that. My lips are sealed."

"And don't shoot him or gas him or fry his hair with your stun gun."

"You got a lot of rules," Lula said.

"He's harmless."

"That's what those stalkers want you to believe, and then *wham*—they get naked pictures of you and put them on the Internet."

"You have personal experience?"

"No, but I heard. Well, okay, maybe a little experience. But not with a stalker."

My mother was at the door waiting for me. "How do you attract these strange men?" my mother asked. "They're never normal."

"He's a stalker," Lula said. "He might even be dangerous."

I turned and looked at Lula. "What about the sealed lips?"

"I forgot. I got carried away."

"He's confused," I said to my mother. "I just need to talk to him. Where is he?"

"He's in the kitchen. I have a full house today. Your grandmother is in the dining room with Betty Greenblat and Ruth Szuch. They're all insane. They each have a computer, and they're playing that game. They don't even take bathroom breaks. I think they're all wearing Depends. They said they're ganging up on the griefer. They don't like being disturbed, so you have to sneak past them."

My mother, Lula, and I tiptoed past Grandma, Betty, and Ruth. They were all dressed like Zook, and they were all hunched over their computers.

"We got a bad snert here, girls," Betty said. "Let's kick ass."

"This looks like the *Queen of the Damned* costume party at the Shady Rest Nursing Home," Lula whispered to me. "Is this what the golden years looks like?"

"I heard that," Ruth said. "The golden years are for pussies. We went straight to brass."

The stalker was in the kitchen stirring a pot of chili. He did a big smile when he saw me. "Surprise," he said.

"So you're the stalker," Lula said, looking him over. "I thought you'd be nastier. You're kind of a disappointment."

"Yeah," he said, "I'm not any good at this. I can't get anyone to pay attention to me."

"You gotta look assertive if you want people to hear you," Lula said. "You gotta talk with authority. You gotta walk the walk and use the language. You see what I'm saying?"

"I guess so. I guess I could try that." He stiffened his spine and pointed his finger at me. "Listen, bitch . . ."

My mother gave him a whack on the head with her wooden spoon. "Behave yourself."

"Don't you have anything better to do?" I asked him. "Don't you have a job?"

"I'm currently between positions. I had a job, but then I had the dream, and I had to give the job up so I could follow Brenda around."

"Okay, now we're getting somewhere," Lula said. "This is about a dream?"

"I told all this to the police and the judge and the psychiatrist," the stalker said.

"Then you should have the story down good," Lula said. "Tell it to me."

"Three years ago, I was struck by lightning in the Wal-Mart parking lot. All my hair fell out, and when it grew back, it was this white color. And I was sort of psychic. Like sometimes people glow and I can see their aura."

"Oh yeah? What's my aura?" Lula wanted to know.

"I'm not seeing one right now."

"Hunh," Lula said. "Some psychic. Can't even see my aura. I bet I have a hell of a aura, too."

"Wait a minute. I think I'm starting to see one. It's . . . red."

"That's a powerful color," Lula said.

"Anyway, sometimes I have these vision dreams that I'm pretty sure mean something. And I started having them about Brenda. And I got this feeling that I was supposed to be protecting her. You know, like staying close by for when I got a vision of danger."

"What's this vision of danger look like?" Lula asked him.

"It's . . . um, a pizza."

"Say what?"

"It's a *big* pizza. It's symbolic. See, there's Brenda, and there's this big pizza she's running away from."

"Maybe you're the pizza," Lula said.

"Or maybe the danger is that she'll get fat if she eats the big pizza," I said.

He shook his head. "No, this is an evil pizza. It's none of those things."

"And you told this to the psychiatrist and he still let you run around loose?" Lula said.

"I'm not considered dangerous," he said. "Just annoying."

"Here's the deal," I said to him. "I promise to keep my eyes open for the big pizza, if you'll go away."

"How about if I just keep a distance?"

"Sure. But it has to be out of sight."

"Okay. And I'll let you know right away if I get any more messages."

"Deal," I said.

I walked him out of the kitchen, past Grandma and the ladies, and into the hall. I watched him leave, and then I locked and bolted the front door.

When I got back to the kitchen, my mother had the spray bottle of bleach in hand and she was disinfecting the counters and the stalker's chair. "Marion Zajak's daughter doesn't have stalkers. Catherine Bargalowski's daughter doesn't have stalkers. Why do I have to be the one with the daughter who has stalkers? Isn't it enough that my mother kills griefers? I mean, what kind of a woman kills griefers? Can she go to jail for that? Am I an accomplice?"

Grandma came into the kitchen. "That no-good son of a peach basket ganked me. I had my bitches here and I still got ganked."

"You didn't kill the griefer, did you?" my mother asked.

"No. Aren't you listening? He *ganked* me."

My mother and I had no clue what happened when someone got ganked, but it didn't sound good.

"Thank heaven," my mother said. And she made the sign of the cross.

"I got big news," Lula said, flashing the ring. "Notice anything new?"

"Wow, that's a pip of a ring," Grandma said.

"I'm engaged to my big sweet potato, Tank," Lula said. "I'm thinking of a June wedding."

"You can't go wrong with a June wedding," Grandma said. "Do you have the hall?"

"No," Lula said. "I only just got started."

"What about flowers?" Grandma asked.

"I was thinking little pink sweetheart roses."

"You could put them on the cake, too. Only make them out of icing," Grandma said. "And then you need table decorations, and what color were you gonna use for brides-maids?"

"Pink," Lula said. "Everything could be pink, like the roses. It could be my theme. I read in one of the maga-zines the best weddings have themes."

"They're more memorable that way," Grandma said.

Lula's eyes got wide. "I just got the best idea. We could put Tank in a pink tuxedo."

"I've never seen a groom in a pink tuxedo," Grandma said. "It might make the news. You could be on television."

"It would look real good with his skin tone," Lula said. "We might have to get it made special, though. I should get started right away."

I wasn't a Tank expert, but I was pretty sure he'd drive his car off a bridge before he'd be seen in a pink tuxedo.

"I'm going back online, and I'm gonna get my chameleon going," Grandma said. "I might even raise my sneak level and go invisible. I got a feeling about the griefer. There's something familiar about him."

Connie called on my cell. "Good news," she said. "Dom

just bailed Loretta out. He got their mother to use her house as collateral."

"I thought her mother was in rehab."

"She is. I didn't look too hard at the signature. Here's the problem. I can't leave the office, and I need someone to spring Loretta and drive her home. Dom won't go anywhere near the jail."

# EIGHT

"I JUST WANT to go home and take a shower and get into clean clothes," Loretta said. "And for the rest of my life, I don't want to ever see a Tom Collins."

I turned down her street, and a block away we could see the disaster. There was a mound of furniture and assorted junk at the curb in front of her house.

"Shit," Loretta said. "It's that bastard slum lord who owns my house. He's evicted me."

I parked and looked at Loretta's front door. It had a board nailed across it and an eviction notice tacked to the board.

"You had to know this was coming," I said to Loretta.

"I was behind on my rent, but I was hoping he'd give me another month. We're coming into wedding season, and the firehouse is booked solid with showers and receptions. I could have caught up this month."

She wrenched the passenger-side door open and got out and stood staring at all her worldly possessions.

"Is this everything?" I asked her.

"Yeah," she said. "Pathetic, isn't it? Most of the big furniture pieces, like the beds and the couch, came with the rental."

"You need to get this trucked out of here. There's not that much. You could haul it in a pickup and store it in your mom's garage."

"I don't have a phone," she said. "My phone went dead in jail."

I gave her my phone, and she called Dom.

Forty minutes later, Dom rolled in driving a rattletrap truck. He pulled to the curb, and I took off. I didn't want another confrontation with crazy Dom, and I was due at the hotel at eleven. I was wearing black slacks and black boots, a stretchy white T-shirt, and a fitted black leather jacket. I was ready to represent Rangeman.

TANK WAS ON guard in front of Brenda's suite when I stepped out of the elevator. I tried to imagine him in a pink tuxedo, but the picture wouldn't come together.

"How's it going?" I asked him.

"Good," he said.

"No trouble with Brenda?"

"No."

So much for conversation.

At precisely eleven o'clock, Ranger arrived, walked straight to Brenda's door, and knocked.

Nancy opened the door a crack and looked out at Ranger.

"The car is here," Ranger said.

Nancy grimaced. "She can't get her eyelashes on."

"And?"

"She can't do television without eyelashes."

Ranger looked over at me. "You want to step in here and translate?"

"*False* eyelashes," I told him. "Doesn't the station have someone doing makeup?" I asked Nancy.

"No. Budget cuts. We have hair and makeup coming in from New York for the concert, but there was a scheduling screwup and they won't arrive in time for this television show."

"Good grief," I said. "This isn't rocket science." I pushed past Nancy and found Brenda in the bathroom, fiddling with her hair. She was wearing a white stretch wraparound shirt that tied in the front and showed a lot of cleavage and a lot of skin between the bottom of the shirt and the top of her jeans. She had her hair in two ponytails. She looked like Daisy Duke.

I looked at the mess of makeup spread out on the bathroom counter. She had individual lashes, which would take an hour to get on, and she had strip lashes, which any idiot could glue to her lids in ten seconds.

"I can do this," I told her. "We'll go with the strip lashes. You don't have time for the individuals."

"Are you a professional?" she asked.

"Even better. I'm from the Burg. I was putting lashes on my Barbie doll when I was seven. Close your eyes."

I glued the lashes to her eyes and swiped on liquid eyeliner. I looked at my watch. Ten minutes late. Could be worse.

We maneuvered Brenda through the lobby to a side exit, where three black Rangeman SUVs idled. Ranger, Nancy, Brenda, and I got into the middle car, and we all cruised off into traffic.

I was in the backseat, and I was thinking I should be sort of excited to be part of Brenda's entourage. After all, she was a star. And she was going to be on television. And I was going to be a backstage insider for the concert. That's a big deal, right? Problem was, she didn't look like a star up close. She looked like she sold real estate to people with more money than brains.

It was a short ride to the station. We signed in at the front desk and followed an intern through a maze of shabby corridors to the green room, which turned out to be painted tan. Some pastries and fruit and coffee had been set out. There were some dog-eared magazines on a side table. The upholstered couch and chairs were leather and slightly shabby. The carpet was the color of dirt.

We all took a seat and watched the television set that was tuned to the station. This was midday news and the anchors and guests were wearing conservative suits. Brenda looked like she was ready to get raffled off at a hoedown.

"How do I look?" Brenda asked Nancy. "Do I look okay?

Is my hair okay?" She reached in and rearranged her breasts. "Are the girls okay?"

"Remember to plug the concert tonight," Nancy said. "We need to sell tickets."

The producer popped in with the soundman, and they hooked a mic to Brenda and led her away.

"I don't have to do this," Nancy said. "I could get lots of good jobs. I could sell shoes at Macy's, or I could clean kennel cages."

Ranger was on his cell phone, conducting business. His eyes were on me, but his thoughts were elsewhere. Nancy and I, smelling disaster, nervously scarfed down doughnuts.

A man and a woman were anchoring the news. They talked a little about the concert, and they introduced Brenda. And then Brenda was suddenly onstage, in a chair next to the female anchor. Brenda's legs were demurely crossed and her bulging breasts looked like polished marble. She was all smiles and white teeth and sparkling eyes. Brenda was stunning. Something happened between Brenda and the camera. Even the whole Daisy Duke thing was working.

Nancy had her fingers in her ears and her eyes squinched shut. "Tell me when it's over."

"It's good," I told her. "You have to see this. She's beautiful."

Nancy opened one eye. "Really?"

"It's magic," I said to her.

"I just love it here," Brenda said to the anchor. "I'm in Trenton, right?"

The anchors laughed. Brenda was adorable.

"Everyone is wondering about your love life," the anchor said. "There's a rumor that you're engaged . . . again."

Brenda clapped her hands over her eyes. "Good Lord," she said. "No way!"

She took her hands away and a feathery black object dropped onto her cheek.

Nancy leaned forward. "What *is* that?"

Brenda's eyes crossed as she focused on the thing on her face, and hysteria jolted her out of her chair. "Spider," she shrieked, jumping around, slapping at her face. "Spider, *spider!*"

Nancy and I were mouths open, eyes wide, watching the television. Even Ranger turned his attention from his phone call to the show.

A stagehand rushed onto the set, tackled Brenda, and dragged her back to her chair.

"What was that?" Brenda asked. "Is it gone? Is it dead?"

One of the anchors picked the thing off the floor and looked at it. "It's a strip of eyelashes."

Brenda blinked and put a finger to her eye. "Oh shit!"

Nancy's face went white. "She just said *shit* on television. And if that isn't awful enough, she looks ridiculous. She's only got lashes on one eye."

"It's not my bad," I said. "I swear. She rubbed her eyes! Everyone knows you don't rub your eyes when you've got lashes glued on!"

"I wouldn't worry about it," Ranger said. "No one looks at her eyes."

Five minutes later, Brenda stormed into the room. "That was so hideous," she said, teeth clenched. "My eyelash fell off. Did you see it? I thought it was a spider." She looked around the room, finally finding me. "You!" she said, pointing her finger. "This is all your fault. You're the one who glued the eyelash. You said you knew what you were doing, but obviously that was a lie."

"You rubbed your eye. The eyelash would have been fine if you hadn't rubbed your eye."

"I'm leaving now," Brenda said, head high. "And I don't want this horrible liar in my car. Does everybody understand that?"

"She's part of your security detail, and she's going in your car," Ranger said.

"Then I'm not going."

"No problem," I said. "I'll ride in one of the other cars, and we'll sort this out later." Hallelujah! With any luck, I'd get fired.

RANGER'S MEN STAYED with the cars at the hotel's side entrance. Ranger, Nancy, and Brenda had taken the elevator to Brenda's floor. And I was waiting in the lobby. Ranger's orders. Hard to tell what would happen next, but I suspected I wouldn't be seeing the concert.

I saw the stalker coming at me from across the room. He was smiling and waving like we were old friends.

"Hi," he said. "Remember me?"

"Of course, I remember you. You're the stalker."

"I just wanted to tell you everything seems to be okay, cosmically speaking."

"Good to know."

"I saw Brenda on television this morning. She did fabulous. And the eyelash bit was funny. Tell her I liked the eyelash bit."

"Okeydokey. I'll pass it on."

The elevator binged, Ranger stepped out, and the stalker scurried away. Ranger crossed over to me, his eyes on the stalker, who was now hiding behind a big potted plant.

"Is he bothering you?" Ranger asked.

"No. He's harmless."

"Let me know if that changes. Tank is on hall duty. Nancy is in the suite with Brenda. You're off the hook for a couple hours, but you need to be back here to get Brenda to her sound check at four. They'll run through the show, and then Brenda will stay there for makeup and wardrobe. Don't let her out of your sight. I won't be able to go to the sound check, so you're in charge until I get there."

"*What?* You aren't serious! I was counting on being fired."

"Why would I fire you?"

"The eyelash."

"Babe, you've gotta do a lot better than that to get fired."

"I can't get Brenda to the sound check. She hates me. She won't listen to me."

"You'll figure it out," Ranger said. "I have to go. I'll see you tonight."

I blew out a sigh and hiked to my car. Easy to find it these days with *Zook* written in Day-Glo paint all over it. I drove to the office and parked at the curb.

Lula was on the phone when I walked into the office. "What do you think about having fireworks go off after the ceremony?" she asked me. "It's part of the package if you have the reception at the VFW hall. They ring the church bells, and then they shoot off fireworks."

"I guess that could be fun," I said.

"Yeah, we'll consider the fireworks," Lula said into the phone. "And maybe while the fireworks are going off, you could serve some of them pigs in a blanket. I love them little things." She listened for another minute and disconnected. "That went real good," she said. "They had a cancellation on a baby shower, and I was able to sneak in."

"Isn't all this going to come to a lot of money?" I asked her. "The gown, the cake, the flowers, the hall, the pigs in a blanket, the fireworks?"

"A wedding is priceless. A girl only gets married once."

"Not the girls in this room," Connie said. "Have you thought about a prenup?"

Lula's eyes widened. "A prenup? You think I need one?"

"He could end up getting your Firebird."

"No way! Not my Firebird."

"And what about your house?"

"I just rent an apartment. I own the couch, though. He better not try to take my couch or my TV."

"You need a lawyer," Connie said.

Lula took a pad out of her purse. "I'll put it on my list.

Now that I'm getting married, I'm more detail-oriented. I'm keeping track of things in my pad."

"How's the Brenda job going?" Connie asked. "What's she like?"

"She's just like she is on television, but she's prettier on television. I need someone to help me get her to a sound check at four. Any takers?"

"Is there money in it?" Lula asked.

"Yeah. You'll be on Ranger's payroll."

"I never been on Ranger's payroll before," Lula said. "I'll do it."

"If you represent Ranger, you have to be dressed in black. I'll meet you in the hotel lobby at three-thirty."

"That don't hardly give me any time," Lula said. "I gotta get home to my apartment and change my makeup if I'm wearing black. And then I got wardrobe decisions to make."

"You have hours."

"Yeah, but this here's important. I'm gonna be mingling with all them entertainment people. This could be my big break. I could get discovered."

Lula left, but I stayed at the office and did some phone work on a couple skips. At three-fifteen, I swiped on some mascara and lipgloss and headed out. At three-thirty, I was in the lobby, waiting for Lula. I didn't see Brenda's stalker, but I knew he was somewhere nearby.

Lula barreled into the lobby through the front door and motored across the floor. She was in black heels and black stockings and a short, totally sequined, tight black skirt.

Her boobs were overflowing out of a black satin bustier, and she had it all topped off with a black satin tuxedo jacket. Her hair was Budweiser red. I suspected she was also wearing a Glock at the small of her back, under the jacket.

"Hey, girlfriend," she said. "Let's rock and roll."

"Brenda might not be too happy to see me," I said to Lula in the elevator. "She had a makeup malfunction on television, and at first glance, it might have seemed to be my fault."

"Are you talking about the eyelash fiasco? Connie and me almost wet our pants."

The elevator doors opened at Brenda's floor, and I looked out at Tank, standing halfway down the hall in front of the suite.

"It's my sweetie!" Lula shrieked, taking off at a run on the stiletto heels.

Tank froze, deer in the headlights. Except with Tank, it was more like rhino in the headlights. Lula grabbed Tank and gave him a kiss, and Tank broke out in a sweat.

"Ranger bailed on the sound check," I told Tank, "so I brought Lula to help out."

Tank almost smiled. He knew Ranger would have a seizure at the thought of Lula working for him.

"I'm all dressed in Rangeman colors," Lula said to Tank.

"Yeah," Tank said. "You look fine."

"And I've been working on our wedding all day," Lula told him. "I've got all the details worked out, so you don't have to worry about anything. I know you want the whole big deal with the fireworks and me in a veil and a gown with a big long train and all, so I've got it all goin' on. And all you gotta do is go for a fitting for your tuxedo."

The sweat was dripping off Tank's chin onto his T-shirt. "Tuxedo?" he said. "Fireworks?"

"And lots of pigs in a blanket. You like pigs in a blanket, right?"

"Yeah," Tank said.

"Then it's all settled," Lula told him.

"I got it covered here," I said to Tank. "Maybe you want to take a break."

Tank nodded but didn't move.

"You aren't going to faint again, are you?" I asked him.

"Tank don't faint," Lula said. "Look at how big he is. He got a circulation system like a steam engine."

I knocked on Brenda's door and Nancy answered.

"Uh-oh," she said when she saw me.

"Ranger is busy," I told her. "Lula and I are here to take Brenda to the sound check."

Nancy looked at Lula and gasped.

"Who's there?" Brenda called from the bedroom. "Is it Mr. Hard Ass?"

I pushed my way into the suite. "Mr. Hard Ass is busy. It's the eyelash expert and her sidekick, Lula. The cars are downstairs, waiting."

Brenda power-walked out of the bedroom. "I am *not* going with you. You destroyed my good reputation. I have an image to uphold. I was a beauty queen. I was America's Sweetheart. I've gone platinum."

"And I was a 'ho," Lula said. "What's that got to do with the price of beans?"

Brenda's eyebrows raised up an inch. "Were you really a 'ho? I've never met a real 'ho before."

"Probably you did," Lula said. "There's lots of 'hos out there, but we look just like regular people."

Brenda and I stared at Lula for a couple beats. Lula didn't nearly look like a regular person.

"So let's get a move on," Lula said. "I don't want to miss nothing on this sound check."

We moved out of the room, into the hall, and hustled into the elevator. We dropped to the lobby, started across the floor, and Brenda spotted the stalker.

"There's Gary," she said. "He's not supposed to be here. I had a restraining order put on him. He should be home with his mother. Ever since he got hit by that lightning, he hasn't been right."

"You know him?"

"He's my cousin. Before the lightning hit him, he had brown hair. Can you imagine that?"

"He said I had a red aura," Lula said.

"You go on home," Brenda yelled across the room to Gary. "I'll get the police after you if I see you again."

"Watch out for the pizza," Gary yelled back.

We climbed into one of the black SUVs and my cell phone rang.

"Where are you?" Zook asked.

"I'm in a car," I said. "Where are you?"

"I'm at school, waiting for someone to pick me up."

"Your mother got bonded out this morning. She was supposed to pick you up."

"She isn't here."

"Okay, stay right there, and I'll get back to you."

I dialed Dom.

"What?" Dom said.

"I'm looking for Loretta."

"She went to get the kid."

"He just called me. He's on the street, waiting."

"She left an hour ago," he said. "Maybe she went to the store or something."

I couldn't see Loretta doing that. She would have been anxious to see her son. She would have gone to the store after she picked him up.

"Oh shit!" Dom said, panic-voiced. "I gotta go." And he hung up.

I redialed. No answer. I called Morelli.

"Something's not right," I said to him. "I can't locate Loretta."

"Do you think she skipped again?"

"I don't know what I think, but I have a bad feeling in my stomach. I got a call from Zook. She never picked him up. I called Dom, and he said she left an hour ago. Some-one has to get Zook."

"Dom?"

"He hung up on me, and I can't get him back."

"Then I guess *you* have to get Zook."

"I can't get Zook. I'm working. You have to get him."

"I can't get him. I'm in the middle of something."

"What?"

"Baseball. You know I play ball with the guys every Thursday."

I rolled my eyes so severely I almost fell off my seat. "Please help me out here," I said. "He's your . . . cousin."

"Okay," Morelli said. "But only because you said *please*."

The SUVs wound their way into the arena back lot, and we off-loaded at the door. The lot held the semis that haul the staging and sound equipment, two band buses, a bunch of cop cars, and a SAT TV truck.

"This is just about the most exciting thing I've ever done," Lula said. "This is better than when Grandma Mazur burned the funeral home down. There were TV trucks from all over the place covering that."

A woman who looked like a Nancy clone led us through the maze of cinderblock corridors to the area set aside for costume changes and makeup. Twenty to thirty people milled around a couple tables of catered food. Electrical cables snaked along the floor, and the whole deal felt like the circus was in town.

Brenda's arrival prompted a flurry of activity. The stage manager, the bandleader, the makeup wrangler, the hairdresser, and the wardrobe specialist clustered around her. I followed Ranger's instructions and kept Brenda in sight, but I did it from a distance. Brenda was suddenly the consummate professional. She answered questions, she made decisions, she followed instructions. People drifted away from the food to do their jobs, and Lula, Nancy, and I waited backstage while everyone walked through the show.

"This here's what I should be doing," Lula said. "I always wanted to be a supermodel, but now I see I should be a singer. I've been doing gigs with Sally Sweet, but it don't showcase my talent. I need to be out there on that stage with a whole bunch of half-naked men dancing behind me."

I gnawed on my lip a little.

"What?" Lula said.

"Nothing."

"Yessir, there's something."

"You can't sing."

"Yeah, but I look real good, and if the band plays loud enough, it don't matter. I think I could be a real star."

My phone rang and I stepped into the corridor to talk.

"I got Zook and I left him with your mother," Morelli said. "Then I rode around the neighborhood looking for Loretta's car. I found it three blocks from her mother's house. No Loretta, but her purse was on the passenger seat and there was blood on the steering wheel and door."

I put my hand to the wall to steady myself. "How much blood?"

"Not a lot. I'm guessing she was wrestled out of the car."

"And what about Dom?"

"Vanished."

"Now what?"

"I have a crime scene guy here, examining the car. And I put out an informal request to look for Loretta and Dom.

The mother's house wasn't locked, so I'm going back there to snoop around. How's it going with you?"

"Could be worse."

The sound check lasted an hour. When it was over, the Nancy clone fetched us back to the dressing rooms and Lula, Nancy, and I mooched food while Brenda settled into a director's chair and the makeup wrangler started working on her. An hour later, the makeup thing was still going on and the hair guy had Brenda's hair rolled up in curlers the size of soup cans.

"You're eating a lot of doughnuts," Lula said to me. "Something bothering you?"

"I'm worried about Loretta. She's disappeared."

"That was fast."

I told Lula about the car.

"That's ugly," Lula said. "I don't like the way that sounds."

My mother's number popped up on my cell screen. It was my Grandma Mazur.

"We're on to the griefer," Grandma yelled into the phone. "We got him on the run. We're moving the operation to Morelli's house, so the griefer can't track us."

"Why would he track you?"

"Griefers are like that," Grandma said. "And anyway, we're driving your mother nuts."

# NINE

I HAD ARRANGED for three comped tickets to be left at will call for Morelli, Zook, and Grandma. I thought it would help to take Zook's mind off his mom. Morelli phoned at seven to tell me they were in the building and so far, no word on Loretta.

"After the show, I'm bringing Zook back to my house," Morelli said. "He's persona non grata with your mother. He spray-painted his name on your mother's sidewalk and front door, and then your grandmother spray-painted *Scorch* on everything, including your parents' ninety-two-year-old neighbor, Mrs. Ciak. They said it was to throw the griefer off."

"You need to talk to Zook. He needs a father figure."

"I know *nothing* about being a father."

"You're good with Bob. Just pretend he's Bob. Remember when Bob ate all your furniture? How did you get Bob to stop?"

"I didn't. He still eats the furniture. He has me trained to live with it."

"You're just a big softy," I said to Morelli.

"Don't tell anyone, okay? I don't want that to get around. I have to go. I can't let Zook wander away from me. I'm afraid he'll redecorate the men's room."

Ranger strolled in at ten after seven.

"Where were you?" I asked him.

"Meetings with house security and checking the building." He glanced across the hall to Lula, who was taking pointers from the makeup lady. "I understand I have a new employee."

"I needed someone to help persuade Brenda to come with me."

"Looks like it worked."

"How's Tank doing?"

"He's confused. If this goes on much longer, I might have to kill Lula."

"You're kidding, right?"

Ranger didn't answer.

"*Right?*" I asked him again.

He hooked an arm around my neck, pulled me to him, and kissed me on the top of my head. "I'm kidding. But it *is* tempting."

"So what's going on out there? Bomb threats? Animal rights activists? Stalkers? Women against boobs?"

"No bomb threats. All the other crazies are in full force. Never have a rock concert on a full moon."

"How were ticket sales?"

"She sold out. Not a lot to do in Trenton this week. And Brenda still has a lot of fans. Mostly your parents' generation."

Truth is, I liked Brenda's music. She had a brassy way of combining country and rock, and she could really belt it out when she wanted. At least, that was true of her last album, but that was a bunch of years ago. I suspected that, in spite of all her efforts, she wasn't capturing the kids. And the kids were the ones who spent money on music. The kids bought sex, and Brenda was good, but she wasn't sexy to a sixteen-year-old. Even the Stones were struggling with that . . . and they were *the Stones*!

Brenda spotted Ranger and blew him a kiss.

"Sorry," I said to Ranger, "you can't kill her, either."

"I'm getting nervous," Brenda said. "I'm gonna throw up. I need a drink. I need a pill. Somebody get me something."

"You'll be fine," Nancy told her.

"I *need* a *pill*."

"Last time you took a pill before a performance, you fell off the stage."

"Yes, but it was a *lot* of pills on that occasion."

Lula stood hands on hips. "You don't need no pills," she said. "You're a professional. Get a grip on yourself."

"You don't know what it's like," Brenda said. "I had a chili dog for dinner. Suppose I fart?"

"You're in Trenton. No one would notice a fart," Lula said.

―――

AFTER THE CONCERT, we immediately hustled Brenda off the stage, through the maze of corridors, out the door to the secure lot.

"I was hot," Brenda said. "I remembered all the words to the songs. And I didn't knock any of the dancers down."

"You were great," Nancy said. "The concert was fabulous."

We wedged Brenda into the SUV's backseat between Ranger and me. Nancy and Lula were behind us. We rolled out of the lot with a police escort. We didn't need the police, but the concert promoter wanted the flashing lights.

"So what about it?" Brenda asked Ranger.

"No," Ranger said.

"I swear, you aren't any fun at all. What's the deal with you? I know you aren't gay. You aren't nice enough to be gay."

The caravan pulled up to the front entrance of the hotel and photographers rushed out to take pictures. Local television was inside, plus a handful of journalists. And scattered in the mix were random fans and special-interest protestors hoping to get a spot on the evening news. Ranger got out first, then Brenda, and then the rest of us. Brenda posed for photos and made her way through the big glass doors into the lobby. The local anchor was waiting for an interview. Brenda stepped up to the anchor, and the circle of fans and photographers closed in.

"We need space," the anchor said.

"I'm on it," Lula told her. "You people better back up, or I'm gonna sit on you. Oops, did I step on your foot with my high heels? 'Scuse me. Sorry I got you with my elbow. Coming back. *Beep, beep, beep.* I got a gun . . . you better listen to me."

"Do you really have a gun?" the anchor asked.

"Sure I got a gun. What kind of half-assed security would I be without a gun? 'Course, I'm just moonlighting here for a friend. Stephanie and me are mostly bounty hunters. And I sing with a band. You might want to have me on your show sometime. I got moves." Lula snapped her fingers and stuck out a hip. *"Woo!"* she said.

Ranger had me by the back of my jacket. "Get her out of here before she tells them she works for me. I'll get Hal to help me with Brenda."

I PARKED IN front of Morelli's house, and Morelli pulled in behind me.

"That was great," Zook said. "Everyone at school's gonna be way jealous. And Joe used the Kojak light to get us through traffic."

Morelli opened the front door, and Bob bounced out at us. He ran to a patch of wilted grass, tinkled, and ran back inside the house.

I followed Bob through the house to the kitchen. I gave Bob a dog biscuit, and I looked in the freezer for ice cream. Hooray! A new tub of chocolate.

Morelli and I sat at the little kitchen table and ate our ice cream. Zook took his into the living room and went online.

"Do you think he should be online at this hour?" I asked Morelli. "It's a school night."

"When I was his age, I was stealing cars at this time of the night, and you were sneaking out your parents' bathroom window."

"Yeah, but we're on the other side now. We're supposed to be smarter than Zook."

"I just spent half a day with him, and I'm not sure I'm smarter. And I'm not sure I feel comfortable being on the other side. It's like I fast-forwarded my life by fifteen years."

"He's not here," Zook said from the living room.

"Who?" I asked.

"The griefer. Moondog. He's always here, but now he's not."

"Maybe you and Grandma scared him off."

The doorbell rang, and Morelli and I did raised eyebrows. It was late for someone to be visiting.

Morelli went to the door, and I trailed behind. With the way things were going, it could be Dom or Loretta or a cop with bad news.

Morelli opened the door, and we both gaped at the guy on the porch. He was my age and just under six feet tall, with shoulder-length, light brown hair, parted in the middle. He was slim and pale, dressed in baggy jeans and a *Fruits Basket* T-shirt.

"I'm looking for Zook," he said.

I switched the porch light on and stared out at him. "Mooner?"

He squinted back at me. "Stephanie Plum?" He turned his attention to Morelli. "And the dude! Whoa, this is too heavy. What's going on? You aren't Zook, are you?"

I'd gone to high school with Walter MoonMan Dunphy. MoonMan was the class stoner and voted most likely to get adopted by a little old lady. He drifted in and out of people's lives, happy to get the occasional bowl of ice cream or cat kibble. He used to live with two other losers on Grant Street, but last I heard he'd moved back home with his mother.

"*I'm* Zook," Mario said from the couch.

Mooner looked in at him. "The little dude is Zook. I can dig it. It's always a little dude."

"Who are you?" Zook asked.

"I'm Moondog."

"No way!"

"Way, man," Mooner said. "I hacked this address. I wanted to see what you looked like. Man, you're harsh. I was having a good run, and you rained on my parade. You and Scorch. I'm, like, all bummed now."

"It's not like we finished you off," Zook said.

"Dude, it was only a matter of time. And Scorch is an animal. Scorch comes on, and I can smell sulfur."

"So, you're the griefer," Morelli said. "How'd that happen?"

Mooner shrugged. "Destiny, dude."

"What are you going to do now?" Zook asked Mooner. "You still have a powerful PC."

"Yeah, but not as powerful as yours. You could go all the

way. You could be the Mega Mage of wizards. You could rule Minionfire."

"Do you really think so?"

"Yeah, but you'd have to make a deal with the wood elves."

"I don't like the wood elves."

"They're okay. They're misunderstood."

"Maybe we could form an alliance, and then *you* could deal with the wood elves," Zook said.

"An alliance would be cool," Mooner said. "We'd need an awesome name . . . like the Legion of Q."

"What's Q?" Zook asked.

"It's everything. It's the big Q. It's, like . . . wind, man."

Mooner dragged his backpack in from the front porch and took his laptop out. "I'll send a pigeon to the king of the wood elves."

"You're going to need a drug test before you run an alliance from my house," Morelli said to Mooner.

"Hey, I'm clean. Swear to God. You gotta be sharp to be a griefer of my magnitude."

We let Mooner send a pigeon, and then we kicked him out, and we all went to bed.

I was so relieved to be off the Brenda job that I fell asleep instantly and slept like the dead. I didn't wake up until Morelli kissed me good-bye the next morning.

"I set the alarm," he said. "You can't oversleep today. You have to get Zook off to school."

I listened to his tread on the stairs and heard the front door open and close. And then two shots from a high-powered rifle shattered the early morning quiet. I flew out of bed and ran to the window. Morelli's SUV was still at the curb, but I didn't see Morelli. I grabbed some clothes off the floor, rammed myself into them, and ran to the stairs. I was halfway down the stairs when I realized Morelli was back in the house, in the foyer, talking on his cell phone.

"What the heck was that?" I asked him. "Are you okay?"

Morelli slid his phone into his pocket. "Yeah, I'm okay. That was crazy Dom. I saw him. He stepped right out where I could see him and opened fire on me! I don't know if he's a lousy shot or if he just meant to scare me. Anyway, he fired two rounds and took off. I called it in to dispatch. If he stays in that same car, there's a good chance someone will pick him up."

I looked up the stairs. No sign of Zook.

"I guess the Legion of Q isn't bothered by gunfire," Morelli said. "He probably sleeps wearing earbuds hooked to his computer so he can listen for the wood elves."

I DROPPED ZOOK off at school and went home to my apartment. I gave Rex fresh water, a bowl of hamster crunchies, and a potato chip. He rushed out of his soup can, twitched his whiskers at me, stuffed the potato chip into his cheek pouch, and scurried back into his soup can. It's easy to have a decent relationship with a hamster. So little is required.

I took a shower and changed into clean clothes. No more Rangeman black. That job was done. I was about to get a pot of coffee going when Connie called.

"You need to come to the office," she said. "We have a situation."

"What does that mean? What's a situation?"

"You have to see for yourself."

I locked up my apartment and went down to the lot to the Zook car. I checked the sky. No clouds. That meant no rain. The paint wouldn't get washed away again today. When I picked Zook up from school, I was going to make him wash my car. And then I'd have him scrub my mom's door and sidewalk.

Ten minutes later, I cruised by the office. Lula's Firebird was parked curbside behind a black stretch limo and a TV news van. Just keep driving, I told myself. This smells like Brenda.

I was two blocks away when my phone rang.

"We saw you drive by," Connie said.

"Maybe it wasn't me."

"How many cars have *Zook* written all over them?"

"I couldn't find a parking place."

"There's lots of parking. Lula's outside waiting for you to turn around. If you don't turn around, she's going to get in her car and come after you."

"I'm pretty sure I could lose her."

"I wouldn't count on it. She's really motivated."

I hung up, hooked a U-turn, and parked in front of the limo.

Lula came running. "Hurry up!" she yelled at me. "Everybody's inside waiting for you!"

She was dressed entirely in black leather. High-heeled

stiletto boots, short black leather skirt, black leather bustier, and a black leather bomber jacket that had CRIME BUSTERS stitched in gold on the back. If you were a guy and you ordered a dominatrix by the pound, Lula would be a wet dream come true.

I got out of the Zookmobile and followed Lula into the office. Brenda was there with her hair teased up. She was dressed in tight black leather pants and a black leather vest. Nothing under the vest but Brenda. Nancy was with her, plus a man and a woman I didn't know. A camera crew sat slouched on the couch, their equipment at their feet.

"What's up?" I asked, not actually wanting to hear the answer.

"This is Mark Bird and his producer, Jenny Walen," Nancy said. "Some suit at Fox was watching the local feed last night and got the brilliant idea of teaming Brenda up with you and Lula on a bust for a Sunday-night special. Mark is going to run point with it."

I put my finger to my eye to stop the twitching. "Don't we already have enough bounty hunter shows on television?"

"Not with Brenda," Mark said. "I think we could really get ratings with this. It would be a cross between *Dog the Bounty Hunter* and Paris Hilton's *The Simple Life*."

Eeek!

"Trouble is, you're not dressed the part," Lula said to me. "You gotta be in black leather."

"I'm not wearing black leather," I told her. "And you shouldn't, either. You look like an S&M ad."

"This is bounty hunter clothes," Lula said. "All the bounty hunters on television wear clothes like this."

I pressed my finger harder against my eyeball. "First off, no real bond enforcer dresses like that. It's like announcing, *Here comes the bounty hunter*. And second, my mother would have a heart attack if she saw me in that getup."

"Yeah, but you're always giving your mother a heart attack," Lula said. "And anyways, you haven't seen the best part. They had jackets made for us. And they got the show's name on the back and our names on the front. It's like we're Charlie's Angels."

"For crissake," Brenda said to me. "You're a bounty hunter. Buy into the stereotype and get it over with. And here's something to consider. I'm getting a crack at reality TV, and I'll kick your ass from here to kingdom come if you screw it up for me."

"I think you should ask Ranger to do this," I said to Nancy. "He'd be a better partner for Brenda."

"We already asked him, and he turned it down," Brenda said.

"This isn't a good idea," I said to Connie.

"They called Vinnie last night, and *he* thinks it's a great idea. It's out of my hands."

"Can I discuss this with you in private?" Lula said to me. "Would you step into my office behind the building for a moment?"

I followed Lula past the bank of file cabinets and through the storeroom to the back door. We stepped outside and stood on the small patch of blacktop that was allocated as emergency parking . . . an emergency usually being when someone is trying to collect money from Vinnie and he doesn't want his car to be seen in front of the agency.

"This here's my big opportunity," Lula said. "I could get discovered. I could have my own reality TV show with Brenda. Even my horoscope said I was gonna look to new horizons today."

"This is a disastrous idea! Think about it. We're like Lucy and Ethel out there. We never know what the heck we're doing. And now we're going to drag Brenda around with us? And it's going to be documented. Remember when that mop fell out of the closet and you thought it was a snake? Do you want that picture to go into a million homes?"

"Maybe not that picture."

"And what about the time you fell in the grave and couldn't get out and freaked?"

"Yeah, but anyone would have. I figure we just have to pick a good bust. Like the old naked guy would have been okay."

"You can't put an old naked guy on national television. Anyway, we already brought him in."

"Connie said she had something we could use. And besides being my big break, they're gonna pay us."

That caught my attention because I needed a new car . . . bad. "How much?"

"A couple thousand. And they thought we'd only have to do two days of filming."

"Okay, I'll do it, but I'm not dressing in black leather."

"You're gonna be sorry. You're gonna look like a amateur. You're not gonna fit in with Brenda and me. You should at least wear the jacket."

"Fine. I'll wear the jacket."

Lula hustled back inside. "We're ready to roll. We just cleared our schedule for you. And Stephanie's all excited about wearing the jacket."

"What have you got?" I asked Connie.

"Susan Stitch. Just came in. She had a fight with her boyfriend and tried to leave, but he climbed onto the roof of her SUV and wouldn't get off, so she drove him to Princeton. Actually, she didn't quite make Princeton. The police finally stopped her on Route 1 about a half mile from the interchange."

"Jeez," I said. "Was he hurt?"

"Not from the ride, but he sort of flew off the car when Susan stopped short, and then she kind of ran over him."

"Kind of?"

"He tried to scramble to his feet, but she gunned the car and clipped him in the leg."

"She sounds dangerous," Lula said. "We want to make sure we're packin'."

"*No!* No packing," I said. "No packing *anything*. This is a domestic disturbance."

"Sure. I know that," Lula said.

"Why did she miss her court date?" I asked Connie. "Did you call her?"

"She said she forgot, and she said she was sorry. So it

should be an easy pickup. She lives on Bing Street in North Trenton. It's a small apartment building. She's in apartment 212."

"You see," I said to Lula. "She's sorry. We don't want to overreact with this woman."

"This sounds like it's going to be boring," Brenda said. "I think we should hunt down a rapist or something."

"Gee, sorry," I said. "There aren't any of those around right now, right, Connie?"

"Yeah, we already caught all the rapists."

"We gotta have a plan for the takedown," Lula said. "Do you have your cuffs ready?" she asked Brenda.

"Cuffs?"

"You gotta have handcuffs," Lula said. "How're you gonna do a takedown without handcuffs?"

Brenda glared at Nancy. "Dammit, why don't I have handcuffs?"

Nancy was head down, thumbing through the pages on her clipboard. "Wardrobe didn't list handcuffs."

"Isn't it bad enough I haven't got a gun?" Brenda said. "Just because little Miss Goody Two Shoes Stephanie Plum doesn't have the stomach for it. Doesn't want to stress out the disturbed woman who ran over her boyfriend."

"You ran over a cameraman," Nancy said to Brenda.

"He deserved it," Brenda said. "The sonovabitch."

"I always got a gun," Lula said. "I got a big one."

"This just isn't going to work," Brenda said. "How are we supposed to look like bounty hunters if we don't go in with

127

guns drawn? This is *very* disappointing. My fans will be expecting action. They're going to want to hear me say, *Freeze! We're bounty hunters*."

"She got a point," Lula said.

"Yes, but here's the problem," I said. "Television bounty hunters do that sort of thing, but I'm not a television bounty hunter. I'm a real-life bond-enforcement agent. So here's how it's going to happen. I'm going to knock on Susan's door and hand her my card and explain who we are. Then I'm going to ask her to come downtown with us so she can get rebonded."

"Hunh," Lula said. "I guess you could do it that way, but it's not gonna get ratings."

"Humor me," I said. "Brenda can go to a studio and do voice-overs, and no one will know the difference."

"That might work," Lula said to Brenda.

"Freeze, suckah," Brenda said in a crouch position, pretending she had a gun.

"That's pretty good," Lula told her. "You should have your own show. You could do *CSI: Brenda*."

I took the paperwork from Connie and shrugged into my jacket. It was almost eighty degrees outside, and I was going to sweat like a pig in this thing.

"Here's the way it works," the sound guy said. "I'm going to wire you all, and I've also wired the Firebird. We'll be able to hear everything, so switch yourself off if you need to use the bathroom. We've also got a lipstick cam in the Firebird, and we'll be filming from the van. When you enter the lady's house, Jeff will follow you with the minicam."

"What if she doesn't want to be filmed?" I asked.

"Everyone wants to be filmed," the sound guy said. "Just start singing the 'Bad Boys' theme song."

We trudged outside, Lula got behind the wheel, Brenda got in next to her, and I climbed into the back. Brenda and Lula were in full view of the lipstick cam mounted above the driver's side door. The camera didn't cover the backseat. Fine by me. My hair didn't look all that great, and my cleavage couldn't nearly measure up.

Lula drove across town to North Trenton and turned down Bing Street. The film crew van was right behind us. We parked in the apartment building lot, and we all got out. I thought we looked like one of those Publishers Clearing House commercials. The only thing missing was the big check and a bunch of balloons.

I led the parade into the building and up one flight of stairs. The building wasn't fancy, but it was clean and the paint looked new. There were six apartments on the second floor.

"Now, remember," I said to Brenda and Lula. "Let me do the talking."

"I should be the one to do the talking," Brenda said. "I'm the star."

"And I'm almost a star," Lula said. "What about me? I need to get a chance to talk."

"Yes," I said. "But I'm the one who signed her name to the contract to apprehend. I'm the one who gets sued if there's a screwup."

"Okay," Lula said. "That sounds fair."

"I can live with it," Brenda said.

According to my paperwork, Susan Stitch was twenty-six years old, unmarried, and worked nights as a bartender at the Holiday Inn. She had no priors. And she lived alone.

I rang the bell and a young woman answered the door. Shoulder-length brown hair, brown eyes, slim. Susan Stitch. She looked just like her booking photo. I introduced myself and gave her my card.

"I'm here to bring you to the courthouse so you can get rebonded," I told her. And that was partially true. The part I neglected to mention was that she would have to go through the arrest process again and that it wasn't a given she would be released.

She looked over my shoulder at the cameraman and sound guy and Brenda and Lula. "Who are all these people?"

"This is your lucky day," Lula said. "You been selected to be arrested by Brenda. And these are the guys who follow her around and take pictures."

"Freeze, bitch," Brenda said.

Susan squinted at Brenda. "Omigod! Is it really you?"

"Yep," Brenda said. "In the flesh."

"Omigod. *Omigod!*" Susan said. "I've got goose bumps. The lady at the bonds office didn't tell me. I would have worn something different. Omigod, you have to come in so I can get my camera. No one's going to believe this."

Susan ran off to get her camera, and we all shuffled into her small apartment.

Her furniture looked a lot like mine. Inexpensive and without personality. Neither of us was a nest-builder. I always had good intentions of buying throw pillows and arranging pictures in frames and maybe getting a houseplant, but somehow it never happened.

"Hey," Lula yelled into the bedroom at Susan. "Did you really give your boyfriend a ride on the roof rack?"

Susan came in with her camera. "He's *not* my boyfriend. He *used* to be my boyfriend, but he's a total jerk. I'm just sorry all I got was his leg. If he hadn't gotten up so fast, I would have run over him like he was a speed bump." She focused the camera and took everyone's picture. "Now one of me with Brenda," she said, handing the camera to Lula. "This is so cool."

"Why'd your boyfriend jump on the car?" Lula wanted to know. "Guess he didn't want you to go?"

"Had nothing to do with me. It was that I took Carl. He just wanted his precious Carl."

"Isn't that tragic," Brenda said. "You have a little boy. A split is always so hard on the children."

"Actually, Carl's a monkey," Susan said.

Lula snapped her head around. "He isn't here, is he? Nothing personal, but I hate monkeys."

"I have him in the bathroom. He gets excited when strangers come into the apartment."

"I have to see this," Brenda said, crossing to the closed bathroom door. "What kind of monkey is it?"

"Don't open the door!" Susan said.

Too late. Brenda yanked the door open, and the monkey launched himself out at her and draped himself over her head.

Everyone in the room went rigid and sucked air.

Brenda rolled her eyes, trying to see through her skull. "What the heck?"

"Hee, hee, hee," Carl said. And he reached down and pinched Brenda's nose . . . hard.

Brenda slapped his hand away, and Carl shrieked and hunkered down, digging into Brenda's scalp with his monkey fingers and toes. All you could see was monkey tail and brown monkey fur sticking out of Brenda's rat's nest hair.

"Uh-oh," Lula said. "I never seen a monkey hump before, but I could swear Carl's in love."

"Somebody do something, for crissake," Brenda yelled. "Get him off me! Kill him. Get him a damn banana!"

It was the spider all over again, times fifty. The difference was that this time Brenda's freak-out was justified. If I had a monkey humping my head, I'd be freaked, too.

"Don't slap at him," Susan said. "You'll make him mad."

Lula had her gun out. "Hold still, and I'll nail the nasty little bugger."

The sound guy reached for Carl, and Carl latched on to his arm and bit his hand.

"Yow! Shit!" the sound guy said. "Shoot him. *Shoot him.*" He whipped his arm out, and Carl flew off into space, hit the wall, and bounced off like a tennis ball. And he kept bouncing. Onto the table, to the chandelier, to the couch, to an end table, to the television.

Carl rocketed around the room, shrieking and chattering

and baring his teeth. His eyes were black and glittery and bugged out of his head, and he was spraying monkey spit.

"It's a *demon* monkey!" Lula yelled. "Get a priest."

"I'm out of here," the cameraman said. "Life's too short."

The sound guy was already in the hall, and Brenda was at the stairs.

"Wait for me," Lula said, pounding after them.

If I didn't catch up, they'd leave without me. They'd drive away and never look back.

"Turn yourself in," I said to Susan. "Sorry about the monkey."

I sprinted across the lot and got to the Firebird just as Lula put the key into the ignition. I hurled myself into the backseat, and we took off with the camera crew truck right on our ass.

"What the hell was that?" Brenda wanted to know.

Lula gave the Firebird gas. "She said don't open the door, but would you listen? Heck, no. You had to go open the door. What were you thinking?"

"I wanted to see the monkey. Did she say the monkey was rabid? No. Did she say the monkey was on crack? No. I assumed it was a pet. Its name was Carl."

"Right there, it tells you something," Lula said. "Carls are always crazy. You never trust anyone named Carl or Steve."

"That's ridiculous," Brenda said. "Do you have any other theories on names?"

"Yeah. It's been my experience that guys named Ralph only got one good nut."

I was sitting behind Brenda, and her hair was Wild Woman of Borneo, with a couple chunks obviously chewed off by the monkey.

"Is my hair all right?" Brenda asked. "Do I need to comb it or something?" She patted the top of her head. "What's this sticky stuff?"

At the very best, I thought it was monkey spit.

"Jeez," I said. "I don't know. I think it might be your gel or something. Probably you want to wait until you get to a ladies' room to comb it."

# TEN

MARK BIRD AND his producer were waiting for us at the office. The producer gasped when Brenda walked through the door. "H-h-how'd it go?" she asked, her attention caught on Brenda's hair.

"This bounty hunter thing is harder than I thought," Brenda said. "I need a ladies' room."

"There's a powder room straight back," Connie said. "It'll be on your right."

Brenda sashayed off to the powder room, and we all stayed mute until the door closed.

"What the heck happened to her?" Connie asked.

"Monkey," Lula said. "Bugger humped her head."

The sound guy was grinning wide. "We looked at the footage in the truck on the way here. It's great!"

"You couldn't possibly use it," I said to him.

"It would be a crime not to," he said. "It's gold."

Connie looked to me. "I assume there was no capture."

135

I took my cell phone out and punched Morelli's number in. "Your assumption is correct."

Morelli answered with a grunt.

"What's new?" I asked him.

"Nothing worth talking about. I caught a double homicide this morning and haven't been able to do anything about Dom or Loretta. Larry Skid is working Loretta. So far, no one's spotted Dom."

"Larry Skid is an idiot."

"Yeah. My description for him would be sack of shit. I've got to go. You're picking the kid up today, right?"

"Right."

I disconnected and fished around in my bag, looking for my keys. "I have to talk to some people," I said to Connie. "I'll get back to Susan Stitch later. Her monkey needs alone time."

"Where you going?" Lula wanted to know. "I might have to go with you. I don't want to be here when Ms. Monkey Hair comes out of the bathroom."

Ten minutes later, we were in front of Dom's mother's house. I knew Morelli had done a search, but I didn't think it would hurt for me to take a look, too. I knocked on the front door. No answer. I turned the knob and the door swung open. We stepped inside and listened.

"All I hear is the refrigerator," Lula said.

The interior of the house was dark and fussy. Lots of candy dishes and figurines and vases filled with plastic flowers. The dining room table was covered with a lace tablecloth.

"What are we looking for?" Lula wanted to know.

"Clues."

"Good thing I asked. I thought it might have been elephants."

I prowled through the kitchen, and it looked to me like Dom had cleared out in a hurry. There were dirty dishes in the sink and a fry pan on the stove. The refrigerator held the usual staples. Yesterday's paper was open on the small kitchen table. A cup of cold coffee was beside the paper. A cardboard box containing cereal, jars of soup, and canned food was on the floor next to the sink. I was guessing this came from Loretta's stash. There were more cardboard boxes upstairs in a spare bedroom. They were labeled "clothes" and "bathroom." The master bedroom was untouched, the bed neatly made. A second bedroom was a disaster. Linens rumpled into a mess in the middle of the bed. Drawers open with clothes everywhere. Either Dom was a slob or else the room had been tossed.

I checked the garage. No cars. Loretta's possessions neatly stacked in a corner.

"What'd we learn here?" Lula wanted to know.

"Not much. Loretta moved in and then disappeared. Dom made an unplanned departure. Hard to tell how many people have searched the house. I'm guessing at least three . . . Morelli and me and someone else."

THE LIMO AND the film crew van were gone when I returned to the office.

"Guess it's safe to park," Lula said. "Looks like everyone went away."

Not everyone. Gary-the-Stalker was sitting on the curb in front of the bonds office. He stood when I got out of the Sentra and walked over to me.

"Brenda went back to the hotel," I told him.

"I know. I saw her leave. I thought I'd have better luck talking to you."

"I'm not working security for her anymore."

"Yeah, but you talk to her."

"Actually, no."

"I had a dream that she was sitting on a toilet in the southbound lane of Route 1."

"Un-hunh?"

"I thought someone needed to know."

"Why?"

"Just in case," he said.

"Anything else?"

"No. That's it."

"Okay, then," I said. "Thanks."

My phone rang and a strange number popped onto the screen.

"Is this Stephanie Plum?" a man asked.

"Yeah," I said, recognizing the voice. "Is this the Mooner?"

"Affirmative. It's the Moonster, the Moondog, the MoonMan. I'm here at the house, looking for Zookarama, but he isn't here."

"He's in school."

"School! Far out."

"Anything else?"

"Here's the thing, it was real late when we were done playing last night, and I think I might have left my computer in the house, because I don't seem to have it with me. So I was wondering if you could, like, let me into the house."

"Sure," I said. "I'm at the bonds office. I'll be right there."

Morelli's house is minutes from the bonds office. It was close to noon, and there was no traffic. No kids playing. No dogs barking. Only Mooner sitting on the small porch, patiently waiting for me.

I unlocked the door, and Bob galloped over to us. Bob stuck his snoot into Mooner's crotch and took a sniff.

"Whoa," Mooner said. "He remembers me. Cool."

We pushed past Bob and found the computer exactly where Mooner had left it, on the coffee table.

"When's the little dude get out of school?" Mooner asked.

"Two-thirty."

Mooner flopped onto the couch.

"What are you doing?" I asked him.

"Waiting."

I decided some time ago that Mooner fell into the pet category. He was like a stray cat that showed up on your doorstep and stayed for a few days and then wandered off. He was amusing in small doses, fairly harmless, and for the most part, housebroken.

I left Mooner on the couch and went to the kitchen to check out the contents of Morelli's refrigerator. It was noon, and as long as I was there, I figured I might as well eat. If I'd been in my house, I would have made a peanut butter sandwich, but this was Morelli's house and he was a meat guy, so I found deli-sliced ham and roast beef and Swiss cheese. I made a sandwich for me and a sandwich for Mooner, and I dragged a big bag of potato chips out of the cupboard. I put it all on the small kitchen table and called Mooner in.

"Thanks, Mom," Mooner said, sitting down, dumping some chips onto his plate. "This is, like, excellent."

I ate half a sandwich, and I realized Bob was at the table, and he was holding a man's shoe in his mouth. It was a scuffed brown lace-up shoe, and I didn't recognize it as Morelli's. I looked under the table at Mooner's feet. Both of them were stuffed into beat-up sneakers.

"Where'd Bob get the shoe?" I asked.

"He brought it up from the basement," Mooner said. "The door's open."

I turned and looked behind me and, sure enough, the basement door was open. I got up and cautiously peeked down the stairs. "Hello?" I called. No one answered. I took the carving knife out of the butcher-block knife caddy, switched the light on in the basement, and carefully crept down the stairs and looked around.

"What's down there?" Mooner wanted to know.

"Furnace, water heater, and a dead guy."

"Bad juju," Mooner said.

The dead guy was spread-eagle on his back, eyes wide open, hole in the middle of his forehead, lots of blood pooling under him, wearing only one shoe. I didn't recognize him. He looked like he came out of central casting for a *Sopranos* episode.

I took a moment to decide if I was going to throw up or faint or evacuate my bowels. None of those things seemed to be going on, so I stumbled up to the kitchen, closed the basement door behind me, and dialed Morelli.

"There's a d-d-dead guy in your b-b-basement," I told him.

Silence.

"Did you hear me?" I asked, working hard to control the shaking in my voice.

"I know this is stupid, but it sounded like you said there was a dead guy in my basement."

"Shot in the f-f-forehead. Bob took his shoe and won't give it b-b-back."

"Have you called the police?"

"Just you."

"You know what would be good?" Mooner said when I hung up. "Coleslaw. I don't suppose you have any coleslaw?"

"No."

"Just thought I'd ask."

"Aren't you bothered by the fact that someone was killed in Morelli's basement?" I asked Mooner.

"Do I know him?"

"I don't know. Do you want to take a look?"

Mooner stood and ambled down the stairs. Moments later, he strolled back into the kitchen and took a handful of chips. "Don't know him," he said, finishing his sandwich, eating his chips.

I wasn't nearly so calm. I don't like dead people, and I especially hated that someone was killed in Morelli's house. It felt unclean and scary and like the house had been violated.

MOONER HAD TAKEN a lawn chair from Morelli's backyard and set it on the sidewalk in front of Morelli's house, so he could watch the homicide show in comfort. He had a can of soda in one hand and the potato chip bag in the other, and he was kicked back. There were several squad cars parked at angles on the street, plus the medical examiner's meat wagon and a couple other assorted cop cars. A clump of uniforms stood by the meat wagon, talking and laughing. Morelli was on his porch, the front door to his house open behind him. He was talking to Rich Spanner, another homicide cop. Spanner had obviously caught the case. I knew him on a superficial level. He was an okay guy. He was a couple years older than Morelli and built like a barrel.

Just minutes ago, they'd carried the victim out in a zippered bag and stuffed him into the ME's truck. The crime lab guy was still inside, working.

I was leaning against my car, not wanting to be in the middle of all the police activity inside the house. Rich

Spanner and Morelli concluded their conversation. Spanner left, and Morelli walked over to me.

"This is a frigging nightmare," Morelli said.

"Did you know the dead guy?"

He shook his head. "Not personally. His name is Allen Gratelli. The address on his license was Lawrenceville. Spanner ran him through the system, and he has no priors. He worked for the cable company."

"So what's his connection to you?"

"Don't know. Was he the guy who ran out of the basement the other night?"

"Could have been. Seemed like the right size, but I couldn't be sure. I don't recognize the name. Did Spanner know him?"

"No. No one knows him. He's nobody."

"Well, somebody knows him, because they killed him in your basement."

"Let's review my life," Morelli said. "I have crazy Dom shooting at me because he thinks I stole this house out from under him. I have his nephew living with me. I'm not sure why, except that he looks a little like me, and the kid's mother is missing. And in the last three days, I've had my house broken into twice and a guy killed in my basement. Did I miss anything?"

"Does Mooner count?"

"No."

"Do you suppose there's a connection between all those people?" I asked him.

"Yeah, I do. And I think it's all related to the bank job.

We know that four men participated in the robbery. Dom took the fall and the other three men were never identified, and the money was never recovered. I'm guessing when we dig around a little, we'll find out Dom knew Allen Gratelli."

"And maybe Gratelli was involved in the robbery."

"It would explain the hole in his head," Morelli said.

"And maybe the money is hidden in your house!"

"It was a lot of money. They hauled it off in a van. More likely, a key or a clue to the location is hidden in the house."

"We need to comb through the house."

"Little by little, I've been making this house my own, and I've gotten rid of a bunch of things that belonged to Rose. A lot of the clutter has been tossed."

"Yes, but a lot of it is still here. You never throw a key away. You still have your locker key from high school. If you found a key, you'd put it in one of your junk drawers." I looked at my watch. "I have to get Zook. When I come back we'll start looking."

# ELEVEN

Zook settled himself onto the passenger seat and stared down at his shoes.

"Problems in school?" I asked him.

"No."

"Well?"

He bit into his lower lip.

"Your mom hasn't turned up in any of the local hospitals," I told him. "That's a good sign."

"Or the morgue."

"Yeah, or the morgue," I said.

"Maybe she took off."

"She wouldn't take off without you. She loves you."

"Thanks," Zook said. "Do you think she's okay?"

"Yes. I do."

I ran into the deli on the way home and picked up lunch meat and chips and ice cream sandwiches. Marion Fitz was working checkout.

"I hear you found a dead guy in Morelli's basement," she said. "Is this Virginia baked ham or the low sodium?"

"Virginia baked."

"I heard it was Allen Gratelli."

"That's what I'm told."

"Wasn't he dating Loretta Rizzi?"

*Bang.* Direct hit to my brain. "I don't know," I said. "Was he?"

"His truck's been in front of her house a lot. Maybe she just had cable problems."

I carried my bag out to my car, tossed it onto the back-seat, and got behind the wheel. Zook was hooked into his iPod, waiting for me.

"Was your mom dating a guy named Allen Gratelli?" I asked him.

"He's Uncle Dom's friend. He'd come over sometimes to see if we were doing okay. I thought he was sort of a jerk. Sometimes it was like he was trying to put moves on my mom, but she always made a joke about it."

"I ran into him today."

"Lucky you."

"He was in Morelli's basement. Someone shot him."

Zook's eyes went wide. "Get out. Was he hurt bad?"

"Yes."

"How bad?"

"Real bad."

I suspect if I was relaying this information to a fourteen-year-old girl, she would be sad at this point. She'd be re-membering pets and relatives and stuffed animals that had been injured, and the tragedies would be commingled in the frontal lobe of her brain. Zook, being a boy, thought it was cool.

"Oh man," Zook said. "Is he dead?"

"Yes."

Zook was leaning forward, straining against his seatbelt. "Who shot him?"

"I don't know. He was dead when I found him."

"What did he look like?"

"He looked dead. Bullet hole in the middle of his forehead."

"Whoa. That's amazing. Is he still there?"

"No. They moved him out."

Zook slumped back. "Darn. I miss all the good stuff."

"Did your Uncle Dom ever say anything about the money? Like where it was hidden?"

"No. He just kept saying he was going to be living the high life."

"Did he have other friends besides Allen Gratelli?"

"I guess, but I don't know any. Allen was the only one who came around after Uncle Dom went to prison. And Allen just started to come around a couple months ago."

THE POLICE WERE gone when I returned to Morelli's house. Only Mooner in the lawn chair and a single van from an emergency cleaning service suggested something unusual had just occurred.

"Zookamundo," Mooner said. "Been waiting for you, man. We gotta convene with the wood elves."

"Did you see the dead guy?" Zook asked.

"Yeah. He was real dead," Mooner said. "Pooped in his pants and everything."

"Awesome," Zook said.

I left Mooner and Zook in the living room with the ice cream sandwiches and the wood elves, and I went to the kitchen to help Morelli. He was methodically going through drawers, extracting keys and odd scraps of paper. The basement door was open, and the smell of bleach and pine-scented detergent drifted up the stairs.

"Zook tells me Allen Gratelli was friends with Dom," I said to Morelli. "Shazam."

Morelli grinned and wrapped an arm around me. "I'm going to get you naked tonight and make you say *shazam* again."

I knew that wasn't an empty promise. "Having any luck here?" I asked him.

"I've got a pile of renegade keys, and I now know the problem with our plan. It's not enough to find a key. You have to know where it goes."

My cell phone rang, and I answered to Connie.

"I have Brenda back with the film crew," Connie said. "They want more footage."

"Are you kidding me? They want more monkey?"

"No. They want a different takedown."

"We screwed up a simple domestic disturbance. Where do we go from there?"

"How about Loretta? She's disappeared, right? That's a violation of her bond agreement."

"I can't find Loretta. I have no place to look. I have no clue."

"Just lead them around. Make something up. At least no one will shoot at you. And there won't be any monkeys," Connie said.

I hung up and looked at Morelli. "Connie wants me to find Loretta."

"Good," Morelli said. "I want you to find Loretta, too. Loretta probably knows what's going on. She might even know where the money is located."

"I don't know where to begin."

"There were four men involved in the robbery. Go on the assumption that Allen Gratelli was one of the men and find the other two. I'm guessing one of them has Loretta."

"Why aren't *you* looking for Loretta?"

"I'm baby-sitting her kid. And it seems to me it's more dangerous to stay in this house than to be on the streets. So I'm staying here, and you're hitting the streets."

"Okay, fine, terrific, I'll go find Loretta, but you're going to owe me."

"Shazam," Morelli said.

THE BONDS OFFICE looked like it was holding a casting call for *'Ho Bounty Hunters.* Lula and Brenda were there, dressed in their leathers, plus Nancy, Mark Bird, and his producer and the camera crew.

"I can't drag everyone around with me," I told them. "I need to talk to people, and the camera crew is intimidating. They're going to have to stay in the van."

"Okay," Mark said, "we'll wire you for sound and we'll do re-creations."

"What's this Loretta like?" Brenda wanted to know. "What did she do?"

"She robbed a liquor store," I told her.

"Was she armed?"

"Yeah. She had a lightsaber."

"A what?"

"She had her kid's *Star Wars* lightsaber from Disney World."

"But she got a lot of money, right?" Brenda said.

"Actually, she got a bottle of gin. She needed a Tom Collins."

"Been there, done that," Brenda said.

I took the new paperwork from Connie, plus a profile on Allen Gratelli, and we all piled into Lula's Firebird. Lula drove north on 206, past Rider College, to a neighborhood of modest houses. She wound down a couple streets and stopped at a house with a lot of cars parked in the driveway. This was Gratelli's house and it looked like people were arriving to give their condolences. Problem was, according to Connie's computer check, Gratelli lived alone. He was divorced, no children. His parents were deceased. He had two brothers and one sister.

Lula parked on the street, and we walked to the house.

The front door was open, and I could hear people yelling at one another inside.

"Knock, knock," I said, peeking into the house.

Two men were shoving each other around, a guy in a cable uniform was ransacking a chest in the hall, and a woman was yelling at the two men.

"You dumb shit," the woman said to one of the men. "Who cares if he slept with your wife? Your wife is a slut. Everyone's slept with your wife. Stop being a jerk and go look for the stupid directions."

"What directions?" I asked her.

Her head snapped around, and she took in Lula and Brenda and me. "Cripes," she said. "It's the rod squad. I knew Allen was a sicko, but this is ridiculous."

Lula stiffened her spine. "Say what?"

"You heard he was dead, right? And now you're here on the scavenger hunt? Well, back off, because I was here first," the woman said.

I corralled Lula and Brenda and pulled them aside. "Cozy up to the guy in the cable uniform and find out what he's looking for."

The woman made a disgusted gesture at the men and flounced off to the kitchen. I tagged along and watched her open and close drawers.

"Are you his sister?" I asked the woman.

"Yeah."

"I'm sorry," I said. "This must be a terrible time for you."

"We weren't close." She cut her eyes to me. "Have you known Allen long?"

"Long enough."

"I guess men talk when you're, you know, doing things."

"Mmm."

"Like what did he say?" she asked me.

"Uh, mostly he gave instructions."

"Really? What sort of instructions? Did he say where it was located?"

"No. I knew where it was located. He mostly said *hit me harder*. And then *ouch* and *yow* and that sort of thing."

"I don't mean *those* instructions. I mean, did he tell you where the money is hidden?"

"Oh. No."

"Allen was such an idiot. I can't believe he got himself shot. What was he thinking?"

"Do you know who shot him?"

"I imagine it was someone looking for the money, just like him. Probably crazy Dominic Rizzi."

"This is the money from the robbery, right?"

"I guess. He just kept talking about the money he was going to get when Dom got out of jail. And then Dom got out and nobody could find the money. And then last night, Allen said he had directions and today he's dead. I figure I'm next of kin and the money is mine. I just need to find the directions. Me and my two remaining moron brothers."

"Doesn't it bother you that Allen was probably killed over the money and you could get killed, too?"

"Do you have any idea how much money we're talking about?"

"A lot?"

"More than a lot. We're talking a shitload."

"What if you don't find the directions here?"

"I guess I just start digging around the death house. I figure Dom gave the money to his crazy old Aunt Rose, and she hid it somewhere. And then she died before Dom got out of prison."

I left the kitchen, gathered up Lula and Brenda, and herded them outside.

"What did you find out?" I asked them.

"He worked with the dead guy," Lula said. "And the dead guy was always talking about the money he was gonna get when Rizzi got out of prison. And so this jerk-off figured now that the dead guy is dead, he was gonna come look for the money."

"That's it?"

"Yeah."

"Did you get his name?"

"Morty Dill. He was all taken with Brenda here. He would have told us anything."

"He reminded me of my fifth husband," Brenda said. "Sort of cute the way he kept calling me *darlin'*."

"I know all about you from *Star* magazine," Lula said. "I thought your fifth husband was that English guy who got caught with his pants down in the movie theater. You're thinking of your sixth husband, who was the country singer. Kenny Bold."

"Are you sure?"

"There was the guy you married right out of high school. The plumber. Then there was the ice skater who turned out to be gay. The third guy was a stock car driver. Then you remarried the plumber, but that only lasted a couple weeks. And then the English guy."

"You're right," Brenda said. "I'd forgotten about the second marriage to the plumber."

A black Mercedes sedan with tinted windows cruised down the street, stopped in front of the house for a moment, and sped away.

"Guess he don't like a crowd," Lula said. "My opinion is, people gonna be coming out of the woodwork to get that robbery money."

"Morty said Allen had directions to the money," Brenda said. "Morty was looking for the directions."

I looked back at the house. "I suppose we should join in the hunt. Or at least we should wait around to see if anyone finds the directions."

An hour later, everyone cleared out. The house had been searched from top to bottom and the result was a big zero.

"I'm not going to get an Emmy on this episode," Brenda said. "This is a huge yawn."

"You'd get an Emmy if we found the directions," I told her. "Let's just think about this a little. Supposedly, Allen Gratelli had directions to the money, and next thing, he was dead in Morelli's basement. So, if the directions weren't on him, and they aren't in his house . . . where would they be?"

"In his car," Lula said.

"I don't remember seeing his car. It wasn't parked in front of Morelli's house."

"If I was doing B&E on a cop's house, I wouldn't park in front of it," Lula said. "When we break into someplace we always park around the corner."

# TWELVE

A HALF HOUR later, we were back in Morelli's neighborhood. According to Connie's research, Gratelli drove a silver Camry. Lula motored around the block and, sure enough, there was Gratelli's car, parked around the corner, a block away. Lula pulled in behind it, and we all got out and looked into the Camry. There was a briefcase on the backseat. The cameraman panned across the car and went in for a close-up.

"There it is," Brenda whispered into her mic. "There's the briefcase with the directions to millions of stolen dollars."

We tried the doors. Locked.

"No problemo," Lula said. She opened her trunk and removed a slim metal tool. She rammed the tool into the doorframe and popped the lock. "It's not like I steal cars or anything," Lula said, "but a girl needs to be prepared. A girl's gotta have skills, you see what I'm saying?"

I took the briefcase from the car and set it on the hood.

It was a Samsonite hardside attaché case. The kind goril-las can jump on and not make a dent. I released the two locks and everyone crowded close together, excited to see if the directions were inside. I lifted the lid and . . . *Bang!*

Blue dye exploded out of the attaché case.

No one moved. No one spoke. No one blinked. We all just stood there, dripping blue dye.

"What happened?" Brenda wanted to know. "Am I okay? Was it a bomb?"

I looked at the dye on my hands and shirt. "Gratelli booby-trapped his briefcase."

"He's lucky he's dead," Lula said. "I'm wearing leather. Somebody's gotta be responsible for this dry-cleaning bill."

The cameraman looked at his blue lens. "I'm done for the day."

I closed the attaché case and snatched it off the hood of Gratelli's car. "I'm taking this with me. I'll give it to Morelli to check out."

"It's in my hair, isn't it?" Brenda asked. "I feel so funky." She looked down at herself. "I have blue boobies."

Lula carefully eased herself into the Firebird and drove away. Brenda and the camera crew took off in the van. And I walked to Morelli's house.

Mooner answered the door. "Far out," he said. "Off the chain."

I had no idea what "off the chain" meant, and I didn't care. I was blue. I walked through the living room, and Zook never looked up from the computer screen. I got to the kitchen, where Morelli was stirring a pot of spaghetti sauce, and I dropped the attaché case onto the kitchen table.

Morelli gaped at me with the spoon in his hand. "What the hell happened to you?"

"Booby-trapped attaché case."

"Have you seen yourself?"

"No. Is it bad?"

"How do you feel about blue?"

I stepped into the powder room, switched the light on, and stifled a sob. Blue hair, blue eyebrows, blue eyelashes, blue lips, blue face. I soaked a hand towel and dabbed at my cheek. Nothing happened.

Morelli was behind me, smiling. "You look like a Smurf. I think I'm getting turned on."

"Everything turns you on."

"Not everything. Remember the time you fell off the fire escape and rolled in the dog diarrhea?"

"I took the briefcase out of Gratelli's car. There's a chance it contains directions for finding the money from the robbery."

Morelli went to the attaché case and flipped the locks. "Guess I don't have to worry about a dye bomb," he said. He raised the lid and looked inside. Everything was soaked in blue dye.

"Gratelli didn't get the memo telling him to put his important papers in plastic pouches," Morelli said. "If there were directions in here, they're gone."

I got a spoon out of the silverware drawer and tasted the spaghetti sauce. "Yum," I said.

"It needs to simmer," Morelli said. "I like to let the sausage soak in the gravy. It's for tomorrow. We're supposed to have dinner at your parents' house tonight."

I put the spoon in the dishwasher. "I bet I know where the money is hidden. I bet it's in your basement."

"I've looked in the basement."

"I bet it's buried. I bet it's under your floor."

"That floor is poured concrete."

"And?"

Morelli partially covered his sauce. "I'm not going to take a jackhammer to my basement floor."

We trooped downstairs and stared at the floor. It had just been professionally steam-cleaned to remove the bloodstains.

"This is an old house," I said. "The floor down here looks pretty new."

"I had it put in two years ago. It used to be dirt."

"Omigod!"

"I'm going to forget we had this conversation," Morelli said. "I don't care if there's a fortune buried here. It's not like the money would be mine. It's bank money."

"The bank would be happy to see it."

"The bank would think it was a pain in the ass. They've already collected the insurance."

"What about the insurance company?"

"Screw the insurance company," Morelli said.

"You would let nine million dollars sit under this concrete?"

"Yeah." He toed the concrete. "I like my floor. The guys did a good job on it. It's nice and smooth."

"If we got married, and you died, I'd have this floor up before your body got cold."

"As long as you don't slit my throat while I'm sleeping." He looked down at me. "You wouldn't, would you?"

"Not for money."

A HALF HOUR later, I was fresh out of the shower and I was still blue. I got dressed in a clean T-shirt and a pair of Morelli's sweats, and I padded downstairs.

"Help," I said to Morelli.

"I have some turpentine in the garage," he said. "Maybe that'll work."

He opened his back door to go to the garage, and there were two people digging in his yard. They looked up and saw Morelli and took off, leaving their shovels behind.

"Anyone you know?" Morelli asked me.

"Nope."

My cell phone rang. It was Grandma Mazur, and she was excited. "I just saw you on television," she said. "You were on the early evening news. They were doing a report on the murder in Morelli's basement and they said it was believed it was tied to that bank robbery that happened years ago. And then there was this part where Brenda found a briefcase in the dead man's car and it had directions about where the money was buried. And some lady said she was pretty sure Dominic Rizzi gave the money to his Aunt Rose and Rose hid it somewhere before she died. Just think—Morelli could have hidden treasure in his backyard!"

I glanced out the kitchen window at the hole the two diggers had started. "And they said all that on television?"

"Yep. It was a pip of a report."

I hung up and passed the news on to Morelli.

"There might be money buried in my basement," Morelli said. "But I'm pretty sure the only thing anyone is going to find in my yard has been left there by Bob."

Morelli jogged across his backyard to his garage and returned with a small can of turpentine. We dabbed it on my hand and rubbed and nothing happened.

"I'll call the crime lab and see if they have a suggestion," Morelli said.

The doorbell rang and Mooner answered. "It's some dude named Gary," Mooner yelled at me. "He says he's a stalker."

I went to the door, and Gary tried hard not to notice I was blue. He looked at his feet, and he looked above my head, and he cleared his throat.

"It's okay," I said. "I know I'm blue."

"It caught me by surprise," he said. "I didn't want to seem rude."

"Just so you know, Brenda is blue, too."

"Is this some art thing?"

"No. It was an accident. What's up?"

"I had the toilet dream again, only this time a bull came charging down the southbound lane, right at Brenda."

"Jeez. What happened then?"

"I woke up." His attention shifted to Mooner and Zook. "Are they playing *Minionfire*? What's their PC?"

"Zook and Moondog."

"Are you kidding me? They're famous. Zook is like a god. He's a Blybold Wizard."

Gary inched his way in and stood behind the couch, watching over Zook's shoulder. "Feel the power," Gary said. "The dragon's coming. There he is! There he is! Go arcane."

Zook turned and looked at him. "How did you know the dragon was coming?"

"Ever since I got hit by lightning, things happen in my head before they happen on the screen. It's like I'm a step ahead of cable, and I'm way faster than dial-up."

"*Whoa,*" Zook and Mooner said, eyes glued to Gary.

Zook looked over at me. "You're blue."

"It's a long story."

"Who's your PC?" Mooner asked Gary.

"I haven't got one. I just lurk. I thought it wasn't fair for me to play with the lightning advantage."

"Far out," Mooner said. "A dude with honor."

Morelli ambled in. "We need to go to your parents' now." He checked out Gary. "Is this the stalker?"

Gary extended his hand. "Pleased to meet you," he said to Morelli.

"Everyone sign off," I said. "We're going to my parents' house for dinner."

MY GRANDMOTHER OPENED the door, and we all marched in. Zook, Mooner, Gary, Morelli, me, and Bob.

"You better set more plates," Grandma yelled to my mother in the kitchen. "We got a group."

My father was in the living room, dozing in front of the television. He picked his head up and looked at everyone standing in the foyer. He mumbled something that sounded a little like *friggin' mutants* and went back to napping.

Bob bounced around, doing his happy dance.

"Isn't he something," Grandma said. She patted his head, and Bob took off for the kitchen.

A moment later, my mother shrieked, and Bob bounded out of the kitchen and streaked through the dining room with a ham firmly clenched in his mouth. He skidded to a stop in front of my father and dropped the ham.

My grandmother ran in and scooped the ham up off the floor. "Thirty-second rule in effect," my grandmother said, returning the ham to the kitchen. There was the sound of water running, and moments later, my grandmother reappeared with the ham on a plate. "Dinner's ready," she said. "Everyone sit."

We dragged extra chairs to the table, and I shuffled plates and silverware around. Bob took his place under the table, ever on guard for food to fall out of someone's mouth onto the rug.

My mother brought in creamed corn, green beans with bacon, and mashed potatoes. She got to the table, looked at me, and her mouth dropped open.

"Booby-trapped attaché case," I said. "No big deal."

She set the side dishes on the table and made the sign of the cross. "Dear God," she said. And she returned to the kitchen. I heard the cabinet door creak open and moments later, my mother returned with a glass of whiskey.

"Isn't this nice," my grandmother said. "It feels like a party. We even got the stalker here."

My mother tossed some whiskey down her throat.

"Stalker?" my father said, mashed potato bowl in hand.

"Yep," Grandma said. "He's a genuine stalker. He's even got a restraining order against him."

My father considered that for a beat and went back to filling his plate. Clearly, he didn't find a stalker to be especially interesting. Now, if Gary had been a cross-dresser, my father would have had something to work with.

"So how's the treasure hunt going?" Grandma asked Morelli. "Did you find all that money yet?"

This got everyone's attention.

My mother had a grip on her whiskey glass. "What money?"

"I guess I'm the only one who watches television," Grandma said. "The early news ran a piece on the dead guy in Morelli's basement."

"Why don't I know about this?" my mother asked.

"I guess I forgot to tell you, being that I was so busy answering all the phone calls," Grandma said.

"You didn't kill him, did you?" my mother asked me.

"No! I just discovered the body."

"The dead guy's name was Allen Gratelli," Grandma said. "Stephanie broke into his car and found his suitcase, and that's how she got blue. And it turns out Allen Gratelli and Dominic Rizzi were friends, and the television reporter said Allen Gratelli was in Morelli's basement looking for all that money that was never recovered from the robbery. Nine million dollars, and Joseph's Aunt Rose, rest in peace, hid it somewhere and now everyone's looking for it."

"Sweet," Mooner said. "You could get high-def TiVo with nine million dollars."

"I could get a lawyer for my mom," Zook said.

"I could get a sports car," Grandma said.

"You don't have a driver's license," my mother told her.

"I could get a driver," Grandma said. "A hot one."

My father had his head down, shoveling in ham. My father would like to see the hot driver deliver Grandma Mazur to the old people's home in Hamilton Township.

"Maybe I could find the money," Gary said. "I could divine it."

"Dude," Mooner said. "That would be awesome. Can you, like, really do that?"

"I found a chicken salad sandwich once. I found it in my sock drawer," Gary said.

"*Badass,*" Mooner said. "Wicked cool."

"What are you doing now?" Grandma asked Mooner. "Are you still involved in the pharmaceutical industry?"

"I mostly gave that up. I was getting stiff competition from the Russians. I've been reviewing my options, and I thought I might open a Japanese teahouse. Either that or a nudie bar."

My father picked his head up. "Don't you need money to open a nudie bar?"

"Yeah, dude, isn't that a bummer? Where's the justice? I mean, where's the incentive for the little businessman?"

"I think you should open a nudie bar for women," Grandma said. "There's lots of bars for men where they can see naked women, but there's no place us women can go to see ding dongs."

"I dig it," Mooner said. "You want private parts parity. Far out."

My mother chugged the rest of her whiskey.

Morelli was slouched back in his chair, taking it all in. He draped an arm across my shoulders and whispered into my ear. "Do women really want to see ding dongs?"

"Yeah," I said, "as long as they don't have to touch them."

"Is it sexual?"

"No. Morbid curiosity."

"How about mine?" he asked.

"Yours is definitely sexual . . . and touchable."

He nuzzled my neck. "Can we go home now?"

"No!"

"Why not?"

"We haven't had dessert. And besides, I feel funny shazaming with Zook in the house."

"We could shazam in the garage."

"I don't think so."

"The SUV?"

"No!"

"I'm becoming more motivated to find Loretta," Morelli said.

# THIRTEEN

IT WAS A little after eight when Morelli pulled to the curb in front of his house. A small crowd was gathered on the sidewalk, watching two men dig in Morelli's tiny front yard. Morelli got out of his car and joined the onlookers.

"Excuse me," Morelli said to the guys digging. "What are you doing?"

"Digging," the one guy said.

"This is private property," Morelli said.

"What?"

"Private property."

"I think there's something about digging," the guy said. "Like people only own the top of the property."

"I think you're wrong," Morelli said.

The guy kept digging. "And why would I give a rat's ass what you think?"

"Because I own this house, and if you don't stop digging, I'm going to have you arrested for destruction of personal property."

169

"Look at me—I'm so scared," the guy said. "Call the cops. Call the cops on me."

Morelli badged him. "I am the cops."

The guy looked at Morelli's badge. "Oh. Sorry."

Everyone dispersed after that, and Morelli, Zook, Mooner, Gary, and I trooped into the house. Morelli walked straight through and swore when he looked out his back window. His backyard was filled with people digging, and his garage door was open.

"This is unbelievable," Morelli said.

"Dude," Mooner said. "You should sell tickets. Like, it would be a hundred dollars to dig for a half hour. We could be, like, rich, dude."

Morelli walked out his back door, unholstered his gun, fired a shot into the ground, and the diggers scattered like roaches when the light goes on. He crossed the yard to his garage and returned with a roll of yellow crime scene tape.

"Do you think that's going to help?" I asked him.

"It's worth a try."

Ten minutes later, Morelli's entire property was behind the yellow tape. Zook, Mooner, and Gary were in the living room making deals with the wood elves, and Morelli and I were sitting out on the back stoop, watching Bob sniff around the holes in his yard.

"I'm going to have to jackhammer my basement," Morelli said. "This isn't going to stop until we find the money."

"If we found the money, Loretta might even turn up."

"I wouldn't count on it. I think Dom did the time and

figured he didn't owe his partners anything. Problem was, for whatever reason, Dom couldn't put his hands on the money right away."

"Maybe because it was buried in Rose's basement and you came along and inherited the house and poured concrete down there."

"Yeah. And it keeps getting worse. Dom's nephew is living in this house, so he can't just blow it up, and thanks to the early news, half of Trenton is on a nine-million-dollar scavenger hunt."

"And Loretta?"

"I'm guessing Loretta is being held hostage by one or both of the partners until Dom forks over the money. I'd feel a lot better if we could get to her before the money is found. There's no guarantee she won't be disposed of the instant she's no longer useful."

"We need to get Dom," I said. "He can take us to the other two partners."

"Any ideas?"

"I'm sure he's worried about his nephew. He hates the thought that Zook is with you. Plus, he wants him away from this house. And maybe he's thinking there's a possibility that whoever has Loretta will decide to hedge his bets and snatch Zook, too. So I think Dom isn't far away. I think he's keeping his eye on the house and on Zook. He's only been out of jail for a week, and he doesn't have a job. We know he hasn't got a lot of money."

"He has a gun," Morelli said.

"True. And a car."

"The car he was driving belongs to his mother. We found it abandoned."

"Where's he sleeping? Is he sneaking back into his mother's house?"

"No. We've been doing random checks," Morelli said.

"It's warm enough to sleep outdoors. Just another street person if he migrated downtown."

"Yes, but he has a rifle. It would make him conspicuous if he carried it with him."

Bob was digging in one of the holes. He had his head below ground level and dirt was flying between his hind legs.

"I think Dom's in the neighborhood, waiting for a chance to get into the house," I said. "So maybe we can set a trap. Make it look like no one's home, but you could be in a closet or something, waiting to jump out and capture Dom."

"Gee, that sounds like lots of fun."

"You have a better plan?"

Morelli blew out a sigh. "No."


MORELLI WOKE ME up out of a sound sleep. "Did you hear that?" he whispered.

"I was sleeping. I didn't hear anything."

"Shush," he said. "Listen."

It was warm and the windows were open. The white gauzy curtain still left from Aunt Rose moved on a gentle breeze.

"There," he said. "Did you hear it?"

"It sounds like someone's digging."

"What does it take to discourage these idiots?"

"I don't know, but I don't care if they're digging. Go back to sleep."

"I can't go to sleep," Morelli said. "This is making me nuts."

He rolled out of bed and moved toward the door.

"Where are you going?"

"I'm going to shoot the digger."

"That's not a good idea. Not to mention, you're naked."

"The digger won't care. He'll be concentrating on his bullet hole."

"You needed a new lawn anyway," I said to him. "Think of this as soil preparation."

He found a pair of boxers and pulled them on. "How's this? Does this meet your dress code for shooting trespassers?"

I dragged myself out of bed and grabbed some clothes off the floor. "Let's at least see who's out there before you shoot them. If we're lucky, it'll be Dom. Do you have a flashlight?"

"In the kitchen."

We padded downstairs and tiptoed through the dark house. I found the flashlight, and Morelli had his Glock in hand. We stood in the pitch-black kitchen and looked out the window. Someone was clearly digging in the backyard, but it was too dark to see much of anything.

"Okay," Morelli said. "On the count of three, I'm going to open the door, and you shine the flashlight on this bastard. One, two . . . three!"

Morelli yanked the back door open, and I hit the button on the flashlight and caught the digger in the act.

"Good God," Morelli said.

It was Grandma Mazur.

"Howdy," Grandma said. "Hope I didn't wake you."

"Of course you woke us," I said. "It's two in the morning. What the heck are you doing?"

"I felt lucky," Grandma said.

"I don't think the money is buried in the backyard," Morelli told her.

"That's okay," she said. "I still feel lucky. It isn't everyday I get to see a man in his underwear."

"How did you get here?" I asked her.

"I drove the Buick."

"You're not supposed to drive," I told her.

"I'm old. I've got rights," she said.

That could be true, but Grandma Mazur was the worst driver ever. She knew only one speed. Foot to the floor.

"I'll drive Grandma home," I said to Morelli.

I dropped Grandma off at the door and locked the Buick up in my father's garage. Morelli was waiting curbside in the SUV when I got to the front of my parents' house. I slid onto the passenger seat and looked over at him. He was only wearing the boxers.

"I thought you might have changed your mind about the SUV," Morelli said.

I checked out his underwear, which was imprinted with pictures of bunnies. "Where did you get those shorts?" I asked.

"Wal-Mart. They came in a pack."

I blew out a sigh. Morelli was irresistible in his bunny boxers. "I haven't changed my mind about the SUV, but I've changed my mind about your bedroom."

MORELLI IS AT his best on a Saturday morning. His body temperature is a little higher and his blood pressure is a little lower than on a Monday. Everything about him is a little softer, a little more sensual. He was at the kitchen table in faded navy sweatpants and a matching sweatshirt that had the sleeves cut short. I suspected he was commando under the sweatpants. He'd showered, but he hadn't shaved, and he looked like he could give a dead woman an orgasm.

He glanced up from his paper and smiled at me. "Shazam."

I smiled back at him. It had been a multiple shazam morning.

I sipped my coffee. "What's going on today?"

"I'm getting someone to demo the basement floor. And I'm going door-to-door looking for Dom. I think you're right. He's nearby."

It was a little after eight, and Zook was still sleeping. Mooner and Gary hadn't yet appeared on Morelli's front doorstep. The sound of car doors slamming shut and people talking carried in from Morelli's backyard.

"It's Saturday morning," Morelli said. "Don't these people take a day off?"

I peeked out the window. "Brenda is in the yard with the film crew."

Morelli took his coffee to the door and stepped out.

"*Hell-o!*" Brenda said, eyeballing Morelli. "You are *hot*. Hold me back!"

Morelli turned and looked at me. "Is she for real?"

"Yes. And you want to keep arm's distance, or she'll give you a pat-down."

"You're trespassing on private property," Morelli said. "And you've ignored the crime scene tape."

"We didn't ignore it," the cameraman said. "We got a real good shot of it."

Brenda was in another black leather outfit. She was wearing four-inch spike-heeled shoes, and her hair and her face and her chest were blue. She had a handheld mic, and she was having a hard time navigating because her heels were sinking into the freshly dug dirt. She climbed onto a dirt mound and looked down into the hole. The cameraman focused on Brenda.

"Here we are at Aunt Rose's house," Brenda said to the camera. "And as you can see, digging for the stolen money has already begun."

"Excuse me," Morelli said. "You're going to have to leave."

Brenda stumbled over to Morelli with the mic. "Are you by any chance the handsome owner of the property—"

"That's it," Morelli said. "I've had enough."

He set his coffee cup on the stoop, reached over the railing, grabbed the garden hose, and turned it on Brenda and the cameraman.

Brenda hit high C at the first blast of water. "Eeeeeee!" she shrieked. "Dammit, shit, sonovabitch!"

The dirt instantly turned to mud, and Brenda lost her footing and went down. The sound guy rushed in to help, and he went down, too.

"Maybe you want to turn the hose off," I said to Morelli.

Brenda had one shoe on and one shoe in her hand. "What *is* your *problem*?" she yelled at Morelli. "Do you know who I am? I'm *Brenda*. I'm doing the news here, and the news is *sacred*, for cripe's sake. You can't turn the hose on the news, you moron!"

Morelli shut the water off and retrieved his coffee cup. "This is going to be another one of those days," he said.

We backed into the house, closed and locked the door, and pulled all the shades down.

Morelli stood in the middle of his kitchen. "I hate this," he said. "I hate bringing this shit into my home."

"We need to find Dom."

Morelli nodded agreement. "I'm going to change my clothes and canvass the neighborhood."

"We'll split it in half."

Morelli smiled down at me. "Nice offer, Cupcake, but you're blue. You'll scare the crap out of everyone."

"I forgot."

"Stay here with Zook. Keep people out of my yard. Get me some estimates on jackhammer rentals."

Morelli went upstairs, and I crept to the window and looked out. No Brenda. No cameraman. No film crew van. I went to the front of the house. No one was there, either. Good deal.

Bob was sleeping in a patch of sun in the living room. He was still spray-painted. He didn't seem to care. While I was standing, looking out the window, Lula's red Firebird slid to a stop in front of Morelli's house. Lula hoisted herself out of the car and marched to Morelli's front door.

"Hey," I said, opening the door to her. "What's up?"

"I need you to help me with my prenup. I got a lawyer appointment this afternoon, and I gotta have this ready."

"I don't know anything about prenups."

"You just gotta help me make out my list. I'm supposed to list all my assets. And then Tank lists all his assets. And we got what we got."

"So Tank is doing this, too?"

"I left a message on his phone. I said if you got anything you want to keep, you better list it out or I could get it in case of divorce. Not that I intend to get a divorce, but I guess you never know, right?"

"Right."

"Do you think Tank and me would ever get divorced?"

"I'm still struggling with you and Tank getting *married*."

"Hunh," Lula said. "Anyways, I got this list. You want to hear it?"

"Sure."

"I got a television, a DVD player, a cable box." Lula cut her eyes to me. "I hate those cable fuckers."

"Everybody hates them."

"I got my Firebird, my Glock, a fur coat that's almost mink, a clock radio, a whip."

"Wait a minute. You have a whip?"

"Don't everyone?"

"I don't have a whip."

"Hunh."

"What do you do with the whip? What does it look like? Is it one of those long black ones like Zorro uses?"

"No," Lula said. "It's the kind a jockey uses. It's for bad boys."

"Eeuw."

"Okay, if you're gonna be squeamish about it, I'll skip over my collection of professional experience enhancement tools. I never used the whip anyway. It went with a Halloween outfit."

Morelli came down the stairs in jeans and running shoes, and a sweatshirt over a T-shirt.

"What's up?" he said to Lula. "I see you're a member of the Blue Girl Group."

"Blue isn't my best color," Lula said.

Morelli grabbed me and kissed me and went off to do his cop thing.

"He looks like he got some last night," Lula said. "Where's he going?"

"He thinks Dom is somewhere in the neighborhood. He's going to look around."

"How come you're not helping him?"

"I'm blue."

"Oh yeah, I forgot. I'm starting to get used to it."

"And someone has to stay here with Zook. I don't want to leave him in the house alone."

"I could baby-sit him," Lula said. "I'm taking the morning to put my prenup in order. I could just as leave do it here."

"I'd really like to go back to my apartment and check on Rex and get some clothes."

"Go for it," Lula said.

I ran upstairs and knocked on Zook's door.

"Yeah?" he said. A moment later, he was at the door, looking almost awake.

"I have to go back to my apartment for an hour or so. Morelli is working, so Lula is going to stay here with you."

"No way! She scares the crap out of me."

"You'll be fine as long as you don't tell her she's fat. And you might want to avoid mentioning the blue dye."

"I'm not going out of my room."

"That would be okay, too."

I grabbed my purse and ran downstairs. "Don't let anyone dig in the yard," I told Lula. "Morelli takes it personally. And Zook is a good kid, but it would be great if he didn't paint anything."

"I'm on it. You can count on me. Do you think I should list shoes in the prenup?"

"Do you and Tank wear the same size?"

"No."

"Then probably your shoes are safe."

My apartment isn't that far from Morelli's house. Too far to walk but fast to drive. I parked the Zook car, bypassed the elevator for the stairs, and let myself into my apartment. I tapped on Rex's cage, and he peeked out at me. I dropped a baby carrot and a piece of cheese into his food dish and gave him fresh water. I stuffed clean jeans and a couple shirts into a tote bag. I didn't need much. Just enough to get me through a couple more days while we straightened out the Zook arrangements.

I took one last look at myself in my bathroom mirror. I wanted to believe that the blue was fading, but truth is, it wasn't. I was hideously blue. I was like Dom . . . conspicuous. A bunch of people were looking for Dom, and Dom didn't want to be found. And Dom didn't have the luxury of taking off for Rio. Dom had to hang close. Dom had his own agenda.

So let's step into Dom's shoes. I'm ultra-recognizable, and I'm confined to a small area. How would I move around? In disguise or at night. Second problem, I have no money. So either I mooch from someone I trust or else I hold up a convenience store. I'm going to guess he's mooching.

I called Connie. "Would you run a personal history on Dom for me?"

"What do you want to know?"

"Where was he living when he was sent to prison?"

"That's easy. He owned a house on Vine Street. When he was sentenced, his wife divorced him and got the house. So far as I know, she's still living there and has remarried."

I got the house number from Connie and hung up. I'd forgotten about the ex-wife. This was great. Ex-wives loved ratting on their ex-husbands.

THE VINE STREET house was a small single-family cape with a detached single-car garage. It had a green Subaru sitting in the driveway.

I parked and knocked on the front door. A woman answered and gasped when she saw me.

"Sorry," I said. "I know I'm blue. I had an accident with some dye."

"I know who you are," she said. "You're Stephanie Plum. There was a piece on you on the late news last night. They said you were involved in the robbery treasure hunt, and you and Brenda got sprayed with blue dye. Do you really know Brenda?"

"Yes."

"What's she like?"

"She's like Brenda. Could I ask you some questions about Dom?"

"Sure, but I don't know much about him anymore. I haven't seen him since he got out."

"I'm interested in the guys he used to hang with."

"Mostly they were from his old neighborhood. Victor Raguzzo, Benny Stoli, Jelly Kantner. And the guy who was shot. Allen Gratelli. Allen and Dom worked together."

"Did you think any of those guys pulled the job with him?"

"I could see Allen doing it. Victor, Benny, and Jelly, no."

"Dom's hiding out somewhere. Do you have any ideas?"

"He's not with his mom?"

"No."

"Jelly would be dumb enough to take him in. Or maybe he's still seeing Peggy Bargaloski. That's why I divorced him. I found out he was spending a *lot* of time at Peggy's house."

I gave her my card and told her to call me if she saw Dom.

I drove around the corner, pulled to the curb, and got addresses from Connie. Jelly was living in a second-floor apartment two blocks from Dom's mother's house. Peggy was in Cleveland.

I wanted to do a drive-by on Jelly's house, but I was too obvious in the Zook car. There was a car wash minutes away on the corner of Hammond and Baker, but I didn't want to put up with the car wash crew and their comments on my blueness. I know that's chickenshit of me. What can I say? I'm blue, and I'm feeling fragile.

I drove back to Morelli's house, thinking I'd check on Lula and trade my Zookmobile for Morelli's SUV. I let myself into the house and couldn't find anyone. Mooner's laptop was on the coffee table beside Zook's, but there was no Mooner or Zook. I walked to the back of the house and looked out. Mooner and Zook were digging in the backyard with Bob. Lula was standing guard with her gun drawn. A small crowd had formed on the perimeter of the crime scene tape. Gary was sitting on the stoop, watching.

"What the heck is this?" I asked Lula.

"We figured it wouldn't hurt to look. There's still some undisturbed ground here. And if we find it, we'll share it with Morelli."

"Are you insane? If you find it, you'll hand it over to the authorities! You're looking for stolen money."

"Hunh," Lula said. "You sure got a stick up your ass. When did you get so play-by-the-book?"

"I've always been play-by-the-book. *You're* the one who doesn't play by the book."

"Well, I knew it was one of us."

"Anyway, I don't think the money is buried in the backyard."

"Me, either," Gary said. "I'm not seeing anything. I told them it was a waste of time, but no one would listen."

"Yeah, but you might be a nut," Lula said.

"Hey," I yelled at Zook and Mooner. "Stop digging. The money isn't in the backyard."

A murmur went up from the people pressed against the crime scene tape. Two of them had shovels.

"It isn't in the front yard, either," I told everyone. "Go home!"

Mooner, Zook, Bob, Gary, Lula, and I left the yard and huddled in the kitchen. I gave everyone an ice cream sandwich, except Bob. Bob got a slice of ham.

"How come you think the money isn't in the yard?" Lula wanted to know.

"People wouldn't be breaking into Morelli's house if the money was in the yard. The only people digging in the yard are idiots who saw Brenda on television."

Lula peeled the wrapper off her ice cream. "So you think the money's in the house?"

"I'm not sure there *is* any money. I suspect it was here at one time, but Dom was in prison for almost ten years, and there were a lot of changes. Rose died. Morelli moved into the house. Things were thrown away. Rooms were renovated. For all we know, Rose could have found the money and given it to the church."

"I don't think so," Gary said. "I'm getting a sharp pain in my forehead."

"It's the ice cream," I told him. "You're getting a brain freeze." I herded everyone into the living room and found some Saturday morning cartoons on television. "I need to go out again, but I'll be back by noon."

I found the keys to Morelli's car and left my keys in their place. I drove to Jelly's house and idled across the street. It was a small two-story house that had been converted into two apartments. There was only one front door, so I assumed the owner had made a small foyer with two inner doors. I looked up to the second floor. Four windows going across. The shades had been raised on all four windows. It would be easier to snoop if Jelly lived on the ground floor. I drove around the block. Sometimes older neighborhoods in Trenton have alleys intersecting the blocks. This block wasn't divided by an alley. I parked around the corner, walked to Jelly's house, and tried the front door. Ordinarily, if you look like you belong somewhere, no one pays attention. Unfortunately, I was blue, and I looked like I belonged in some distant galaxy.

The front door was unlocked, so I stepped inside. Just as I'd thought, there was a small foyer. The door to my left led to the ground-floor apartment. The door directly in front of me led upstairs. I rang the bell. No answer. I rang again. Nothing. I tried the doorknob. Locked. I looked under the mat. No key. I felt the top of the doorjamb. Eureka . . . a key. I plugged the key into the lock, the door clicked open, and I stepped inside. I closed the door and stood listening, hearing nothing but quiet.

I crept up the stairs and cautiously peeked into the apartment. Living room with a galley kitchen at one end. A small hall leading to a bedroom and a bathroom. Dirty dishes in the sink. A cereal box on the counter. A pillow on the couch in front of the small television. An open half-empty bag of chips on the coffee table. I moved to the bathroom. Not clean. Two toothbrushes. Two razors. Towels on the floor. Toilet lid up. Ick. The door was open to the bedroom. Bed unmade. Sheets looked like they'd been on there since Christmas. Socks and underwear on the floor. Top bureau drawer open. Big mess.

I thought there was a good chance Dom was crashing here. I was tempted to do a more thorough search, but I wasn't sure what it would produce. And the longer I lingered, the better my chance of getting caught in the act. I decided to sneak out and do a background search on Jelly and turn the whole mess over to Morelli.

I walked out of the bedroom into the short hallway, and I heard the door open and close at the foot of the stairs. Instant panic! I was trapped. I wasn't in a position where I felt I could successfully detain Dom, and I didn't want to blow his cover and have him run. I did a ten-second imitation of a cat on roller skates. I pulled myself together, scurried into the bedroom, and dove under the bed.

The reality of hiding under a bed is that it's uncomfortable, it's terrifying, and you feel like an idiot. I inched to the middle, so there was less chance I'd be seen, and I tried to breathe quietly.

There were two sets of footsteps on the stairs and then there was a moment of quiet, and I knew they were in the living room.

"Nobody home," a male voice said. Not Dom's.

"Yeah, but I know he was here. I can smell him."

The second voice was also male. And again, not Dom's.

"Look around. Maybe he left something laying out that would tell us something."

"He wouldn't do that. He's living with Jelly. He's not going to let Jelly see anything."

"Look around anyway. People are stupid. They do stupid things. And maybe if we stay here long enough, he'll come home, and we can persuade him to talk to us."

"We've got his sister on ice. How much more persuading can we do? Personally, I don't think he knows where the money is."

"For crissake, just look! Would it kill you to look?"

Holy crap. Dom's partners. And I was stuck under the bed. I went cold inside. I could feel everything liquefying in my intestines. How does this happen to me? How do I get myself into these situations? I heard them rummaging through the living room and kitchen. They came into the bedroom, and my heart rate picked up.

"These guys are such slobs," one of them said. "It's like two pigs living in their own slop."

"You should talk. I've been in your apartment and it isn't that great."

"Wait until I get my hands on the money, and you'll see great. I'll be out of that shit-hole apartment. I'll be cruising the islands in my boat. Did I ever show you a picture of my boat?"

"Only about a million times."

They were walking around the bed, and I could see their shoes and the bottoms of their slacks. The one guy was wearing scuffed brown tie shoes, worn down at the heel, and tan slacks with cuffs. The other was in jeans and beat-up CAT boots with a gash in the toe. They went through the bureau drawers and rifled the single drawer in the bed-side chest.

"There's nothing here," the one guy said. "What do you want to do now?"

"I don't feel like waiting. I got stuff to do. My wife's on my ass."

"I wouldn't know about that."

"Yeah, no one would marry you."

"Lots of women would marry me."

"Oh yeah? Who?"

"Lots of women. And I'm not paying through the nose for a woman I'm not even getting anything from."

They left the bedroom, and moments later, I heard them on the stairs. The door opened and closed, and the apartment was quiet. I didn't know what to do. I was afraid to crawl out from under the bed. I was pretty sure they were no longer in the apartment, but what if I was wrong? I waited a couple minutes more and slithered to the edge, where I had a better view. I held my breath and listened. I carefully looked around. Now or never, I thought. I belly-crawled out, got to my feet, and forced myself to creep down the hall to the living room. I almost keeled over with relief when no one was there. I hurried to the foyer at the bottom of the stairs and hesitated. If the two bad guys saw me leave, they might think I was coming from the down-stairs apartment. Unless they watched the evening news. Then they'd know who I was because I was *blue*.

I locked the door, placed the key on the top of the door-jamb, opened the front door a crack, and looked out. No one standing there with a gun in his hand. No black mafia staff cars with tinted windows lined up at the curb. I casu-ally walked away from the house, down the block to the corner, around the corner, and angled myself behind the wheel of Morelli's SUV. I two-handed the key into the ig-nition and pulled away from the curb with a white-knuckle grip on the wheel. Okay, so I was a little freaked, but I hadn't messed my pants. That was pretty good, right?

By the time I got to Morelli's house, I'd calmed down a little but not entirely. It was almost noon and Morelli was sit-ting on his front step with Bob. I plunked myself down next to him, he put his arm around me, and I collapsed into him.

"Either you like me a lot, or you've had a bad morning," Morelli said.

"It's both. I did some legwork and ended up at Jelly Kantner's apartment."

"*At* his apartment or *in* his apartment?"

"In."

"Were you *invited* in?"

"No, but I also wasn't told to stay out."

"Nobody home," Morelli said.

"Mmm. Anyway, it was obvious someone was staying with Jelly, and it wasn't a woman."

"You think it was Dom?"

"Yes. And I wasn't the only one to reach that conclusion, because just as I was about to leave, two guys showed up."

I felt Morelli tense against me and go silent for a beat. "You told them you were the maid?"

"I didn't tell them anything. I was under the bed."

"This is why our relationship is stressful," Morelli said.

"I think they were Dom's two remaining partners. They were looking for him because they wanted the money. And they have Loretta. They're holding her hostage, but so far Dom hasn't come through."

"Did you get to see them? Do you have names?"

"No names. One is married and one isn't. One of them lives in an apartment. One was wearing beat-up CAT boots and jeans, and the other was wearing tan slacks with cuffs and brown shoes. I couldn't see more than that."

What I didn't say was that the voice on the single guy sounded familiar. It had a slight rasp, like a smoker. And there wasn't a lot of inflection. I couldn't associate a name or face with the voice. I just felt like I'd heard it before.

"I'll bring Bob in and then I'll go to Jelly's and wait for Dom," Morelli said. "Where's Zook?"

"Zook's in the house with Lula."

"I got back about ten minutes ago, and Lula's car was here, but no one was in the house."

"Did you look in the backyard?"

"Yeah," Morelli said. "No one's in the backyard. It's wall-to-wall mud. I think if I keep turning the hose on it no one will dig there."

"That's weird," I said, "because I could swear I hear digging."

Morelli listened. "It doesn't sound like digging. It's more like drilling and . . . oh shit."

"What?"

Morelli was on his feet. "That's a jackhammer."

I followed Morelli to the kitchen and down the cellar stairs. Mooner was wailing away at the concrete floor with a pickax, and Lula had a jackhammer propped against her belly. She gave the jackhammer a blast of juice, and I was afraid her breasts were going to break loose from their moorings and knock her out. Gary and Zook were in a corner, mesmerized by the spectacle.

"This is my basement floor," Morelli yelled. "You can't just go into a man's house and jackhammer his floor!"

Lula jiggled to a stop. "Well, *excuse* me. It's not like we weren't gonna share the money with you."

"There's no sharing," Morelli said. "The money was stolen."

"It was over ten years ago," Lula said. "Isn't there some kind of time limit and then it's finders keepers losers weepers?"

"No," Morelli said. "Where'd you get the jackhammer?"

"I sort of borrowed it."

"Oh great," he said. "A hot jackhammer."

"It's a Saturday. You can borrow these things on a Saturday," Lula said.

"This is a lot of floor to demo," Morelli said. "And after we demo the floor, we still don't know where to dig."

"Guess that's why there were directions," Lula said. "Probably it was like a treasure map. Seven paces north and two paces west and the treasure is buried under the piece of floor with the X marked on it."

"I thought you had an appointment with your lawyer," I said to Lula.

"Yeah, I guess I better get going." She turned to Morelli. "You want me to come back and jackhammer some more when I'm done with the lawyer?"

"No," Morelli said. "But I appreciate the offer."

"So, like, now what?" Mooner asked Morelli. "This is majorly disappointing. I was counting on some moola, man. Like, being a griefer doesn't pay a lot, you know what I mean? And a man has needs, right? Like, what happens when I have a craving for a Big Mo candy bar or a crab puff?"

"Here's a deal," Morelli said. "I could use some security in the house. Suppose I pay you guys to protect the house. That means you have to keep people from digging in my yard, pickaxing my basement, spray-painting my dog . . ."

"Whoa, cool," Mooner said. "And how about the Zookduder and me? Can we do those things?"

"No," Morelli said. "You have to protect the house from everyone, including yourselves."

"How much?" Zook asked.

"Five dollars a day."

"No way," Zook said.

"Ten."

"Twenty," Zook said. "Apiece."

"Ten," Morelli said. "Apiece."

"Take it, dude," Mooner said to Zook. "It's a cool gig."

"Me, too?" Gary asked.

"Yeah, you, too," Morelli said.

"Should we be, like, packing heat, or something?" Mooner wanted to know.

"No!" Morelli said. "If someone comes to the house, you politely tell them to go away. If they won't go away, you call me."

"Gotcha," Mooner said.

"Looks like we're done in the basement," I said. "Everyone upstairs for lunch."

Gary had been quietly standing in his corner. "I think it might be here," he said.

Everyone looked at him.

"I feel like I have a vision coming, but it's still in the back of my head. Sometimes it's like that. It's like brain constipation."

"Oh man, I hate when I get that," Mooner said.

"Maybe lunch will help," I said to Gary.

Gary didn't budge from the corner. "I think I should stay here."

I made sandwiches for Zook, Mooner, Morelli, Bob, and me, and I brought Gary's sandwich down to the basement.

"How's it going?" I said to him. "Anything coming through?"

"I had sort of a tingle before, but it went away."

"Okeydokey. Shout out if you need anything."

Lula left, and Mooner and Zook checked in on Minion-fire.

"I'm going to get my cousin Mooch over here to finish the basement," Morelli said. "Part of it's torn up. I might as well finish the job."

Mooch owned a small construction company. He specialized in renovation, and fitting people into cement overcoats. His Yellow Pages ad read MOOCH MORELLI, DEMO AND DISPOSAL.

"Can you trust Mooch to let you know if he finds the money?" I asked Morelli.

"I'll keep my eye on him."

"What about Dom?"

"You can watch for Dom," Morelli said. "Stake out Jelly's apartment and call me if Dom shows up."

# FOURTEEN

FOUR HOURS LATER, I was still watching for Dom. My ass was asleep, and I had to tinkle. I got Jelly's phone number from Connie and tried calling him. No one answered, so I called Morelli.

"What's new?" I said to Morelli.

"Mooch and his guy Tiny have gone through two six-packs and have destroyed almost my entire basement. I think they only have maybe four or five more bottles of work left to do."

"What did they find?"

"Dirt."

"Are they going to dig up the dirt?"

"No. They're wasted. Mooch is lucky he hasn't jackhammered his foot."

"I need a bathroom break."

"No activity?"

"None. It looks to me like no one's even in the bottom half of the house."

"I'd take your place, but I'm afraid to leave Mooch alone with the kids."

"Afraid he'll plant them in the cellar?"

"No. I'm afraid he'll share my remaining beer with them."

So I had a dilemma. I had to tinkle. *Bad.* And I had no one to relieve me. I could drive around and look for a gas station or convenience store with a bathroom, but that could take time. Or I could run across the street and use Jelly's bathroom. If I used Jelly's bathroom, I ran the risk of getting trapped again. Not to mention contracting a disease.

I did a mental coin toss, and Jelly's bathroom won. I pulled the key out of the ignition, shoved it into my pocket, and crossed the street. I let myself into the apartment, went straight to the bathroom, and lined the seat with toilet paper. Even with the toilet paper, I tried to be careful not to touch anything. This wasn't a bathroom that inspired confidence, and better safe than sorry. I was about to squat when I heard a crash and a sizzle, and an explosion rocked the building. I yanked my pants up and ran out of the bathroom. I got to the hall and saw a wall of flames race around Jelly's living room, creating an instant inferno. No way to get to the stairs. I ran back to the bedroom and slammed the door shut. I shoved the window up and crawled out. I hung by my hands, took a deep breath, closed my eyes, and let go. My feet hit first and then I was flat on my back with the wind knocked out of me.

I dragged myself to my feet and took a couple deep breaths. This wasn't good. I didn't want to be found here. I limped through the house's little backyard and half climbed, half fell over the split-rail wood fence, into his neighbor's yard. I crept between houses and came out on the street behind Jelly's.

A big black glob of smoke rose above the housetops, into the sky. Two police cruisers raced past me, and I could see the flashing lights of a fire truck farther down the street. I walked around the block and stood by Morelli's SUV, across the street and two houses down. My face felt flushed from the heat of the fire, and the realization that I could have died on the toilet.

My back ached and my arm was scratched and bleeding. I was having a hard time breathing, and I could feel tears collecting in my throat and behind my eyes. I managed to get into the SUV, but I was paralyzed by the horror and unable to drive. Jelly's house was completely engulfed in flames. Firemen were spraying water on neighboring houses and the fire didn't seem to be spreading. Thank goodness for that.

Emergency vehicles clogged the street. Fire trucks, cop cars, EMS trucks. Even if I was capable, I couldn't leave. One by one, the surplus trucks began moving out. I waited for my opportunity, and then I left, too.

Morelli, Mooch, and Tiny were in the kitchen, drinking coffee and eating sandwiches, when I walked in.

"We need to talk," I said to Morelli.

Morelli looked at my scraped arm. "Are you okay?"

"Marginally. Somebody blew up Jelly's house while I was in his bathroom."

Everyone went slack-jawed and stared at me.

"I was staking it out, and I had to go," I told them.

"Jeez," Mooch said. "Blowing up a house is serious stuff. Not in Trenton, but in most places."

Morelli paled. "You couldn't find a gas station? You actually broke into his house to use his bathroom?"

"It seemed easier. Until the house blew up."

"Was anyone hurt?"

"I don't think so. I think the downstairs apartment was unoccupied. And I was alone upstairs. It must have been a firebomb shot into the front window. I heard the glass shatter, and then the explosion, and then everything was in flames. I was able to escape by dropping from the bedroom window."

"Why were you watching Jelly?" Mooch asked.

"I was watching for Dom," I told him. "It's possible Dom's been bunking with Jelly."

"Do you have any ideas about Dom's partners?" Morelli asked Mooch.

"There's been some talk lately about Stanley Zero. The fourth partner is a big mystery."

The name sounded familiar, but I couldn't place him. "Who's Stanley Zero?"

"Football player," Morelli said. "He was a couple years ahead of us. Probably in Dom's class. Not good enough to make pro and too dumb to get into college."

"He's in construction," Mooch said. "He does framing for Premier Homes. He's been working for them for years."

"Why is he suddenly linked to the robbery?" I asked.

"I don't know," Mooch said. "Hard to say how these things start going around. A guy shoots his mouth off in a bar, or talks to a girl, and next thing it's public."

I looked at the cellar door. "Is Gary still down there?"

"No. He went home," Morelli said.

"Kentucky?"

"No. Home here in Trenton. I'm not sure where that is. He said he had a headache. I imagine it was from listening to the jackhammer."

"I got a headache, too," Tiny said.

Morelli took the SUV keys from me. "I'm going to take Mooch and Tiny home. They can come back for the truck tomorrow. We need to finish carting the concrete chunks out anyway."

Tiny was about a thousand pounds. I had no idea how Morelli was going to get him into the SUV, and if he did succeed, I had a mental image of the tires going flat.

"We're out of food," I said to Morelli. "You need to stop on the way home and get something for supper."

"This is getting expensive," Morelli said. "I'm paying protection money to three guys so they don't destroy my home, *and* I'm feeding them. Plus, I've now got Mooch and Tiny on the payroll."

"I had Connie run a check on Jelly," I told Morelli. "He's driving an orange Corolla. I have the plate number, but I don't think you need it. How many orange Corollas are there in Trenton?"

"I'll watch for it," Morelli said, herding Mooch and Tiny through the house and out the door.

Miraculously, Morelli got Tiny into the SUV and the tires didn't buckle. I watched them drive away, and I called Ranger. I wanted information on Stanley Zero, and Connie only worked a half day on Saturday.

"Babe," Ranger said.

"I need information on Stanley Zero. Place of residence, car, anything personal . . . like friends, wife, whatever."

"How do you want it? Can I e-mail it to you?"

"No. I'm at Morelli's house. I don't have my computer."

"I can send it to Morelli."

"That would work. How's Tank doing?"

"He's distracted."

"Why doesn't he just break it off?"

"The man is confused," Ranger said. "Sometimes it's difficult to tell what you want to do with a woman."

"Are you speaking about yourself?"

"No. I know exactly what I want to do."

I knew what he wanted to do, too.

"Is there anything else you need from me?" Ranger asked.

"Not right now."

"There will come a time," Ranger said. "Let me know when." And he disconnected.

I opened the freezer and stuck my head in to cool off. If there'd been any more innuendo in that conversation, I could have fried an egg on my forehead. Ranger was a successful bounty hunter because he was exceptionally intuitive and doggedly aggressive. And that was also his description as a lover.

I removed my head from the freezer, and I brought an ice cream sandwich out with me. Morelli's computer was upstairs in his office. I was eating the last of the ice cream, so I sneaked past Mooner and Zook and tiptoed up the stairs.

Ranger's office was ultra modern and very high tech. Polished glass, stainless steel, and black onyx surfaces with black leather chairs. It was dust and clutter free. The computer and phone system was state of the art and there was a plasma television on one wall.

Morelli's office was a mess. A red plastic milk crate held his baseball mitt, bat, and some tennis balls he'd collected for Bob. Stacks of dog-eared files hunkered in corners and against the wall. Smaller stacks of books he'd been given as presents or he thought he might like to read but never seemed to get to were tucked between the files. A dead houseplant on a small table by the window. Coffee cup rings everywhere. A yard sale desk and chair. Running shoes that had seen better days, kicked off under the desk and forgotten. And his computer, which was a nice new MacBook Pro. Plus a DeskJet printer.

I turned the computer on and brought up Morelli's mail program. I'm not a computer whiz, but I can do the basics. I knew it wouldn't take Ranger long to run the background check, but I relaxed in Morelli's chair for a moment before checking in. Truth is, I like Morelli's office. Okay, it could be a little cleaner, but it felt warm and comfy, like Morelli.

I could see across the hall into Zook's room. It was a typical teen disaster. Rumpled bed and every piece of clothing he had with him was on the floor. I thought he was doing remarkably well, considering his mother was missing. I imagined there might be some tears when he went to bed at night, but during the day he managed to hold his own. Mooner was helping. Mooner wasn't the world's best role model, but he kept Zook occupied.

I hit the GET MAIL button and Ranger's file came up. I printed it out and sat back to read it. Stanley Zero was married with two kids but not living with them. He was living alone in a low-rent apartment complex off Route 1. He worked for Premier Homes. I already knew that. So maybe he was Work Boots, and he was the partner with the crapola apartment. He'd run up his credit cards, but he wasn't in collection. He drove a red F150 truck. Four years old. No prior arrests. His wife was a nurse. Worked at St. Francis. She was living in a house that was owned jointly by Stanley and her. Heavily mortgaged. The kids were five and nine. The typical American family. Except Stanley might have robbed a bank, blown up a house, and shot a guy dead.

So I had Stanley Zero, Allen Gratelli, and Dom. If I could find the common thread, the one thing that brought them together, I might learn the identity of the fourth man. Or maybe there was no common thread. Stanley and Dom had gone to school together. Dom and Allen had worked together for the cable company. Maybe Dom was the organizer.

I straightened Morelli's bedroom, made the bed, and did a superficial cleaning of the bathroom. I peeked in at Zook's room and decided not to invade his privacy. Stephanie Plum, Ms. Sensitivity and half-assed housewife.

I heard Bob gallop from the kitchen to the front door, and I knew Morelli had arrived with food.

"Steph," he yelled. "I'm home."

Ricky Ricardo brings Lucy her dinner.

I met Morelli at the bottom of the stairs and took a grocery bag from him. He handed the other bags over to Zook and Mooner.

"Meatball subs, potato salad, coleslaw for all of us," he said to Zook and Mooner. "The beer is for me."

I took the bag into the kitchen and put the lunch meat, milk, orange juice, and sliced cheese in the fridge. Morelli'd also gotten bread and a cake that said HAPPY BIRTHDAY KEN.

"A birthday cake?" I said to him.

"I know you love birthday cake, and apparently Ken didn't need his."

We brought napkins, plates, silverware, and soda to the living room and Morelli remoted the television on. We crammed ourselves onto the couch and ate our food and watched the early evening news.

"And now we bring you our special report from that special person . . . Brenda," the anchor said.

Brenda popped onto the screen. Her face was blue, she was in full black leather bounty hunter mode, and she was in Morelli's backyard.

"Here we are at Aunt Rose's house," she said. "And as you can see, digging for the stolen money has already begun."

There was a shot of Morelli telling her to leave, and there was a full thirty seconds of Morelli turning the hose on her. The screen went black for a moment, and then Brenda reappeared in dry clothes, free from mud. "Here we are back at Aunt Rose's house," Brenda said. "We aren't going to bother the hot guy who lives here, because he might turn his hose on us again, and while I wouldn't mind seeing his hose in private, I'm not taking any chances in his backyard. As you can see, there's this big dump truck parked behind his garage. I had one of my crew climb up on the truck and look inside, and he said it's getting filled up with chunks of concrete. And even as we speak I can hear the jackhammer working in Aunt Rose's basement." Brenda aimed the microphone at the back of Morelli's house, and there was the faint sound of the jackhammer, which at that distance sounded like a woodpecker. "As you all know, it's been thought the missing nine million dollars was last seen by Aunt Rose, and maybe this new development will bring us closer to all that money. This is Brenda signing off and saying . . . see you soon!"

Zook gave a howl of laughter.

"Dude," Mooner said. "Awesome. Ratings fabuloso."

The next shot was Brenda in the studio sitting opposite the anchor.

"That was an interesting piece of film," the anchor said

to her. "I understand you've been an insider on this investigation."

"Yes, I have," Brenda said. "In fact—"

And at that instant, Gary crept up behind Brenda and tapped her on the shoulder.

"I have to talk to you," he said. "I had a headache, so I went to my bedroom to lay down, and I had another one of those dreams. You know, the big pizza dream. Only this time, the pizza was pepperoni and black olives, and it was very disturbing because it could fly! I saw it *flying through the air*."

Brenda rolled her eyes. "Gary, how many times have I told you to go home? Have you stopped your medication again?"

The anchor was on his feet. "How did he get in here? Who is he?"

"I'm her cousin on our Grammy Mim's side," Gary told him.

The anchor had his hand waving in the air. "Security!"

"You have to beware of the big pizza!" Gary said to Brenda. "It's not an ordinary pizza, and it's out to get you. And it might be when you're sitting on the toilet on Route 1."

"I swear," Brenda said. "You are *such* a *nut*."

Two uniformed guards appeared on the set and the station went to commercial.

"That was primo," Mooner said. "The dude was, like, a real celebrity stalker. And the white hair is a good look for him. Au courant but raging retro. Like totally Warhol."

Morelli cut his eyes to me. "The really scary part of all this is I'm starting to understand Mooner."

"Just think of it as learning a foreign language," I said to Morelli. "Pretend you're visiting the Republic of Moon."

We finished the subs, potato salad, and coleslaw, Mooner sang happy birthday to Ken, and we dug into the cake.

We ate half a cake and the phone rang.

"I'm at the police station bonding out Gary-the-Stalker," Connie said. "Someone needs to take him somewhere and get him to shut up about the big pizza before he gets carted away and shot full of Thorazine. And it's not me, because I'm late for JoAnn Garber's baby shower."

"I'll come get him. How do you want to do this?"

"I'll take him with me, and we'll make the switch at the firehouse," Connie said.

"I'm on it."


I took possession of Gary fifteen minutes later.

"How did you get to the television station?" I asked him.

"I drove. I followed Brenda from her hotel. I tried to talk to her before she got into the car, but she was moving too fast. And then she parked in a special lot at the station, and I couldn't get in. So I had to find a place on the street, and then it wasn't easy getting into the building. I had to climb in through a window in the back."

"Most people would leave a message on Brenda's cell phone."

"I'm not most people."

No kidding.

"And she keeps changing her number," Gary said.

"Because she doesn't want you bothering her?"

"She's very brave. And she doesn't want to impose."

"Has it ever occurred to you that you might be delusional?"

"That's what the psychiatrist said, but I think he's wrong. There's an evil flying pizza out there, and it's got Brenda's name on it."

"I'm assuming your car is still parked on the street."

"Yes."

"I'm going to take you to your car, and then you're going to go home."

"Yes."

"Where is home?"

"Morelli's garage," Gary said.

"Excuse me?"

"I have a little camper that I tow behind my car. I parked it in Morelli's garage yesterday, and it's still there."

"Does Morelli know this?"

"I don't think it ever came up."

We located his car, he followed me to Morelli's house, and we both parked at the curb. I got out and looked at his white Taurus.

"I thought this was a rental," I said to him. "No one *buys* a white Taurus."

"It matches my hair," Gary said. "And it's my zodiac sign."

It made as much sense as anything else in my life. "Have you had dinner?"

"No."

"Prowl through the fridge and make yourself a sandwich. If you're lucky, there's still some birthday cake left."

"Whose birthday?" he asked.

"Ken's."

I brought him into the house, and he settled in with Zook and Mooner, so he could lurk. Morelli was in the kitchen loading the dishwasher.

"I brought Gary back here," I told him. "He's helping out with the wood elves."

"That's a comfort."

"Yeah, I knew you'd be excited. I had Ranger run a check on Stanley Zero. I have the printout upstairs. One of us should take a look at him."

# FIFTEEN

THE PHONE RANG at two in the morning. Morelli came awake first, a bare arm reaching across me to get at the bedside phone. Not the first time he'd gotten a call in the middle of the night.

"Yeah?" he said.

There was a short conversation, and Morelli hung up and flopped back onto his side of the bed.

"You're not going to believe this," he said. "On second thought, it makes perfect sense. That was your friend and mine, supercop Carl Costanza. He's working a shift with Big Dog, and they got a report that there were lights in the cemetery. Turns out it was a bunch of people who all got the idea to dig up Rose. One of them was your Grandma Mazur."

"Is she in jail?"

"No. Everyone ran away when Carl and Big Dog drove up, but your grandmother recognized Carl and told him she needed a ride home."

"Omigod."

"Yeah. Carl said they're bringing her here. She didn't want to get dropped off at your parents' house in a police car because people would talk."

I rolled out of bed, scuffed through the clothes on the floor, and found what I needed.

Zook was in the hall when I opened Morelli's bedroom door. "I heard the call," he said. "Was it about my mom?"

"No. It was about my grandmother. She's having a friend drop her off here, and then I'm going to give her a ride home."

Zook smiled. "I bet she did something bad and she's afraid your mother will ground her."

"Close enough," I said.

I padded downstairs in the dark and looked out the front window. No police car yet. I walked through the house to the kitchen to get a bottle of water and checked on the yard. No one digging, but there was a bar of light under Morelli's garage door. Gary was still up. Or maybe Gary was afraid of the dark. Lucky for Gary there was electric in the garage. Unfortunate for Morelli, since he was paying the bill.

I returned to the living room, and Morelli joined me.

"You didn't have to get up," I said to him.

"No way was I going to miss this."

We saw headlights glide to a stop in front of the house, and we went out to say hello to Carl and Big Dog.

"Here she is," Big Dog said to me, opening the door for Grandma. "Maybe your mother should put a bell around her neck." He looked at Grandma and shook his finger. "No more sneaking out at night. It's dangerous."

"Thanks for the ride," Grandma said. She looked in the car at Carl. "My regards to your mother."

Carl smiled and nodded.

"Thanks," I said to Carl and Big Dog. "I really appreciate this."

"We would have hauled her in, but it was too embarrassing," Big Dog said. "She was the only one we could catch."

Morelli waved them off, and I buckled Grandma into the SUV.

"Where's your shovel?" I asked her.

"I didn't have one. I was just supervising. I went to Elmer Rhiner's viewing and Marion Barker was there with Bitty Kuleza. And Marion said she heard Rose was always saying how she was gonna take her fortune to the grave. And one thing led to another, and it ended up that we thought it would be a good idea to dig Rose up and take a look. So Bitty gave me a ride, and we met Marion and her two grandsons at the cemetery. Her grandsons are real big guys, and they were doing the digging."

"That's crazy!"

"Yeah. I don't know what it is about that money, but it's just got ahold of me. It's a beaut of a mystery."

Morelli drove the short distance and parked in front of my parents' house. We watched Grandma sneak in, and we waited a couple minutes to make sure she didn't sneak back out.

"You should snap me up," Morelli said. "Not many men would marry you after meeting your grandmother. You're lucky to have me."

I looked over at him. "Is that a proposal?"

There was total silence for a couple beats. "I'm not sure. It just popped out."

"Let me know when you're sure."

"Would you say *yes*?" Morelli asked.

"I'm not sure."

"I bet I could convince you it would be a good thing," Morelli said. "How about taking a look at my assets?"

Oh good grief.

It took us about twenty minutes in the alley behind the bonds office to appreciate his assets. When we finally returned to his house, all the lights were blazing and two squad cars were angle-parked at his curb. Morelli slid to a stop, and we hit the sidewalk at a run.

"What's going on?" he said to the cop at the door.

"Your houseguest heard someone break in and called 911."

Zook was standing in the hall, hanging on to Bob's collar. "Right after you left, I heard someone at the back door," Zook said. "Bob heard them, too, and he started barking, and he never barks if it's someone he knows, so I grabbed Bob and brought him into my room, and then I locked my door and called 911. I put all my lights off and looked out the window at the backyard, and just before the first police car showed up, I saw two men run out of the house and across the yard."

"What did they look like?" Morelli asked.

"I don't know. Just average. I couldn't see. It was real dark. But one of them had a shovel."

"You have forced entry on the back door," one of the cops said to Morelli. "And the basement door was open. Other than that, everything seems okay."

After everyone left, Morelli walked through the house, checking windows and doors. He searched the basement, the closets, all nooks and crannies and under the beds.

"Tomorrow we get the alarm system up and running," he said.


MORELLI TOOK HIS cereal bowl and coffee mug to the sink. "I'm going to take a look at Stanley Zero this morning. Do you have any plans?"

"I'm doing laundry."

"That's pretty exciting."

"I'm washing sheets," I told him.

Morelli slid an arm around me and kissed my neck. "I love when you talk about sheets."

Now, here's the thing I like about Morelli. There's a lot of variety to his sexiness. He can be hot, he can be funny, he can be loving, he can be short on time and hungry. This morning, he was playful.

"Would you like to know what I'm going to do to you to-night when you slide between those sheets?" I asked him.

The depth of his eyes instantly changed, and he left playful behind. "Yeah," he said. "I'd like to know."

"You have to wait."

"I'm not good at waiting."

"No kidding!"

Morelli broke out in a wide grin. "Have I just been insulted?"

"Only a little. Did you get the background report on Zero? I left it on your desk."

"Got it. Thanks. Keep your eyes open here."

"You betcha."

Ten minutes after Morelli left, Zook shuffled down the stairs and into the kitchen. He helped himself to a bagel and took it into the living room.

Moments later, Gary was at the back door. "I thought I smelled coffee."

I pointed to the coffeepot. "Help yourself."

He looked at the bag of bagels sitting on the counter.

"Would you like a bagel?" I asked him.

"Yeah! That would be great."

Morelli was going to have to find the nine million and take a cut just to pay his electric and food bills.

Sunday mornings are quiet in the Burg and surrounding communities. The women go to church, and the men take the Sunday paper and sit on the can. I've never understood the attraction of sitting on a toilet, pants at your ankles, newspaper in hand. I could think of a million better places to read the paper. And yet this is a firmly adhered-to Sunday ritual for Burg husbands. My father couldn't imagine a Sunday morning without this quality bathroom experience. Unmarried men seem to be exempt.

After Morelli's car left his neighborhood, there was no more street traffic. No dogs were walked. No kids on skateboards. Just Sunday morning quiet. And that's why it was twice as startling when the brick sailed through Morelli's living room window.

Zook and Gary were on the couch, deep into the world of Minionfire, I was walking though the living room, on my way to collect the laundry, and the glass shattered. We all jumped and there was a collective gasp of surprise.

Jelly's apartment explosion and fire were still fresh in my mind. I looked at the brick, which had a small box attached, and my first thought was *bomb*. I rushed over, picked the brick up, and threw it back outside via the broken window.

Gary and Zook were frozen on the couch, eyes huge, mouths open. I went to the front door and looked out. The brick was just sitting there on Morelli's postage-stamp lawn. The box attached to the brick looked small to be a bomb, but heck, what do I know? I watched it for a couple minutes and cautiously crept out to take a closer look. I was standing there, looking at the brick, when Mooner strolled up and stood next to me.

"Whoa," Mooner said. "That's a brick."

"Yep."

He bent down to see it better. "It's got a box attached to it."

And before I could stop him, he picked it up and shook it to see if the box rattled.

"It's got the dude's name on it," Mooner said.

I craned my neck and read the writing on the box. JOE MORELLI.

"What's it doing sitting here in the yard?" Mooner wanted to know. "There's no mail delivery today. It's a Sunday. Even I know that."

"Someone tossed it through Morelli's window."

"Get the heck out," Mooner said. "Was the window open?"

"No," I told him.

"Get the heck out," he said.

The box was held to the brick with electrician's tape. I took the box upstairs, set it on Morelli's desk, and called Morelli.

"How's it going?" I asked him.

"Not good. I got a call from dispatch. Two gang killings in the projects. I'm on my way there now. I don't know when I'll get home. Sometimes these things take time to sort out. What's up with you?"

"Someone pitched a brick through your living room window. And attached to the brick was a box with your name on it."

"Is this for real?"

"Yep."

"Put the brick and the box in the garage. Don't leave it in the house. Better to blow up the garage than the house."

"Do you think it's a bomb?"

"I think it doesn't hurt to be careful. I'll deal with it when I'm done here," Morelli said. "And I'll call Mooch and get him to replace the glass. And I'll make arrangements to have an alarm system installed."

I disconnected and stared at the box. I was faced with a dilemma. Gary was living in the garage. I didn't want to explode Gary. No big deal, I thought. Just ask Gary to pull his camper out of the garage.

The doorbell chimed, the door opened and closed, and I heard Lula ask for me.

"I'm upstairs," I yelled at her. "Come on up."

Lula was dressed down. Running shoes, black stretch yoga pants, and a black stretch T-shirt that looked like it was going to burst at the seams.

"What's the occasion?" I asked her.

"I went to try some wedding gowns yesterday, and it was a depressing experience. First off, they only had itty-bitty sizes for those skinny bitches. Like us big and beautiful women don't get married? And then they said they were gonna have to charge extra on account of they were gonna have to order so much material. What the heck is that about? It's not like I'm getting a circus tent. So anyway, I decided I'd join a gym. I figure with the money I save on less material, I could pay for the membership."

"That's a terrific idea. I should do something like that. What gym did you join?"

"I didn't exactly join a gym yet. I just got the clothes."

"It's a start," I said to Lula.

"Damn right," Lula said. "What's this package with Morelli's name on it? And why's it on a brick?"

"Someone pitched it through his living room window just now."

"Get the heck out. What are you going to do with it?"

"Morelli wants me to put it in the garage for safe keeping until he gets home later today."

"I don't think that's a good idea." Lula picked the box up and tested its weight. "It could be something important that requires immediate attention. I think you should open this sucker."

"It could be a bomb."

"Okay then, let Gary open it."

I did an eye roll.

"Nothing wrong with that," Lula said. "He's always saying how he knows things. Let's see if he knows it's a bomb. Anyway, it don't look like a bomb."

"It's all wrapped up. How could you tell?"

"Well, if it was a bomb, it would be a little one."

I heard Bob jump off the bed and head down the stairs.

"I need to get the glass cleaned up before Bob steps in it," I told Lula. "Put the box down and look up some gyms in the phone book and we'll check some out."

Five minutes later, I walked back into Morelli's office and found Lula unwrapping the box.

"It's not a bomb," Lula said. "There's a note in here and something all wrapped up." She handed me the note.

"That was addressed to Morelli," I said to her.

"Yeah, but I didn't want him to get hisself all blown up. Besides, I kicked the box around some and nothing happened, so I figured it was safe."

I unfolded the piece of paper and read the printed message.

I KNOW YOU HAVE THE MONEY. GIVE ME THE MONEY AND I'LL GIVE YOU LORETTA. JUST SO YOU KNOW I'M SERIOUS I'M ENCLOSING A PRESENT. EVERY DAY I DON'T GET THE MONEY YOU'LL GET ANOTHER PRESENT. HANG A RED SCARF IN THE UPSTAIRS WINDOW WHEN YOU WANT TO MAKE A DEAL.

"I like getting presents," Lula said, "but this one don't smell too good."

I had a bad feeling about this present. I carefully peeled away the tissue paper, and we stared at a pinkie toe with red toenail polish.

"Good pedicure," Lula said.

I clapped a hand over my mouth and told myself I wasn't going to throw up. I was sweating at my hairline and little black dots were floating in front of my eyes. They'd chopped off one of Loretta's toes, and they were going to keep chopping until they got their money.

"Maybe we should give them the money," Lula said.

"We don't have the money," I whispered.

"Oh yeah. I forgot."

"I don't want Zook to see this," I told her. "He's just a kid. He doesn't need this. And I can't stand around and let them chop off Loretta's body parts. We have to find either Loretta or the money."

"And we're gonna do this how?"

"I have a lead."

"Okay," Lula said. "But what about the pinkie toe?"

"It's evidence. I'll put it in the freezer for now."

————————

I'D SEEN ARMY barracks that were more attractive than
Stanley Zero's apartment complex. Hummingbird Hollow
consisted of six cement-block, three-story buildings clustered around a large macadam parking lot. As far as I could
see, there were no trees, no flowers, no hummingbirds.
And the only hollow was an empty, sick feeling in the pit
of my stomach. The mailboxes would lead me to believe
that there were twenty-four units to each building. Zero
lived on the second floor, in unit 2D, with his windows
facing the lot. According to my report, he lived alone. I
found his truck in the lot, and I checked the plate to make
sure.

"He's home," I said to Lula.

We were in Lula's Firebird. It wasn't the best surveil-
lance vehicle, but it was better than my Zook car. Lula slid
into a space behind and to the left of the F150.

"Now what?" Lula asked.

"Now we wait."

"I hate to wait. He don't know me. How about if I go up
and ring his bell and ask if he wants some Lula? Then I
could look around and see if he got Loretta tied up without her toe in his closet."

"They don't have Loretta here," I said. "It's not private
enough. You can probably hear everything through these
walls. I'm hoping he'll go out and lead us to his partner."

We sat for an hour, looking up into his windows, watching the building's back door. Nothing.

"He might not even be in there," Lula said. "Maybe someone came and picked him up, and we'll sit here 'til the cows come home."

"Then we'll check out the car that drops him off, and maybe that car will belong to the partner."

"You sure you don't want me to go up there and poke around?" Lula asked.

I cut my eyes to her. "You're not going to give up, are you?"

"I should have brought my bride magazines to read. I got nothing to do here. I sit here much longer, I'm gonna get that thing they were talking about on the morning show . . . restless leg syndrome."

"Okay already, go see if he's home."

Lula marched across the lot and into the building. Five minutes later, she was back at the car.

"Nobody home," Lula said. "I tried the door, but it was locked."

"That doesn't usually stop you."

"I fiddled with the lock a little, but I couldn't get anything to work. Too bad, because this here's a good opportunity to snoop."

I called Ranger. "I'm watching an apartment off Route 1, and I'd like to get in but it's locked up tight."

"I'll send Slick."

I gave Ranger the address, and Lula and I waited with slightly elevated heart rates. Breaking and entering was always tense. Especially since it was a crapshoot if Lula could squeeze under a bed. A shiny black Rangeman SUV pulled into the lot and Slick got out and went into the building. He was out of uniform, dressed in jeans and a baggy shirt. Wouldn't be good if he was seen picking a lock in Rangeman black. Five minutes later, he walked through the door, looked my way, and nodded. He got into the Rangeman SUV, and drove away.

"Rock and roll," Lula said.

We took the stairs to the second floor and went directly to Zero's apartment. I turned the knob, and the door opened. We stepped inside and closed the door.

"Hello," I called out.

No one answered.

We were standing in an area that was living room, dining room. Beyond was the kitchen and a hall that would lead to the bedrooms. The furniture was old and collected for comfort with no thought to design. Empty beer cans and Styrofoam coffee cups with days-old coffee still in the bottom were left on end tables. A couple newspapers had been tossed to the floor. Mud had been tracked onto the rug. Not that it mattered. The rug looked like it hadn't been vacuumed in a long, long time. Maybe never.

We glanced at the kitchen and moved into the hall. It was a one-bedroom, one-bath apartment, and the bedroom door was open. Lula and I looked through the open door and froze. There was a man on the floor, toes up, eyes open, bullet hole in the middle of his head. Dead.

"I *hate* when we find dead people," Lula said. "Dead people give me the heebie-jeebies. I'm not doing this no more if we keep finding dead people. And I'm getting out of here. I'm not staying in no room with a guy with a hole in his head."

Don't panic, I told myself. Take it one step at a time. I followed Lula back to the living room, did some deep breathing, and punched Morelli's number into my cell phone.

"Talk," Morelli said.

"I found another dead guy."

"You want to run that by me again?"

"Lula and I decided we'd talk to Stanley Zero, so we knocked on his door, and the door swung open, and we found a dead guy in the bedroom."

There was a moment of silence, and I knew Morelli was either popping Rolaids or counting to ten. Probably both. "The door swung open when you touched it," he finally said.

"Yeah." No need to go into details on how the door got unlocked, right? I mean, he didn't ask how it got unlocked.

"Where are you now?"

"In the living room," I told him.

"Anything else I need to know before I call this in?"

"Nope. That's the whole enchilada."

I disconnected and noticed Lula had her keys in her hand.

"Are you going somewhere?" I asked Lula.

"I figure you don't need me anymore, so I thought I'd go home. I got things to do. I gotta think about a honeymoon. And this place is gonna be swarming with cops, and I hate cops. Except for Morelli. Morelli is fine."

"If you leave, I have no way to get home."

"What about Morelli? What about Ranger? What about calling a cab?"

"What about waiting in your car in the parking lot?" I said to her.

"I guess I could do that."

She hotfooted it out of the apartment, and I thought there was a twenty percent chance she'd be in the lot when I was ready to go home. Not that Lula was unreliable, more that her cop phobia overrode her best intentions.

I figured I had five to ten minutes before the first cop showed up, so I told myself to get over the dead guy and think about rescuing Loretta. I did a quick run through the kitchen, being careful not to leave prints. I found leftover fast-food chicken and expired milk in the refrigerator, and dots of blue mold on the bread that was sitting on the counter. Not enough mold to slow down a big, tough construction guy from Trenton. No scraps of paper lying around with a phone number or address.

I walked back into the bedroom, and as best I could, I avoided looking at the body. A pair of beat-up CAT boots had been kicked off beside the bed, and a framed photograph of a large powerboat was propped on the dresser. I'd found the third partner's apartment. And probably the guy on the floor was the third partner, since he was in socks. I guess I could have seen if the boots fit, but I didn't want to know who he was that bad. Let the police figure it out.

There were clothes all over the place. Hard to tell if the apartment had been tossed, since Zero wasn't the world's best housekeeper. I went through all pockets, omitting the ones attached to the dead guy, and I looked through drawers. I did a fast bathroom check.

I looked out the bedroom window and saw the first police car angle to a stop in the lot. He'd come in without a siren, probably at Morelli's suggestion. A second squad car followed. Eddie Gazarra got out of the second squad car. That was a relief. We'd grown up together and he'd married my cousin, Shirley the Whiner. Eddie wouldn't come at me with a suspicious, hostile attitude, and that would make my life much more pleasant.

I stepped out of the apartment and waited in the hall. I got an eye roll from Gazarra when he walked out of the elevator, and then concern.

"Are you okay?" he asked.

"Yes. The door was open when I got here. He was dead on the floor in the bedroom. No one else was here. I assume it's Stanley Zero, but I don't know for sure."

Gazarra went about securing the crime scene, and a couple minutes later, Rich Spanner showed up.

"We have to stop meeting like this," Spanner said to me. "People are gonna talk." He entered the apartment, checked out the body, and returned to the hall. "What do you think?"

"I think he's got one too many holes in his forehead."

"Yeah," Spanner said. "I noticed that. I also noticed he reminds me a lot of the dead guy in Morelli's basement."

"Because of the hole in his head?"

"Mmm. And because you found him."

"It's getting old."

"I bet," Spanner said.

I repeated my mostly true story for Spanner. The ME slipped past us, followed by two paramedics and a forensic photographer.

"Do you have anything else you want to share?" Spanner asked.

I shook my head. "No. Do you think that's Stanley Zero on the floor?"

Spanner moved into the doorway. "Hey, Gazarra, you have a tentative ID?"

"Looks like Stanley Zero. We got a driver's license here. He matches the photo, except for the hole in his head."

# SIXTEEN

I WAS SHOCKED to find Lula still in the lot.

"What are you doing here?" I asked her.

"Waiting for you."

"It's been over an hour and you're still here."

"I have stuff to ask you. I want to know about the honeymoon. I'm thinking Paris or Tahiti."

"Can you afford that?"

"Don't the groom pay?"

"Can Tank afford that?"

"He better," Lula said. "I don't come cheap."

"I thought the groom planned the honeymoon."

"That was in the Dark Ages. And besides, Tank's busy. He don't got a lot of time for that stuff. He's gotta watch Ranger's ass."

"If it was me, I'd go to Paris," I told her. "Better shopping, and it's a shorter plane ride. Italy would be good, too, if you're interested in handbags and shoes."

"I never thought of Italy, but that's a good idea. I could always use a new handbag."

"Why do you want to get married?" I asked Lula.

"I don't know. It just sort of popped into my head. And then one thing led to another, and before I knew it, I was at the lawyer drawing up my prenup. I guess it was one of those snowball things. You don't think I'm rushing into it, do you? I could postpone it to July, but I got a good deal on the hall for the reception. I'd have to give the hall up. And the fireworks wouldn't be the same. This way, I get the jump on July Fourth." Lula cranked her car over. "Where we going now?"

"Back to Morelli's house. I should make sure Zook is okay."

EVERYTHING LOOKED STATUS quo at Morelli's. It was early afternoon, but there was no activity. The crime scene tape was in place. No gawkers present. Lula pulled to the curb, took the key out of the ignition, and there was a sound like a grenade getting launched, and then *thud*, something hit the passenger-side door.

"What the bejeezus was that?" Lula yelled. "Incoming! We're under attack. Call SWAT. No, wait a minute. I hate those SWAT guys."

Mooner waved at me from Morelli's small front porch. "Sorry," he said. "My bad."

I got out and examined the car door. There was a dent in it, and something was splattered from one end to the other. I cautiously touched it with my finger.

"Potato?" I asked Mooner.

"Yep. Yukon Gold."

Lula was around the car and next to me, and there was a frightening amount of white showing in her eyes. The whole eyeball was about the size of a tennis ball. "My baby!" she yelled. "My Firebird! Who did this? Who made this mess on my Firebird?" The big eyes narrowed, her face scrunched up, and she took a closer look, her nose just about touching the potato splatter. "Is this a dent? This better not be a dent I'm seeing."

"I didn't recognize you," Mooner said. "Good thing I was all out of Russet. Russet is, like, atomic."

Zook and Gary were standing behind Mooner.

"We've been guarding the house," Zook said. "Mooner is so cool. He knows all about homegrown security. He knows how to make potato cannons."

Mooner tapped the top of his head. "No grass growing here."

"What's a potato cannon?" Lula wanted to know.

"All you need is PVC pipe and hairspray and a lighter," Zook said. "And you can shoot *anything* out of it. You can shoot eggs and apples and tomatoes."

"See, that's the thing about a potato cannon," Mooner said. "You can stuff anything into it. You could shoot monkey shit out of a potato cannon. All you gotta do is find a monkey."

"I know where there's a monkey," Lula said.

"Whoa," Mooner said. "Far out. You want to go get some shit?"

Great. Just what I need. Mooner shooting monkey shit at passing motorists.

"It's illegal to shoot monkey shit on a Sunday," I told him. "Have you had lunch?"

Zook was grinning. "We didn't *eat* lunch. We *launched* lunch."

"I got a deductable, and I don't know if I'm covered for potatoes," Lula said, her eyes still narrowed.

I was having a hard time getting worked up over the dent in Lula's Firebird. I had bigger fish to fry. I had a pinky toe in Morelli's freezer. And tomorrow I'd have *two* toes if I didn't hang a scarf in the upstairs window.

"Everyone inside," I said. "You stay out here too long, and some new griefer will take over."

"We're not playing *Minionfire* anymore," Zook said. "We're in charge of homegrown security now. We got weapons to make and posts to man. We're keeping the integrity of the crime scene. We're protecting the house."

"Yeah, but what about the back?" Lula asked. "You can't see the back from here."

"Dude, she's right," Mooner said. "Man your potato cannon. Secure the yard!"

Mooner, Zook, and Gary ran inside. Lula and I followed at a slightly slower pace.

"You got a loony bin," Lula said to me.

Mooner was already at the living room window when we walked into the room. He was holding a two-foot section of white PVC pipe that had a smaller pipe glued toward the base.

"Lieutenant Zook," he said into a two-way attached to his shirt. "Are you in position?"

"Yessir, Captain," Zook answered from the kitchen.

"Munitions Expert Gary, are you ready?"

"Yessir," Gary said.

Gary was in the dining room, halfway between Mooner and Zook. He was wearing a utility belt that carried a can of hairspray and a grill lighter. And he was holding a basket of potatoes. Tucked into the potato basket was a large bag of M&Ms and a large order of fast-food fries still in the cardboard container.

"What's with the M&Ms and the fries?" Lula wanted to know.

"It's in case we need a shotgun."

"Makes sense," Lula said. And she turned and looked at me and made the crazy signal with her finger going around alongside her head.

Zook's voice whispered over the two-way. "I got a bandit at two o'clock. I need a partial baked."

Gary ran into the kitchen and handed Zook a potato. Zook dropped it into his PVC pipe and rammed it down. Gary sprayed hairspray into the pipe and jumped back. Zook pointed the spud gun out the door and *phoonf!* Zook got knocked on his ass from the kick, and the potato rocketed out of the pipe and caught the digger in the back of his leg. The guy went down like a house of cards and rolled around yelping. He got up and half limped, half ran out of the yard.

I was dumbstruck. I didn't know whether to burst out laughing or be truly horrified.

Zook got to his feet. "We only use raw potatoes on cars

and stuff. We use half-baked on poachers. It leaves a good bruise, but it isn't lethal. We tried using eggs, but the gun kept misfiring."

I called Morelli and got his voice mail. "Just checking in," I said. "And by the way, no reason to get alarmed, but do you have personal liability insurance tacked on to your homeowner's?"

Lula had her head stuck in the refrigerator. "Where's the fried chicken? You gotta have fried chicken on Sunday."

"I want to talk to Stanley Zero's almost-ex-wife," I said to Lula. "We can stop at Cluck-in-a-Bucket on the way."

"Why do you want to talk to his ex?"

"I had good luck with Dom's ex. I thought it wouldn't hurt to try Zero's."

Lula looked at Gary, standing in the dining room. "You think we should leave the homegrown idiots alone?"

I was between a rock and a hard place. I didn't trust the three potato heads to make the right decision on *anything*, but I was panicked over Loretta's fingers and toes.

"You stay here," I said to Lula. "I'll have a little conversation with Zero's wife, and I'll stop at Cluck-in-a-Bucket on the way home."

"You aren't going to be long, are you? I don't have a lot of patience when it comes to fried chicken."

"An hour, tops."

"Okay," Lula said. "I guess I could last. I want a large bucket of extra spicy, extra crispy fried chicken. I want a order of biscuits with gravy and some coleslaw."

"I thought you were trying to lose weight."

"Yeah, but I don't want to waste away to nothing. And anyway, everyone knows you don't gain weight on Sunday. Sunday's a free day."

LISA ZERO LIVED in a nice little house in Hamilton Township. The nine-year-old answered the door and Lisa immediately showed up behind him. She was wearing makeup and a skirt, and I guessed she'd gone to church this morning. She was a couple inches shorter than me and a couple pounds heavier. Her eyes were red, as if she'd been crying. I supposed she'd heard about Stanley.

I introduced myself and apologized for being blue and for intruding.

"It's okay," she said. "Let's step outside. I don't want the kids to hear. I haven't told them yet. Stanley was an asshole, but he was still their father."

"Did you know he was involved in the bank robbery?"

"I suspected. Not at the time, but the last couple years he started drinking too much and he'd say things. I guess you're after the money."

I shook my head. "No. I'm looking for the fourth partner."

"I'm afraid I can't help you there. Stanley never said anything about the partners. He only talked about the money. How when Dom got out, they could put it all together, and they'd all be rich."

"Put it all together?"

"Yeah, I don't know what he meant by that, but I got the

233

feeling there was a map or something. Or maybe a bank account in all their names. Like they each had a piece of a puzzle. I didn't figure I'd ever see it, so I didn't pay close attention. He'd drink, and then he'd get real talky, and then he'd get mean."

"I'm sorry."

"It's okay. I got the house, and we're moving ahead with our lives."

"Do you know a guy named Allen Gratelli?"

"No."

"But you knew Dom."

"Not really. I only knew him from the newspaper articles when he robbed the bank, and then when Stanley started talking about him."

"You must have been surprised to learn Stanley was mixed up in a bank robbery."

"Stanley was always mixed up in something. He was always looking for easy money. One time, he held up a convenience store and stole lottery tickets. *Hello.* Like they couldn't figure that one out if he won?"

I gave Lisa Zero my card and told her to call if she thought of anything helpful. I wound my way through her subdivision, hit Klockner, and drove on autopilot to Cluck-in-a-Bucket. I parked in the lot, under the big rotating chicken. I stuffed a couple twenties into my jeans pocket and got out of the Zook car.

Cluck-in-a-Bucket is a zoo on Sunday. It's the lunch of choice for the lazy, the fat, the salt-starved, the emotionally injured, the families on budgets, the cholesterol-deprived, and the remaining ten percent of the population who just want a piece of chicken.

The tables and booths were filled and there were lines in front of all the registers at the counter. Clucky Chicken was making balloon chickens for the kids and handing out coupons for Clucky Apple Pies. I went to the end of a line and zoned out. No one seemed to notice I was blue.

I was thinking about Lisa Zero and her comment about the puzzle pieces. Suppose Dom was the one who hid the money, and to make sure it was still intact when he got out of prison, he didn't tell his partners the exact location. But maybe it was a concern that Dom might not make it through his term, so each partner got a piece of the treasure map. No. That didn't work. They could put their pieces together any time they wanted and cut Dom out. Okay, suppose a fifth person, like Aunt Rose, hid the money? And then she gave each of the partners a piece of the map. I shuffled forward in the chicken line, still thinking about the map. The fifth-person theory didn't totally hold up, either. The partners were ruthless. They were killing one another off and mutilating Loretta. They would have gotten the money location out of Rose.

I absentmindedly looked around as I took another step forward. Two people in front of me. Three lined up behind. There were five registers working. I was in the line farthest from the door. I looked over and saw a stocky guy push in. Big head, balding, curly black hair. Unibrow. Looked like he slept in his clothes. Dom.

I had nothing on me to help subdue him. Stun gun,

pepper spray, cuffs were in my purse in the car. He was bigger and meaner than me, and I had no legal reason to apprehend. I moved out of line, keeping my eye on him, trying to be invisible. My plan was to work my way around to the door and try to follow him when he left.

Dom was rumbling around, looking for the shortest line. My line moved forward, Dom elbowed his way over and spotted me. Our eyes locked for a moment, and Dom whirled around and shoved his way to the door. His effort was misconstrued as line-breaking, and this was an unfortunate thing, since line-breaking doesn't go down well in Jersey.

"Asshole," some woman said, giving him a hard shot to the kidney.

Dom instinctively turned on her and coldcocked her with a punch to the forehead. The woman went down to the ground and the rest was pandemonium. I dove for Dom and missed him by inches. Mothers were grabbing for their children and dropping food. Clucky Chicken was in the mix, waving his wings, trying to keep his footing. I slid on mashed potatoes and took Clucky down with me. A pack of people piled on top of us.

"I hate this lousy job," Clucky said, kicking people off him. "This is the third time this has happened this month."

I was on hands and knees, and I saw Brenda and her crew at the door. Brenda had a mic in her hand and the camera guy was filming.

"This is Brenda reporting from Cluck-in-a-Bucket," Brenda said. "Bringing you a live update on the latest developments in the hunt for the missing nine million dollars. We're here to interview Stephanie Plum."

I dragged myself to my feet and picked mashed potatoes out of my hair. I was drenched with soda and covered with gravy. I looked around, but I didn't see Dom.

"So," Brenda said, pointing the mic at me, "are you making any progress at locating the money?"

"How did you find me?" I asked her.

"We were driving by and saw the Zook car in the parking lot."

Great. The Zook car.

"No comment," I said, easing my way past the film crew.

"Jeez," Brenda said. "Give me a break here. I'm trying to get something going. Do you have any idea what it's like for a sixty-one-year-old woman in show business? The only parts you can get are witches and grandmothers."

"What about the stage show?"

"The stage show sucks. I'm playing Trenton, for crying out loud! All the men in the act are gay and all the women are forty years younger than me. Okay, I know I don't look my age, but I'm busting my ass on maintenance. I don't know how much longer I can keep this up before I need more work."

"What kind of work?"

"All kinds of work. My facelift is eight years old. I've got two years, tops, and then the warranty runs out. The implants are shifting in my breasts, and these young guys I'm fucking are killing me. I'm going to need a vagina transplant."

"Maybe you should consider a man more your own age."

"Have you ever seen a man my age naked? It's frightening. It's like everything has stretched. And then you do the deed with him and it's like fucking Rubberman. And halfway through, you're wondering what the heck that noise is and you realize he's fallen asleep and he's snoring. You have to have football playing on television to keep him awake."

"Sometimes Joe watches football after."

"Joe. Is that the Italian Stallion who turned the hose on me?"

"Yep."

"No offense, but I wouldn't mind doing him."

"No offense taken. Almost everyone wants to do him." I looked down at my shirt. The gravy was congealing. "I need to get home and change my shirt."

"Well, there you have it from Stephanie Plum," Brenda said to the camera. "It looks like the money is still up for grabs, folks."

I hurried to my car, rammed myself behind the wheel, and motored off. Depressing news about sixty-one-year-old men. Probably it didn't apply to Morelli and Ranger. I called Lula when I was half a block away.

"Don't let anyone shoot vegetables at me," I told her. "I'm about to park in front of the house."

"Copy," Lula said. "Cease all operations," she yelled out.

This wasn't a desirable sign. I was hoping Lula would confiscate weapons, but it sounded like she'd signed on to Star Fleet.

"Where's my chicken?" Lula wanted to know, opening the door to me. "I don't see no bags or buckets. All I see is you wearing dinner."

"It's complicated," I said.

"I bet. Is that my mashed potatoes in your hair?"

"I never got that far. I was in line and there was a riot."

"Yeah, but after the riot you should have tried the drive-through."

Mooner was holding his position at the front window.

"He hasn't shot anyone, has he?" I asked Lula.

"Since you been gone? He lobbed a tomato at an old guy with a shovel. Got him in the head and it was instant salsa. That was about it."

The news van pulled to the curb behind my car.

"Whoa," Mooner said. "It's the news. I hate the news. It's never good."

"I'll get rid of them," Lula said. "Give me the big boy."

Gary ran forward and handed Lula a monster spud gun. It was made from wide bore black pipe and had to be four feet long. Lula opened the door, set the pipe on Mooner's shoulder, Gary dropped a honeydew melon into the pipe, rammed it down, and sprayed it.

"Fire in the hole," Lula yelled, and turned the ignitor knob.

*POW!* The melon exploded out of the pipe, Lula and Mooner were knocked off their feet, and the melon sailed over the news truck like a cannonball and took the top off a flowering crabapple tree on the other side of the street.

"Did I hit the target?" Lula asked.

"No, but you scared the crap out of them. They're already in the next county."

"I need a sight," Lula said to Mooner. "All us expert marksmen have sights."

"It would be awesome if we had monkey shit," Mooner said.

"Forget the monkey shit," Lula told him. "I'm not getting you no monkey shit. I hate monkeys."

"This isn't a good idea," I said. "Someone's going to get hurt with this stuff. I want it all put away. Put it in the cellar."

"Mooch and some other guy are in the cellar digging," Lula said. "Zook accidentally beaned Mooch with a half-baked when he saw him in the yard, and we might not want to get too close to Mooch until he calms down."

"Then put the spud guns someplace else. Just stop using them."

"Yeah," Lula said, "but what if we see people trespassing? Morelli's paying these men good money to protect his property. You wouldn't want them to be derelict in their duties."

My eye was twitching like mad. I put my finger to it and looked at Lula out of the other eye. "I'm going to take a shower. Use some common sense."

"Sure, I got lots of common sense," Lula said. "You can count on me."

I threw my clothes into the laundry basket in Morelli's room, wrapped myself in his robe, and ran across the hall to the bathroom to take a shower. When I came back to the bedroom with clean hair and body, I found Bob eating my clothes. Couldn't blame him. They smelled like fried chicken and gravy.

I wrestled what was left of the clothes away from Bob and assessed the damage. T-shirt half there. Jeans had chunks missing. Socks and underwear, gone. Not the first time Bob had eaten my underwear, so I knew the drill. Bob would be spending a lot of time in the backyard tomorrow, letting nature take its course.

I got dressed and blasted my hair with the hair dryer. I took a close look at myself in the mirror. The blue was fading. I was now a ghoulish shade of pale. I went back to the bedroom and dialed Morelli.

"Yep," Morelli said.

"Have you got a minute to talk?"

"Thirty seconds, tops. This is a royal mess. Two kids dead. A shooter who is related to a councilman. Two more at large. And the neighborhood is in a state of siege. What's up?"

"You have three lunatics guarding your house, there are a bunch of fortune hunters creeping around your yard, someone sent you Loretta's pinky toe, and Bob ate my underpants."

"Lucky Bob."

"I put the toe in your freezer."

"Shit," Morelli said. "I'm out of Rolaids. Are you sure it was a toe?"

"Either that or a giant garbonzo bean with a toenail."

"I'll be home as soon as I can, but it will probably be late tonight."

"Should I report the toe to someone?" I asked him.

"I'll tell Spanner about it. I'm sure it's all related. Gotta go."

I flopped onto the bed and covered my eyes with my hands. The day was grinding on, and I wasn't making any progress. Loretta was suffering somewhere, and I couldn't get to her.

Let's list all this out, I thought. What do I know about the fourth partner? I know he's single. I know what his shoes look like. I might remember his voice. That's it. That's all I know.

No it isn't, I thought. I know more. None of it good. I know he robbed a bank and let his partner take the fall. I know he killed one or more of his partners and blew up a house. I know he has Loretta and is capable of doing most anything to her. I know for sure that he wants the nine million real bad. And either he thinks Morelli has already found the money, or he's decided his best shot is to force Morelli to find it for him. What else do I know? I know Dom is still in the neighborhood.

I carted my half-eaten clothes downstairs and tossed them into the garbage. I ate a bowl of cereal and a banana, and I went into the living room. Zook, Mooner, and Gary were back to the world of Minionfire. The spud guns were lined up along the wall.

Lula was on the phone. "What do you mean he don't want to talk to me? Of course he wants to talk to me. I'm his honey. We're engaged to get married. Did you tell him it was Lula?" She listened for a minute, tapping her toe, looking really pissed off. "You're a big fibber. I've got a mind to come over there and hit you alongside the head. How'd you like that, you little pissant?"

I gave Lula raised eyebrows.

"Hunh," Lula said. "He hung up on me."

"You called him a pissant."

"I just learned that word yesterday. It was on one of them game shows. I bet he don't even know what it means."

"Who were you talking to?"

"Some guy at Rangeman. Hal or Cal or something."

My cell phone rang.

"Babe," Ranger said. "*Do* something with her."

And he disconnected.

I called Ranger back. "No," I said. "And I need information on Jelly Kantner. His apartment got blown up, and I need to find him."

"And I should do this why?"

"Because you like me."

There was a full beat of silence. "I do," Ranger said. "I like you a lot. Sometimes I'm not sure why. Give me a couple minutes."

I slid my phone into my pocket and waited. Five minutes went by and finally Ranger called.

"What do you mean you're not sure why you like me?" I asked him.

"Liking you doesn't seem to be getting me where I want to go."

"Maybe you need to change the destination."

"Maybe," Ranger said. "But not today. I have a personal information report for you on Jelly Kantner, also known as Jay Kantner."

"E-mail Kantner's report to Morelli."

"Ten-four."

I moved to Morelli's office and waited for the e-mail to come in. I printed the report and sat in his chair to read it. Kantner's parents were deceased. He had a sister living in the Burg. She was married with two kids. Kantner had no derogatory information. His credit was good. He'd worked as a maintenance specialist for J. B. Management Associates for ten years. Probably didn't make a lot of money, but his work history was solid. He'd never married.

I called the sister's number and asked for Jelly.

"Jelly," she shouted. "It's a *girl*!"

"Hello?" Jelly said.

"Hey, it's Stephanie Plum."

"Oh no!"

"Don't hang up. I just want to talk to you."

"Okay," Jelly said. Tentative. Not sure if it was a smart thing.

"I'm trying to find Dom," I told him.

"I don't know where he is. He got my apartment blown up. And I haven't seen him since."

"You're friends. You must have some idea where he went."

"We *were* friends. In the past. No more. Not ever again. He took off as soon as I didn't have an apartment. He never even said *thank you* or *gee, I'm sorry*. All he thinks about is himself. He used to be fun, but now he's crazy. All he ever talked about was the money and how he hates Morelli. He blames Morelli for everything. He said Morelli swindled him out of his house and his future. He never said, but I figured the money had to be in that house somewhere. He was obsessed with the stupid house."

"Did he have a map or directions that led to the money?"

"No. He said it was in his head."

"What about Victor or Benny? He used to hang with them. Would they take him in?"

"Are you kidding? Those guys are locked down. Their wives would kick their asses if they had anything to do with Dom."

"Relatives?" I asked him.

"Maybe. He's related to half the Burg. He used to be close to his cousin Bugger, but I don't know about now."

"Bugger Baronni?"

"Yeah, there's only one Bugger."

Thank heavens for that.

# SEVENTEEN

I LEFT MOONER, Zook, and Gary home alone with detailed instructions. They were to wash my car. They were to stay close to Morelli's house. They were *not* allowed to shoot *anything*. They were to stay away from Mooch.

We were in Lula's Firebird, and Lula was in a mood. "First off, I never got no chicken. And now I'm driving you to check out some guy named Bugger. I don't even want to know how he got that name."

"Sixth grade," I said. "On a class trip to a petting zoo."

"What's he doing now?"

"He's a lawyer."

"Figures," Lula said.

Bugger lived a little north of Trenton, in an affluent neighborhood close to the river. He specialized in messy divorce cases, and the word on him was that everyone took it up the ass when he got involved. Literally and figuratively.

I thought chances were slim that Dom was here, but no

stone unturned. Bugger was a relative and sometimes that meant something. As would the possibility of getting cut in on nine million dollars. There was no Mrs. Bugger. No Mr. Bugger, either. Just Bugger and a big dog named Lover.

Lula drove by the house and gave a low whistle. "This guy does okay."

The house was a redbrick colonial that looked like about ten thousand square feet under roof. It was on a large landscaped lot with a gated drive. Much of the house and yard was obscured by a privacy hedge.

The house was impressive but felt excessively large for one person. I guess you have a big house like that, you get used to living in it, but all I could think of was keeping toilet paper in all those bathrooms.

"What's this guy look like?" Lula wanted to know.

"I only met him once when I was at a party years ago, but I remember him as a slim Dom."

If my life wasn't so complicated, I'd stake out the house. It was as good a place as any for Dom to hide. He'd be relatively safe behind the gates. Bugger obviously had guest rooms and probably had a couple cars. Plus, Bugger had no scruples and loved money. It was a match made in heaven.

"I don't suppose you'd want to do a stakeout for me?" I asked Lula.

"Don't suppose I would," Lula said. "Who you want to stake out?"

"Bugger."

Lula looked up and down the street. "How are you gonna do a stakeout here? Everyone parks their car in their garage. I don't even see any cars in driveways. We're sitting here looking like we're planning a robbery."

She was right. A car parked at the side of the road was painfully obvious.

I had my hand on the door handle. "I'm going to sneak around in the bushes and look in some windows. You can circle the block and pick me up when I'm done."

"Better you than me," Lula said. "This is one of them snooty neighborhoods, and they probably got all kinds of dogs and alarms and shit like that."

"I've heard rumors about Bugger's dog, and as long as I don't bend over, I think I'll be okay."

I was out of the car and about to cross the street when the gates to Bugger's driveway swung open. A silver Lexus rolled from behind the hedge, through the open gate, and turned left. Only one person in the car. Dom. We locked eyes, and Dom floored it.

I ran around and jumped into the Firebird. "Catch him!"

He had a good head start, but in his panic he turned down a cul-de-sac. Lula angled her car across the road and blocked his exit. He swerved coming at us, jumped the curb, and took out about five thousand dollars' worth of hedge. The house behind it looked like pictures I've seen of Versailles.

The Lexus stalled in the hedge, and Dom wrenched the door open and took off for the faux chateau. I ran flat-out after him and tackled him halfway to the house. He was heavier and stronger than I was, but I was willing to fight dirty. I brought my knee up and rearranged his private parts so that they were halfway into his intestines.

Dom grabbed himself and went into a fetal position. He was sweating and gasping for air, and for a moment I was afraid he might throw up. I removed a gun from him and stood.

"You're out on parole," I told him. "You're not allowed to carry a gun."

He sort of nodded. Still trying to get it together.

"Be a shame to have to shoot you with your own gun," I said. "So I want you to move nice and slow and not get me excited."

Another nod.

"You need to listen carefully, because this is serious," I said. "Your fourth partner has Loretta."

"I know. I'm trying to help her," Dom said, "but I can't get to the money. If I let Morelli in on it, he'll turn the money back to the bank, and I'm afraid Loretta will be killed, just like Allen."

"And Stanley Zero."

Dom locked eyes with me. "What do you mean?"

"Someone put a bullet in Zero. I found him earlier today."

"Do you know who did it?"

I shook my head. "No. But I'm thinking your fourth partner."

"Bastard," Dom said. "I never felt good about him."

"I need a name."

Dom was on his feet, still holding himself and a little stooped over, but starting to get color back in his face.

"I don't have a name," he said. "He was the inside guy. I never even saw him. Stan brought him in. Said he had a sensitive job and no one could know who he was. I always figured he worked for the bank, because he was able to get information. He had access to files and schedules. Or maybe he was one of those computer hackers."

"How did you get in touch with him?"

"Stan got in touch with him. They were buddies. Stan was friends with *everyone*."

I wanted to get Dom someplace more secure. I wanted him in cuffs and shackles so he couldn't get away. I wanted him talking to Morelli. There was a lot at stake, and I was well aware that I wasn't entirely competent. Problem was, he was talking, and I didn't want to give him pause to reconsider and shut up. So I held my breath and pushed on.

"Obviously, something is hidden in Morelli's basement. What is it?" I asked him.

He pulled his pants waistband out and looked down at himself. I guess making sure they were actually still there. "It's two keys on a keychain. I knew I was spotted at the bank, and I'd be locked away for a while. I saw the camera pan to me before we took it out. I wasn't sure I trusted the guys, so I changed the plan. I was supposed to drive the van to a warehouse where we were going to keep it on ice until the money was safe to use. Instead, I drove it to a garage I knew about. Then I buried the keys to the garage and the truck in Rose's basement. Rose was old, and she'd always promised the house to me. She always told me I was in her will."

"But she was disappointed that you robbed a bank, and she changed her will."

"That would be Morelli's version. My version goes that he sweet-talked her out of the house and screwed me like he screwed my sister."

He'd stopped holding himself, but he was still standing bent and bowlegged. "I'm gonna have cramps for days," he said. "You should register that knee as a lethal weapon."

"It was an accident."

"Yeah, right. And if I stop talking, it's gonna be an accident that you shoot me."

"Let's skip to where you get out of prison."

"That was a real kick in the head. I break into the house and what do I find? Asshole Morelli has poured concrete in the basement. I can't get the friggin' keys. So I tell everybody, but they don't believe me. They think I'm juicing them out of the money. And the truth is, I was thinking about it. I did the time. I figured I deserved extra. I never ratted on anyone."

"And?"

"It just got more and more fucked up. Everybody was hungry for the money and nobody trusted anybody else. And Gratelli thought he was James Bond. He was carrying a gun and planting bugs he bought at the Spy Store and going around at night wearing infrared goggles. This is the guy who pissed his pants as soon as we got into the bank. As a joke, I gave him a map with directions and told him he couldn't show anyone. I said it was top secret and it would take him to the money, but he had to guard it and wait for things to settle down. I told him we'd cut the other guys out and get more for ourselves. It was directions to Starbucks, but Gratelli took it serious. Poor dumb, dead shmuck."

Oh great. I got dyed over directions to Starbucks.

"Anyway, I'm up shit creek because my nephew is now living in Morelli's house, so I don't want to give away that the keys are in Morelli's basement. I'm afraid these sons of bitches will go in there like World War III. So I'm telling them not to get their shorts in a bunch and they get all pissed off and snatch Loretta."

"How did Gratelli get shot?"

"They had Loretta. So I said I would take them to the keys, but they had to go with me, and we had to wait for a time when I knew the house was empty. So the three of us wait until everybody goes out of the house, and then we all go in and troop into the basement, and I show them the nice, new, perfect concrete floor. It's in that corner, I say. Under six inches of concrete that asshole Morelli laid down. And this is sort of the funny part. I mean, it's not really funny, but . . . Anyway, Gratelli is sort of freaking because he has a map in his car that I swear leads to the money, and he knows it doesn't take him here. He knows it takes him to Starbucks. And he actually thinks the keys are hidden somewhere at Starbucks. Stan doesn't know what to make of any of it, but he has plans for the money, and he's tired of the whole thing. And I haven't mentioned this before, but Stan has done the occasional job."

"Job?"

"Wet work."

"Yikes."

"Yeah. So to make an impression, and because Stan has already figured out Gratelli isn't an asset, he pulls his gun and pops Gratelli in the forehead. We both look at the stairs and decide it's too much of a pain in the ass to get Gratelli out of the basement, so we leave. And on the way out, Stan tells me his friend is getting real restless, and if I'm messing with them and this isn't for real, I'm going to look like Gratelli real soon."

"Turned out he was the one who looked like Gratelli."

"I don't know what to make of that. I thought they were tight. I guess when it comes to nine million, things change."

"So where are we now?"

"The keys are in the corner by the water heater. You had the cellar dug up. I'm surprised you didn't find them."

"Morelli had the cement broken up, but he didn't dig through all the dirt."

"You should be looking happy because you know where the keys are," Dom said. "Why don't you look happy?"

"Two men broke into Morelli's house last night while Morelli and I were out. Zook heard them come in the back door and called the police, but it looks like they were in the cellar before leaving."

"That's not good news," Dom said. "And now Stan's dead and the fourth partner is left. But at least he don't know how to find the garage where I stashed the van. He still needs me. So he still needs Loretta to be alive. Otherwise, I'd never deal with the prick."

This was making me feel a little less panicky. We could still bargain for Loretta. We could arrange a hostage swap.

"This is great," I said to Dom. "We can give your partner the money and get Loretta back."

"I don't want Morelli involved. Morelli will never do it. He'll do his cop thing and turn the money in to the bank. He walked away from my sister before, and he'd do it again."

Dom was agitated. He was pacing around. Obviously, his equipment had dropped back into place, and he wasn't feeling so vulnerable. Not the time to argue paternity, I told myself. Let it slide for now. Just find out where he's got the money.

"Okay, we won't involve Morelli," I said. "We'll do it without him. Where's the money?"

"I hate Morelli," Dom said. "I've always hated him. Rotten S.O.B. He's not even bald."

"Excuse me?"

"*Bald!* Go ahead, tell me you didn't notice I'm going bald."

Oh boy. He'd flipped out. Just like that. One minute normal, and the next minute rabid bald guy.

"Maybe you're a little bald on the top," I said, "but it's not unattractive."

"Is Morelli bald?"

"No."

"Damn right he's not bald," Dom said. "He's the golden boy. Has he got hair on his back? On his ass? Does he have hair on his knuckles? On his toes? No. He's perfect. He's got hair on his *fucking head*."

I thought about Morelli. "Maybe a little on his ass," I said. Hell, he was Italian. It was practically *required* for him to have hair on his ass.

We both paused for a moment, our attention caught by high-pitched whining.

"What's that?" Dom asked.

The whining changed to yelps, and the realization hit us.

"Dogs," Dom said.

The pack rounded the back corner of the house and raced toward us. Five Dobermans with "killer" written all over them.

"Run!" I yelled at Dom.

We had a large expanse of rolling lawn between us and the dogs, and an equally large expanse between us and the road. We took off, and I could hear Dom pounding after me, his breath wheezing through his teeth.

"Shoot 'em!" he was shouting at me. "Shoot the fuckers."

I was running with Dom's gun in my hand, and while a small corner of my panicked, terrified brain wanted to stop the beasts in their tracks, the rest of my brain was seeing them as Snoopy. No way could I shoot them. Probably if they caught us, they wouldn't hurt us, I told myself. But just in case, I was running like hell.

We reached Dom's car with the dogs at our heels. I scrambled onto the car and perched on the roof, and Dom kept running. He crossed the street and disappeared behind another huge mansion-type house. The dogs stayed with me, surrounding the car, barking and snarling.

Lula had been waiting in the Firebird all this time. She rolled out of the car, pointed her Glock skyward, and fired off a shot. The dogs gave one last yip, turned tail, and ran back to the house.

I climbed down from the Lexus, walked shaky-legged to the Firebird, and collapsed into the passenger seat.

"That was almost it," I told Lula. "I thought for sure I was going to be dog food."

"Where'd you get the gun?"

"I took it from Dom."

I dropped the gun into my purse and sat back with my hand over my heart. "I've gotta join a gym," I said. "I almost died back there."

# EIGHTEEN

IT WAS ALMOST eleven when Morelli dragged himself through the front door. I'd sent Mooner home. Gary was tucked away in his camper in the garage. Zook was in bed. Bob and I were on the couch pretending we were watching television when really we were just waiting for Morelli.

Morelli gave both of us a kiss on the top of the head and kept going into the kitchen. We followed after him and watched him knock back a beer. He dropped his jacket on the floor and threw his gun on the counter and belched.

"Beer," he said by way of explanation.

"Tough day?"

"Unh."

He took a tub of deli potato salad out of the refrigerator and forked some into his mouth.

"Did you get anything resolved?" I asked.

"It's a process." His gaze went to the small table. "What's with the gun in the plastic bag?"

259

"Test it out to see if it matches either of the murder weapons."

"Where'd you get it?"

I gave him the short version.

Morelli tossed the empty potato salad container into the trash. "Have you looked in the basement?"

"Yes. Big hole in the corner where the keys were supposedly buried. No keys."

"Good riddance. Let's go to bed."


MORELLI WAS STILL in the kitchen when I got back from driving Zook to school. Morelli was showered and shaved and looked relatively civilized in a blue button-down shirt and jeans. He had his gun clipped to his belt, the phone cradled against his neck and shoulder, and he was taking notes in a small pad he always carried. I poured myself a second cup of coffee and waited for Morelli to get off the phone.

"You're getting a late start," I said when he disconnected.

"I want to talk to you, and I didn't want to do it until Zook was out of the house. There was a padded envelope stuck under my windshield wiper when I went out this morning. I put the contents in the freezer."

My heart stuttered in my chest.

"I've been talking to Larry Skid and Spanner and the Fed who headed the bank job, and they're going to set up a sting. I doubt Dom will go back to Bugger's house. And it doesn't seem likely he'll get in touch with you, so we're going without him. Hang the scarf in the window and tell the fourth partner you talked to Dom and you know everything. Tell him you want to swap what you know for Loretta. Let the partner suggest how to make the exchange. He'll be less suspicious of a trap if he sets it up. The Feds have a garage in place." Morelli handed me a page from his notebook. "This is the address. Make sure he passes you Loretta before you give him this information."

"Was it another toe?"

"Yeah." He poured coffee into a travel mug, and took two bubble-wrapped packages from the freezer and dropped them into a plastic bag. "I'm taking these in with me, along with the gun. Don't call me on your cell phone if you want to talk about this. Call me on something that's secure." He kissed me and left.

I gave him twenty minutes and hung a red scarf in the window. It was cashmere and had been a Christmas present from Morelli's mom two years ago. He'd never worn it. He wasn't a red scarf kind of guy.

I got a call on my cell phone ten minutes after I hung the scarf.

"Who hung the scarf?" he said.

I recognized the voice. Slight rasp. Flat. "I did," I told him.

"And?"

"I know everything. I had a conversation with Dom yesterday. He wants to make a deal for Loretta."

"Why isn't he talking to me?"

"Afraid, I guess."

"But you're not afraid?"

"I'm not involved like Dom."

"What about Morelli?"

"He's not part of it."

I sat out a full sixty seconds of silence. I suppose he was debating whether to go forward. Or maybe he was waiting to see if I'd get nervous and start blabbering.

"Here's the deal," he finally said. "You tell me where the van is located, and I give you Loretta."

"I need Loretta first."

"Not gonna happen, sweetie."

I hated this guy. I hated his voice. I hated his arrogance and his ability to kill and maim in cold blood. And I hated that he called me sweetie.

"You're going to have to come up with a plan we can both live with," I told him.

"I'm a reasonable guy," he said. "I'll call you back in twenty minutes."

By the time he called, my eye was twitching and my stomach was clenched in a knot. The phone rang and I jumped in my seat. I took a moment to breathe and steady my voice, and I answered the phone.

"The keys are taped to the underside of a bench in front of the train station," he said. "Look for the bus stop with the Nike ad. When you get the keys, you can use them to get the van. After you've secured the van, you can call me. The phone number is in the envelope with the keys. You need to remember two things. If anything goes wrong, I'll kill Loretta. Then I'll kill her son. And then I'll kill you. And don't doubt for a moment that I won't."

"What's the second thing?"

"Be careful not to set off the detonation device."

Oh boy. "Dom didn't tell me about the detonation device."

There was a moment of silence. "Allen booby-trapped the van. Allen loved doing that sort of thing. In this case, it wasn't a bad idea, since none of us could really be trusted. The key is necessary to disarm the mechanism. So, while Dom has always known where the van was located, he had no access to the money without the key. Allen probably could have bypassed his system, but he didn't know the location of the van. Once Zero was convinced he knew where the key was located, he eliminated Allen. And then, of course, I eliminated Zero after we retrieved the keys. Nine million is much better than four and a half. And I'm telling you this so you will be careful when inserting the ignition key, and also so you understand that I'm ruthless."

I didn't respond.

"Well?" he said.

"I'll get the van."

"No police. If you bring the police in on this, I'll know. And it won't be good for Loretta."

"I have to make sure she's okay."

"She's as okay as anyone could be who just had two toes removed, and that's as close as you're going to get to her."

My newly washed car was at the curb. No more Zook

decorations. Just rust and faded paint and a bunch of dings and dents. I drove to the office and got there just as Connie was unlocking the door. No sign of Lula. I called Morelli on the office phone, and he called me back from a landline.

"He's left the keys on a bench at the train station. I'm to pick them up and get the van. When I have the van, I'm supposed to call him. His number will be with the keys."

"We can do this," Morelli said. "We have video of the van. We can duplicate it and have it in the garage. Get the keys and I'll get back to you when we're ready."

The door to the bonds office banged open and shut and Lula stormed in.

"I swear," she said. "I have a mind not to get married. That man came to my house stinking drunk last night. I opened the door, and he called me Charlotte. Who the hell is Charlotte? He said it was his mother, but I don't believe it for a minute. And then when I said I wanted to meet his mother, he said she was dead. And I don't think that's true. I think he don't want me to meet his mama."

"We've got a stack of filing," Connie said. "Are you up to filing?"

"I'm up to murder. I'm in a vicious mood. I was ready for a good time, if you know what I mean. And he fell asleep in the bathroom. I thought he was getting ready. You know how sometimes men need to get ready?"

I didn't have that problem. The men in my life were always ready. In fact, I could do with a little less ready.

Connie looked confused by it, too. "Ready for what?" Connie asked.

"Whatever," Lula said. "How the hell do I know what they do in there? Anyway, he's not coming out and he's not coming out, and finally I go in and he's asleep on the floor. So I said to him, *Hey!* And he never even twitched. And then I pushed him around. And that didn't do nothing. So I watched some television and went to bed, and when I got up he was gone. Good thing, too, because I wasn't happy. I'm not marrying no alcoholic."

I couldn't imagine Tank or Ranger drunk. They were always in control. They ate vegetables. They exercised. They didn't eat butter, and they ate whole wheat bread. What on earth could drive Tank to drink? The answer was clear. The answer was . . . Lula. Big, tough Tank was no match for Lula.

"I have an errand to run," I said. "I'll be back."

The train station wasn't far away, and the bench was easy to find. There was only one with a Nike ad. I illegally parked, ran over, and sat on the bench. I had my choice of feeling around or bending over and looking. Neither was appealing, considering what might be stuck there besides the keys. I went with the looking and had good luck. The keys and the phone number were in an envelope held to the seat with electricians tape. I shoved the envelope into my pocket and motored back to the office. Connie was on the phone and Lula was filing when I walked in.

I sunk into the couch and paged through one of Lula's bride magazines. Connie got off the phone and looked over at me.

"Vinnie's coming home on Wednesday, and he's not

going to be happy about the number of skips out there," Connie said. "We have a stack of low-money losers that adds up to a lot of money."

I knew she was right. I had a list in my purse. Loretta had been taking precedent over the job.

"Susan Stitch would be a good place to start," Connie said.

"No way," Lula said from behind a file cabinet. "That's the monkey lady. I'm not going back there. I hate monkeys. And I especially hate *that* monkey. That monkey is the spawn of the devil."

"It was Brenda's fault for letting him out of the bath-room," I said. "I'm sure he'll be fine as long as we don't drag Brenda and a film crew along with us."

Truth is, I was nervous about the ransom sting, and I wouldn't have minded a diversion while I waited for Morelli's phone call. I stood and hung my bag on my shoulder.

"I'm off to North Trenton," I said to Connie. I cut my eyes to Lula. "Are you coming with me?"

"I guess I am," Lula said. "Someone's gotta go along and protect your skinny ass."

"You didn't do a lot of protecting yesterday. You sat in the car when I chased down Dom."

"Darn right. I knew there was gonna be dogs. These people got dogs and all kinds of security shit. Did you think of that? No. You chased Dom into that yard, and next thing, there was a pack of killer dogs running after you."

We got out on the sidewalk, and Lula looked at my car.

"No more *Zook*," she said. "I thought the *Zook* was an improvement."

"It was too recognizable with *Zook* on it."

"Yeah, Connie and me always knew when you were trying to sneak past the office."

I drove to North Trenton and parked in Susan's lot. We took the stairs, and I knocked on her apartment door. No one answered, but the door eased open.

"Uh-oh," Lula said. "There's always dead bodies inside when this happens." She stuck her head in and sniffed. "I smell monkey," she said.

I rapped on the open door. "Anyone home?" I yelled.

No one answered, but I could hear a television squawking somewhere. I stepped into the apartment and scanned for the monkey. No monkey in sight.

Lula was pressed tight behind me. "I better not get attacked by no monkey," she whispered. "I'm gonna be mad at you if I get a monkey on my head. There was lots of other losers we could have gone after."

The living room and kitchen area was unoccupied. The television was blaring from the bedroom.

"Hello," I yelled again. "Anyone home?"

"Who could hear over that television?" Lula said. "Sounds like one of them music video stations."

We cautiously crept to the bedroom and peeked through the open door. Susan was naked on top of some guy with a cast on his leg, and she was going to town on him, grinding and pounding away in time with the music.

"Oops," I said. "Sorry."

Susan paused for a moment and covered her breasts with her hands. "We made up," she said.

I was telling myself not to look, but my eyes weren't co-operating. "Great, but you still have to get your bond straightened out."

"It was for Carl," she said. "He was unhappy."

"Un-hunh."

I could hear Lula making choking sounds behind me.

"We'll wait in the hall until you're done," I said to Susan.

"Okay," she said. "It never takes long."

"Cripes," the guy said. "What's that supposed to mean?"

Lula and I almost knocked each other over trying to get out of the bedroom.

"I gotta get outta here before I bust from trying not to laugh out loud," she said. "I didn't want to be rude, but I was a 'ho for a bunch of years, and I never seen anyone bouncing around on a wanger like that. That woman still got some anger left in her. He's lucky if she don't bend something and do permanent damage."

Lula was looking at me and not paying attention to what she was doing. She opened the powder room door instead of the front door and Carl lunged out at her and grabbed her face.

"Eeeeee," she squealed. "I got a monkey on my face. Help! Do something."

Carl backflipped off her and ran around the room.

"Get me out of here," Lula said. "Where's the door? Someone open the door!"

She found the door, yanked it open, and Carl scampered

out. He ran down the hall, jumped up, and punched the elevator button. The elevator doors opened, Carl leaped inside, and the doors closed.

"I didn't see that," Lula said. "I had nothing to do with it, and I never was here."

I didn't want to go back into the bedroom, so I yelled as loud as I could. "Susan! Your monkey just got into the elevator."

"Oh *yes!*" Susan shouted. "Yes, yes, yes. Yippie-ki-yay, cowboy!"

"I'm gonna pretend she heard," Lula said.

"I did my best to tell her."

Lula nodded in agreement. "Nobody could ask for anything more from you."

The racket was still going on in the bedroom.

"Probably we shouldn't wait for Susan to get done," I said.

"Yeah. I just remembered I got something to do."

We hurried down the stairs and slunk through the lobby to the lot. We didn't see Carl.

"I hope Carl's okay," I said to Lula.

"Carl's probably on his way to stick up a 7-Eleven."

# NINETEEN

I DROPPED LULA at the office and went to my apartment to check on Rex. I leaned over his cage and told him about my day so far. He was in his soup can and probably wasn't listening, but I talked to him anyway. I gave him an olive and a corn chip, and I called Susan Stitch.

"Did you find Carl?" I asked her.

"Yep. He escapes like that all the time. He's such a clever little dickens. He was on the first floor visiting with Mrs. Rooney. He likes to play with her beagle."

"Would this be a good time to get rebonded?"

"It's perfect, but you don't have to worry about it. Ron and I are going to the courthouse together. We're meeting his lawyer there, and hopefully this can all be worked out."

"That's great," I said, assuming Ron was the guy with the leg cast and stiffy. "Good luck."

I hung up, and I took a moment to enjoy being in my own space. Morelli's house had ice cream sandwiches, but my apartment was home. My apartment was quiet and sane and was free from überelves and bank robbers.

My cell rang, and I saw on the screen that it was Morelli. I was tempted not to answer, but I knew he'd keep calling until I connected.

"Hola," I said to him.

"Do you have a landline?"

"Yes. I'll get back to you on my kitchen phone."

"Here's the deal," he said when we reconnected. "The address I gave you earlier is actually a storage facility down by the river. The lockers are big. Garage-size. People keep furniture and boats and ATVs in them. It's not a stretch to drive a van into one. It's locker number twenty-four, and it's rigged with a lock that will open with any key. Inside is an exact replica of the van used in the robbery. The key is in the ignition. We've got nine million in dummy money in the back of the van. All you have to do is go along with the deal."

"How am I going to communicate?"

"I'll put a wire on you. Give me twenty minutes."

I put the phone down and went back to talking to Rex.

"I hate this," I said to him. "I don't know if you've noticed, but I'm not the hero type. I wanted to be Wonder Woman when I was a kid. Now that I'm an adult, I think kicking ass leaves a lot to be desired. For one thing, I'm not that good at it. And wearing a wire makes my stomach feel squishy. I'm always afraid I'll get found out, and I'll end up with a bullet in the head like Allen Gratelli."

It was a sobering thought when said out loud.

"Not that it would happen," I said to Rex.

I refilled Rex's water bottle and gave him an extra bowl of hamster food, just in case. And then Rex and I waited in silence in the kitchen for Morelli to arrive.

Ten minutes later, Morelli knocked and opened the door. He had a key.

"I'm not supposed to be doing this," he said. "I'm still working the gang thing, but I didn't want anyone else feeling you up when they taped the wire."

"If something happened to me, you'd take care of Rex, wouldn't you?"

"Nothing's going to happen to you."

"Yes, but if it did."

"If anything happened to you, I'd be so destroyed they'd have to strap me to a bed and feed me through a tube. After five or six years, I might be capable of taking care of Rex. In the interim, you should assign a guardian."

Morelli had his hands under my shirt and supposedly was installing the wire, but his thumb kept tracing a line across the tip of my breast. I was starting to lose focus.

"If you're trying to get my mind off the ransom, it's working," I told him.

"Yeah, sometimes I love my job," he said, giving me a whole-hand fondle. He took a small receiver out of his pocket, put the attached earbud into his ear, and stepped back. "Push the button and switch it on."

I felt along the battery pack and pushed the button.

"Testing," I said. "Mary had a little lamb. Yada, yada, yada."

"Perfect," Morelli said. "You're going to be transmitting to the Fed. Unfortunately, he won't be able to talk to you, so you'll have to run with it. If you feel like you're in trouble, do whatever you have to do. It's okay if you abort."

"I'm a little weirded out," I said.

Morelli looked down at me. Serious. "You don't have to do this."

"Yes, I do."

He kissed me on the forehead. "You'll be fine."

I went to the window and watched him cross the lot to his car. He opened the driver's side door, stood for a moment, and then slammed the door shut without getting in. My window was closed, so I couldn't hear what Morelli was saying, but clearly he was talking to himself. He was waving his arms and pacing and his face was getting red. He punched the car and stood hands on hips, starring down at his shoes. I've seen him do this a million times. Getting a grip.

I called him on my cell. "I'll be fine," I told him.

"This really sucks," he said. And he got in his car and drove away.


THE STORAGE FACILITY chosen by the Feds was down by the river, off Lamberton Road. I took Hamilton and passed by the bonds office and the hospital. I turned at the junction of South Broad and felt my way around until I hit Lamberton. I was watching my mirror for a tail, but I didn't pick one up. I turned onto a private road leading to a small industrial park, and kept driving until I saw the sign for the storage facility. The facility itself was about a half acre in size and protected by a chain-link fence. The gate to the fence was open. There was a one-room cinderblock building that served as office. So far as I could see, the office was vacant. Beyond the office were rows of storage lockers, each the size of a single-car garage.

I drove down the second row of lockers and stopped at number 24. I got out of my car and looked around. Very quiet. No sign of the fourth partner. No indication of police presence. I had the wire switched on, but I wasn't saying anything.

I walked to the garage door, took a deep breath, and shoved the key in. The door rolled up to reveal a dark maroon Econoline van with Pennsylvania plates.

I looked in the driver's side window. The key was in the ignition, as promised. I wrenched the door open and climbed in. I was feeling calmer now that everything was in motion. Piece of cake, I said to myself. Cool as a cucumber. Wonder Woman on board.

I cranked the engine over, backed the van out, put my car in the garage, and rolled the garage door down. I carefully drove the van out of the storage facility, parked on the side of the road, and dialed the number the fourth partner gave me.

"Long time no hear," he said.

"I had things to do. I had to look in on a skip."

"Is that all you had to do?"

"Pretty much."

"What about waiting for the police to set the trap?"

"Nope. Didn't do that."

"I told you I would know. I know everything."

"Not *everything*," I said.

"I know you've got phony money in the back of that phony Econoline. I know you got the van out of a phony garage off Lamberton. I know you're wired. Now, here's the deal. Hang the scarf in the window when you're ready to make a trade without police involvement. If I don't see the scarf by noon tomorrow, I'm cutting Loretta's hand off."

"But I don't . . ."

He was gone.

"He knew," I said into the wire. "He knew the whole deal. You need to clean house. He's on the inside."

I RETRACED MY route back to the garage and traded the van for my car. Still no one walking around, but I knew police were planted somewhere. I drove out of the industrial park and went straight to Morelli's house. School was still in session. Just me and Bob at home.

I took the red scarf from the upstairs window and set it on Morelli's desk. All the way home, I'd been boiling inside, seething mad that this had gotten screwed up. I wanted it over and done. I wanted Loretta to be safe. I was angry at Dom for running away from me, and I was angry at the police that they couldn't manage a secure operation.

I sat in Morelli's chair and forced myself to think. Who is this fourth partner? A cop? A computer whiz? A professional crook? I looked at the red scarf. He wanted it hung from the second-floor window. Why the second floor? Wouldn't it be easier to see it from the *first* floor if you were walking or driving past the house?

I swiveled around and stared out the window. The houses on the opposite side of the street were all two-story, like Morelli's. Easy to see into their bedroom windows from here. The convenient assumption would be that the partner lived in one of these houses, but Morelli had already gone door-to-door in his neighborhood and hadn't found anything odd.

I called Morelli, but got his voice mail. I called my mother, and got my grandmother. She said my mother couldn't come to the phone because she'd taken a pill and fallen asleep after seeing me wrestling with the chicken on *News at Noon*. I called the office and was transferred to Connie's cell. She was at the courthouse trying to help resolve the Susan Stitch mess.

My modus operandi when investigating is, if you have no ideas . . . eat something. It doesn't help to get ideas, but it passes the time. So I trekked downstairs and nuked a tray of mac and cheese.

This got me to feeling very mellow, because it's impossible to stay upset while eating mac and cheese. Here's the positive side, I told myself. You continue to make little inroads on the fourth partner's identity. If you can't find Dom and get your hands on the money, maybe you can find the fourth partner. He's kind of full of himself, and that confidence could be his undoing.

I called Ranger.

"I want to get into Stanley Zero's apartment again," I told him.

"That's a sealed crime scene," Ranger said.

"And?"

"It would be safer if we went in at night."

"I can wait."

"I'll meet you in his apartment parking lot at eleven."

I REACHED THE school just as it was letting out. Zook ambled over to the car with his usual cluster of misfits and pulled the passenger-side door open. He slouched into the seat, dropped his backpack on the floor between his feet, and looked over at me. "The kids at school are talking."

I gave the Sentra some gas and moved into the stream of traffic. "What are they saying?"

"They're saying my mom cut out on me. Like maybe she found the nine million and took off with it."

"They're wrong."

"I sort of wouldn't blame her. That's a lot of money."

"Your mom is okay. She's just not . . . accessible right now."

"What's that mean?"

"I can't tell you, but we're trying to work it all out."

He pushed his backpack around with a foot that seemed way too big for his slim frame. He was like a puppy that hadn't grown up to his feet yet. "I'm not some dumb little kid," he said. "I deserve to know what's going on with my mom."

I turned onto Hamilton and slid a sideways glance at him. He wasn't dumb, and he wasn't a little kid. He was a *big* kid. And he had a point. He needed to know what was going on with his mom.

"You're right," I said. "You deserve to know. But you can't tell anyone. No one at school. Not Mooner. Not Gary. No one."

He nodded his head.

"Three men robbed the bank with your Uncle Dom. Two are dead, and your uncle is in hiding. The fourth partner has your mom and is holding her for ransom. He wants the nine million dollars. Problem is, we don't have it, and we don't know where it's located. The police are involved, and we're making progress at getting your mom back, but you have to be patient."

"That is *so sucky*," he said.

"You're right," I said on a sigh. "It is totally sucky."

Mooner and Gary were waiting on Morelli's front steps when I pulled to the curb with Zook. They were dressed in Army fatigues, and they stood and saluted when I parked the car.

Zook and I burst out laughing.

"I know they're goofy," I said to Zook, "but I like them. They're in the moment."

I unlocked Morelli's front door, and Bob rushed out and ran around in circles. He did some yelping and grunting, and then he hunched and pooped out my underwear.

"Whoa," Mooner said. "Victoria's Secret colonic, dude. Far out."

Bob ran back into the house the instant he was done, and we all followed. Eventually, I'd come out in rubber gloves and contamination suit and scoop up the deposit, but for now I was walking away from it.

"Where did you get the clothes?" I asked Mooner.

"Army surplus. We got some for the Zookster, too."

"We changed the patches," Gary said. "We made them say 'Homegrown Security.'"

I got everyone settled in the living room with chips and pretzels and sodas. I phoned for pizza. I asked about Zook's homework.

How bizarre was this? It was like running a day-care facility. Makes you wonder, doesn't it? I mean, who am I? I was raised to have traditional values, but I screwed up on my first marriage big-time, I took an odd job, and now I love two men. One is definite husband-and-father material. The other . . . I don't know what to think of the other. And now here I was, doing my "mother cat" impersonation.

The doorbell rang and I went to answer it. I opened the door and didn't bother to hold back the grimace. It was Brenda and her film crew.

"How about it?" she said. "Have you thought of anything?"

"No."

"Make something up. You've got an imagination, right? This is the news. It doesn't have to be real."

"I thought that was the whole purpose of the news . . . to report real stuff."

"Oh puhleeze. You don't actually believe that crap. You think we could get ratings with real stuff? The news people make up entire wars. Listen, all you have to do is find something sexy to say about the money. Like, 'Tall, dark and handsome Morelli was taking a nap, and he woke up and thought he heard a noise in the yard, so he rushed out naked and tackled some guy who was digging with a shovel, and Morelli saw a couple hundred-dollar bills sticking out of the ground.'" Brenda smiled. "See? It's easy."

"I'd like to help you, but I don't think I could pull that off."

"Of course, you can. Look at me. I can do it, and I'm not that good. I'm just motivated. I've got a three-million-dollar house in Brentwood with a mortgage big enough to choke a horse." She looked at the guys on the couch. "Is that Gary?"

Gary waved at her. "I'm lurking."

"No shit," she said. "What's with the uniform? Did you join the Army?"

"Homegrown Security," Gary said. "I'm a gunnery officer."

"Great," Brenda said. "Perfect. A gunnery officer. That makes me feel real safe."

"Yeah, but you still have to watch out for the pizza," Gary said.

Brenda's face brightened. "Maybe I could do a feature

on stalkers. We could film you stalking me," she said to Gary.

"I appreciate the offer, but no, thanks," Gary said. "I haven't got time to stalk right now. I promised the guys I'd lurk, and I'm on standby with Homegrown."

Brenda narrowed her eyes at Mooner. "You stole my stalker."

"No way, the Mooner doesn't steal. He, like, borrows sometimes, but he's got a code. He's protecting his oneness."

"Oneness, my ass," Brenda said. "I could own you like a cheap suit."

"Whoa," Mooner said. "Have you been talking to the wood elves?"

The soundman was standing behind Brenda. "If we don't get film to the studio soon, we'll miss our spot."

"I'm not missing my spot," Brenda said, turning from me and storming off the porch.

I closed the door and peeked out the living room window at her. She was standing over Bob's poo while the cameraman zoomed in for a closer look.

"And here we have a suspicious substance on Joe Morelli's front lawn," Brenda said into her mic. "It would appear that the dog in this household has been fed a thong. Clearly a case for investigation by . . ." She looked over at the soundman. "Who investigates this shit?"

# TWENTY

LULA WAS ON my cell phone. "I'm two minutes away," she said. "Be out front. I'm in a consultation for my wedding gown, and I need an opinion. You gotta go back to the bride store with me."

"Okay, but I can't stay away too long. I don't like leaving Zook on his own."

"Don't he have Homegrown Security with him?"

"Yeah, that's part of the problem."

I grabbed my purse, told everyone I'd be back soon and I was on my cell if an emergency arose, and I ran out of the house. The Firebird careened around the corner and slid to a stop in front of me. Lula was behind the wheel in a silky bathrobe.

"I got a hour appointment with these bitches," she said, "and the clock's ticking."

"You're in a bathrobe."

"It took less time than getting back in my clothes."

I fastened my seat belt and we rocketed away. "I thought you were having second thoughts about marrying an alcoholic."

"Yeah, but I had this appointment, and I didn't want to lose it. I might have to wait weeks to get another appointment. I mean, even if I don't marry Tank, chances are good I'll marry someone else someday. Might as well get the gown, I figure."

"You might want to rethink that plan."

"Yeah, it's insane, right? It's that I have momentum. You see what I'm saying? It's all in motion and it don't stop. Turns out, that's how it is with weddings. You just keep getting in deeper and deeper until you want to throw up."

Lula hooked a left, cut across traffic, and zipped into the small parking lot that attached to the bridal salon. We got out and hurried into the showroom.

"You sit down, and I'll put the gown on," Lula said.

I was halfway through a magazine when she rustled out of the dressing room. The gown was brilliant white satin and fit like skin from Lula's ankles to her armpits. It was strapless and had a bustle in the back over her ass and a twelve-foot train that stretched out behind her.

"We like this one because it's so slimming," the saleswoman said. "We think it hugs her curves and is very flattering. She's a lucky lady that we had her size in stock."

"All it needs is some of them crystal beads to make it sparkle," Lula said. "They said they could sew them on."

The gown was slimming because it was two sizes too small

and squished in all Lula's fat and pushed it up until there was no more gown. She was spilling out of the top in rolls of Lula. She had cleavage *everywhere* . . . front, back, side.

"It's pretty," I said, "but there seems to be a lot of you oozing over the top. Maybe you should go up a size."

"They don't got this in a bigger size," Lula said. "And anyway, I don't want it too big on account of I'm planning to lose some weight."

I heard something pop and fly off the back of the dress, and the zipper burst open.

"Hunh," Lula said. "This here seems to be shoddy workmanship."

Ten minutes later, Lula dropped me at Morelli's.

"Boy," Lula said. "I dodged that bullet. Those people don't know how to sew."

"You might consider getting married in a dress instead of a gown," I said. "It wouldn't even have to be white."

"And it could be more representative of my outgoing personality," Lula said. "It could be animal print. You know how I'm partial to animal print."

"And it would be practical because you could wear it even if you didn't get married."

"I'm psyched," Lula said. "I'm going to the mall. You want to come?"

"No. Morelli should be getting off his shift right about now and I need to talk to him."

---

I WAS IN the kitchen, eating pizza, when Morelli rolled in. He helped himself to a piece from the box and went to the refrigerator in search of beer.

"My refrigerator is filled with potatoes," he said, door open, face bathed in refrigerator light. "They're everywhere. I've got potatoes in the egg holder."

"Ammo. I think the beer is behind the half-baked."

He moved some potatoes around and grunted when he found the beer. "Zook's a terrific kid, but I feel displaced. Bad enough Mooner is always here, now we've got Gary. Once, I got up in the middle of the night to get water, and I swear I saw him sitting in a lawn chair in front of my garage."

"Imagine that," I said. "How odd."

"Have you heard from the partner?"

"No. The ball's in our court."

Morelli took a second piece of pizza. "This is bad. Either someone is leaking information or the guy is inside."

"Or maybe he's some genius computer geek that can tap into phones and computers."

Morelli shook his head. "That only happens in the movies. This guy knew about the van and the money. I didn't tell anyone, and Spanner swears he didn't tell anyone. I know the Fed who's running the show, and I can't see him telling anyone."

"What about the sack of shit?"

"Larry Skid? He could leak. And there were some other people working details. Looking at it in retrospect, we should have played it tighter, but there's always all this chain-of-command crap."

"I assume the department is investigating."

"Yes, but there's not much to go on. Truth is, some of this op went through the bureaucracy. The van needed to be requisitioned, the storage facility had to be cleared, yada yada."

I checked to make sure Zook wasn't listening and I lowered my voice. "He said he would cut Loretta's hand off at noon tomorrow if he doesn't have the money."

"He's sick," Morelli said. "He's caught up in the drama. If he was thinking sanely, he'd back off and wait. There's no way he's going to drive away with nine million dollars. It was a good plan when they executed it ten years ago, but it's not a good plan now that the police are involved."

"I suppose he figures he can stay ahead of the game if he can force me to locate the money and drive the van to him without telling anyone."

Morelli cut his eyes to me. "You wouldn't do that, would you?"

"Of course not," I said. And we both knew I would.

Problem was, I had the key but I didn't know what to do with it. And I had no way to reach Dom. I suspected Dom and the fourth partner had the same dilemma. Dom had always talked to Zero and Gratelli.

"I can practically see the wheels turning in your head," Morelli said. "What are you thinking?"

"I'm thinking this is pathetic. There's no communication between the major players here. Dom and I have identical goals right now, but we can't get anything done because I can't get in touch with him."

"Connie couldn't pull up a cell number?"

"No. Nothing for Dom. And the partner has me calling him on Zero's phone. I had Connie run it."

"Let's go obvious," Morelli said. "We think Dom watches the house, so make a sign and hang it in the living room window. 'Have key. Call me.'"

I ran upstairs to Morelli's office and used black magic marker on a piece of computer paper. I brought the sign downstairs and taped it to the window.

"We only have a couple hours of daylight where he can read it," I said to Morelli.

"No problem. I'll hook up a spot."

We moved Zook and Mooner and Gary into the dining room, and Morelli and Bob and I sat in front of the television, waiting for the call.

At ten o'clock, I got a call, but it was from the wrong person.

"You must be kidding," he said.

It was the fourth partner.

"What?"

He sighed into the phone. "You don't have any way of getting in touch with this idiot, either, do you?"

"You mean Dom? No."

"You better hope he sees your sign, because I'm running out of patience."

And he disconnected.

"That was the fourth partner," I told Morelli. "He saw the sign."

At ten-thirty, I had a problem. I didn't know how to get

out of the house to meet Ranger without Morelli going postal. Take the coward's way out, I thought. Go out the bathroom window and deal with Morelli when you get home.

I didn't want anyone to think I was kidnapped, so I wrote a message on the toilet lid with my eyeliner pencil. BE BACK SOON. DON'T WORRY. I climbed out the window onto the small overhang that shelters the back stoop. Morelli's house is almost identical to my parents' house, and this was the route I'd used all through high school to sneak out with my friends. I rolled off the edge of the roof and lowered myself down. I felt hands at my waist, and I got an assist from Morelli.

"Dammit," I said to him. "How did you know?"

"I have the windows attached to the new alarm system. It dings when you open them. What are you doing?"

"I'm meeting Ranger, and you don't want any more information than that."

"Wrong." He glanced at his garage. "It looks like the light is on."

"Gary has his camper parked in there."

Morelli was silent for a couple beats. "Notice I'm not yelling," he said to me.

"Yeah, but I think the roots of your hair are smoking."

"How long has Gary been squatting in my garage?"

"A couple days."

Morelli opened the back door for me. "Get in the house."

Fine with me. My car was parked out front. Now I didn't have to walk halfway around the block. "I won't be long,"

I told Morelli, wasting no time getting through the kitchen and dining room. "Maybe an hour."

Morelli was close behind me. "Is this about Loretta?"

"Yep."

"I'm going with you."

"That's not a good idea."

"Why not?"

"You don't want to know," I told him.

"And Ranger is in on this?"

"He's not *in* on it. I asked him to help me. He has skills I lack."

"Such as?"

"He's good with locks."

"You're right. I don't want to know, but if anything happens to you, I'll go after Ranger, and it won't be pretty."

"Nothing's going to happen." Probably.

I ran to my car and took off. The fourth partner saw the sign, and that meant he was watching the house. I didn't want to be followed, so I wound around in the Burg, looking for headlights behind me. When I felt absolutely safe, I cut across town to Route 1 and headed for Stanley Zero's apartment complex.

Ranger was already there when I pulled into the lot. He was in his black Porsche Turbo, watching the building. I parked next to him, and he got out. He was wearing black jeans and T-shirt and a black windbreaker. Nothing with the Rangeman insignia. He looked at my ghoulish complexion and smiled.

"Long story," I said.

"I know the story. I'm just sorry I missed seeing you before you faded."

We walked to the entrance, and when we got to the door, he draped an arm across my shoulders. We were a couple, home from date night. When Ranger got close to me like this, I could smell his Bulgari shower gel. I've used the same gel, and the scent is fleeting on me. It lingers on Ranger.

Zero's apartment was sealed with yellow crime scene tape. A DO NOT ENTER notice was tacked to the door. Ranger peeled the tape back, used a pick on the lock, and in seconds we were inside. Nothing keeps Ranger out when he wants to get in. I've seen him open a door when a slide bolt was thrown. It's borderline eerie.

We pulled on disposable gloves and methodically moved through the apartment. There were smudges where the crime lab had searched for prints, and marks on the carpet where the body had fallen.

"I'm looking for something that might give me the identity of Dominic Rizzi's fourth partner," I told Ranger.

"Either the killer swept the apartment, or else the crime lab did an unusually thorough evidence collection," Ranger said. "I'm not finding anything. No cell phone, no computer, no address book."

"I had a few minutes to look around after I discovered the body, and I don't remember seeing a computer or phone. I went through all his pockets, with the exception of the clothes he was wearing. I couldn't bring myself to touch the body."

"He was dressed?"

"In jeans and a shirt. His boots were beside the bed."

"They're still there," Ranger said. He walked into the bedroom and picked up one of the boots. "I know it's a cliché, but people really do hide things in their shoes." He removed the padded insert and found a scrap of paper with a phone number on it.

"Damn," I said. "You're good."

Ranger smiled. "That's what they tell me. Do you recognize the number?"

"No, but it's local."

Ranger called his control room and gave them the number. Two minutes later, the answer came back. The number belonged to Alma Rizzi.

So Dom was using his mother's cell phone, and Zero hadn't wanted to share that information with his partner. He didn't trust himself to remember the number, so he hid it in his shoe. This was quite the group of guys.

I dialed the number, but there was no answer.

"Nothing in the other boot," Ranger said. "I think we've done as much as we can here."

We let ourselves out, took the stairs, crossed the small lobby, and walked to our cars.

"Not much of a date," Ranger said.

"Not true. I got a phone number."

He kissed me on the cheek. "You could have gotten more than a phone number."

"I'll take a rain check."

———

MORELLI REMOTED THE television off when I walked into the house. He stood and stretched. "Well?"

"Someone picked Zero's apartment clean."

"You didn't find anything?"

"No."

Our eyes held for a moment, and he didn't ask anything more and I didn't tell. I trusted Morelli, but he was a cop, after all. And the cops didn't have a good track record on this operation.

IT WAS FOUR in the morning, and I was wide awake, trying not to thrash around and disturb Morelli. I couldn't stop thinking about the fourth partner. He was out there, moving through his day as a normal person. This guy who could kill his friends and mutilate a mother. He did his mundane job and talked sports scores while he drank coffee with his friends. And he was watching Morelli's house and monitoring police action. How was he doing that?

When the bedside clock hit five-thirty, I got dressed in jeans and a T-shirt and sneakers. I went downstairs, made coffee, and dialed Dom. Still no answer. I could hear Morelli moving around upstairs. It was a workday.

I was pacing when he came into the kitchen.

"What's the special occasion?" he asked. "You're never up this early."

"I couldn't sleep. Loretta will lose her hand today if I don't figure this out."

"It's not your fault."

"I know that. I just don't want it to happen."

"Me, either. I'm still on the gang killings, but Spanner's keeping me in the loop. The Feds are nuts that the op got blown. They're on everyone's ass."

"You went door-to-door, right? You talked to all your neighbors?"

"Everyone on the street. I covered three blocks." He poured coffee into a travel mug and capped it. "I have an early meeting. I'll grab a bagel on the way in." He kissed me on the top of my head. "I have to go. Be careful. This guy is a real crazy. Don't piss him off. I'll try to keep in touch."

I fed Bob and hooked him to his leash. "Time for a walk," I told him.

I knew we were missing something, and walking Bob would give me a chance to look around. The fourth partner was close. He saw the sign intended for Dom. He saw the scarf. And he was the one who broke into Morelli's house and got the key. He knew when Morelli and I left the house to take Grandma home.

I walked two blocks in each direction, several times. The guy was so close, I could practically smell him, but I couldn't put my finger on him.

Zook was eating breakfast when I returned. He looked up expectantly.

"Hang in there," I told him.

"She's okay, isn't she?"

"Yes." Alive is okay, right? Worse things in life than missing a toe or two. I tried to give him a reassuring smile, but I'm not sure I totally pulled it off.

I drove Zook to school and rode around Morelli's block. I cruised by his house and looked up at the second-floor windows. They were visible from the street, but I was having a hard time thinking this guy was constantly driving by. He was squirreled away somewhere, and he could see the house.

I kept a gym bag in the back. It held bounty hunter stuff. Cuffs, shackles, stun gun, Cheez Doodles, flashlight, and binoculars. I grabbed the binoculars out of the bag and brought them into the house. I ran up the stairs and trained the glasses on the houses across the street. I looked in all the windows. I looked at the front yards and the cars parked in front of the houses. I looked over the roofs to see if line of sight carried to any houses on the next block.

I put the binoculars down and pressed my fingers to my eyeballs. Think, Stephanie. What are you missing? There has to be something.

I raised the binoculars again and ran them across the housetops. And there it was . . . a camera. It was positioned on the roof, directly across from Morelli. I don't know how I missed it. I suppose I just wasn't looking for it before.

I called Ranger on my cell.

"I need some technical information," I said to him. "Can you mount a camera somewhere, like on a roof, and access it from somewhere else? I mean, do you need wires and things?"

"No. You can transmit wireless. If you're going a distance, you need relays. Or you can bounce it off a satellite."

"Suppose you want to run it all day, day after day. You'd need a power source, right?"

"Yes. If it was on a roof, you could tie into the house's electric. It would be easy if the house had a dish."

I used the phone in Morelli's office to call him.

"What," he whispered into his phone.

"I've got it."

"I'm in a meeting," he said. "Is this important?"

"Didn't you hear me? *I've got it.* I know how the fourth partner saw the scarf and the sign, and I know how he saw us leave the house to take Grandma home. There's a camera on the roof of the house across from you."

"Are you sure?"

"I'm looking at it through binoculars. Do you know the people who live across from you? Would they put a camera on their roof?"

"Mr. and Mrs. Geary live across from me. They're nice, but they're about a hundred and ten. I can't imagine why they'd have a camera on their roof. I'm stuck in this meeting, but I'll send Spanner over with a tech."

I was cracking my knuckles now because in a couple hours Loretta would lose her hand. I was calling Alma Rizzi's phone every fifteen minutes and no one was answering. The sign was in Morelli's window. Nothing happening with that. The red scarf was on Morelli's desk. I had no reason to hang it in the window.

I looked up, and Mooner was in the doorway.

"The door was unlocked, so I figured you were open for business," Mooner said.

I had my hand over my heart. "You took me by surprise. Next time, yell when you come into the house."

"I was projecting my aura, but you might have been too distracted to catch it. Probably you were struggling with the feng shui in this room. Major bummer on that one." He looked across the hall. "Where's Zookamundo?"

"School."

"Again?"

"Five days a week."

"Whoa. He must be serious about it."

"Have you had breakfast?"

"No. We were all out of Cap'n Crunch. I have my standards, you know. I was hoping the dude had some."

We trekked downstairs, I pawed through Morelli's cupboard, found a half-empty box of Cap'n Crunch, and gave it to Mooner. I brewed a new pot of coffee and turned to see Gary at the back door. I opened the door and Gary came in.

"How long have you been standing there?" I asked him.

"I just got here. I had a dream you were making coffee."

"You dreamed correct," I told him. "Help yourself."

I went to the living room and looked out the window, and Mooner and Gary followed me.

"What are we looking at?" Mooner wanted to know.

"I'm waiting for one of Morelli's partners to show up."

"Cool," Mooner said, sharing the box of Crunch with Gary.

Spanner finally arrived in a blue Fairlane.

"Bummer," Mooner said. "No lights."

"He's not a uniform," I told Mooner. "I have to talk to him. You stay here."

"Homegrown Security on the job," Mooner said. "You can count on Gary and me."

If you knew where to look, you could see the camera from the street. I positioned Spanner as far back as he could go in Morelli's small yard and handed him my binoculars.

"I see it," Spanner said. "It looks like a camera all right."

We walked across the street and Spanner knocked on the Gearys' front door. The door was answered by a little old man still in his pajamas. Spanner introduced himself and asked about the camera.

"You have a camera on your roof," Spanner said.

"What?" Mr. Geary asked.

"A camera."

"Where?"

"On your roof."

Mr. Geary looked confused. "Where's the camera?"

"I'd like permission to take a look at it," Spanner said.

"What do you want to look at?" Mr. Geary asked.

"The camera."

I looked at my watch. This could take a while.

Spanner had it figured out, too. He jumped in with the bottom line. "Okay, thanks," Spanner said to Geary. "Appreciate you letting us take a look at the camera. I'm going to send a tech up there."

"Sure," Mr. Geary said. "Always happy to help the police."

"I need to run," Spanner said to me. "I'm going to send someone to get the camera. In the meantime, you might want to close your curtains when you get undressed."

Getting caught undressing was the least of my problems. I was counting down to dismemberment. I watched Spanner drive away, and I spotted the news van parked at the end of the block. Brenda was hovering. I couldn't blame her. I understood her problem, and I might have done the same thing. She was trying to make a job for herself. Still, it was annoying.

I paced in the living room, watching for the tech to come get the camera. To pass the time, I called Alma Rizzi's cell phone. And Dom picked up.

"What?" he said.

"Dom?"

"Who's this?"

"It's Stephanie. Don't hang up! I have to talk to you about Loretta."

"What about her?"

"Your partner has amputated two of her toes and sent them here. If I don't give him the garage location by noon, he's going to cut her hand off."

I could hear Dom suck in some breath. "Jesus," he said.

"Morelli isn't involved in this," I told Dom. "It's just me negotiating with your partner, and he's desperate. He wants the money."

"I don't even care about the money anymore," Dom said. "I just want this over. And I want to be the one to talk to him. I want to hear his voice. I want to make sure he isn't going to hurt Loretta anymore."

I didn't trust Dom to keep it together. He wasn't exactly smart, and he wasn't emotionally stable.

"We can call him together," I said. "I can put him on speakerphone, so you can listen, but please let me do the talking. I don't want this screwed up."

"Yeah. You're right. I'd probably screw it up. I want to kill the bastard. I want to rip his eyes out. I want to cut his balls off and shove them down his throat."

"Probably you should do the anger management course that was offered to you," I said to Dom.

"Fuck that. That shit is for pussies. Give me ten minutes. I gotta get a car."

I disconnected Dom, and saw a crime scene van park in front of the Gearys' house. The tech off-loaded a folding ladder, set it against the house, and climbed to the roof.

"You guys stay here," I told Mooner and Gary. "I want to talk to the tech."

I waited on the sidewalk while the tech unbolted the camera and put it in a large evidence bag. He climbed down and walked the camera to the van.

I had his age at late thirties to early forties. He was average height and build. He had brown hair cut short, ears that would lift him off the ground if they caught enough wind, and his eyes were hidden behind Oakleys. He was wearing a wrinkled short-sleeved, collared knit shirt and khakis that were bagged out and creased at the crotch. I was guessing he had no wife, and his mother was either dead or lived out of state.

"What happens to the camera now?" I asked him.

"We'll take it to the shop and have a look at it."

I felt a flash of heat pass through my entire body and my heart jumped in my chest. Major adrenaline rush. It was the voice. I looked down at his shoes. Jackpot.

I was afraid to talk. I didn't trust my voice. I smiled and nodded. "Okay, then," I managed to say.

I backed away and walked stiff-legged across the street. I slipped into Morelli's house and closed and locked the door. I tried to call Morelli on my cell, but my hand was shaking so bad I couldn't get the numbers right. I held my breath and tried again.

"Morelli here," he said.

"It's the crime lab tech," I told him. "He's across the street. He just took the camera down, and I recognized his voice and the shoes. He's the fourth partner."

"Are you sure?"

"Absolutely." Mostly.

"I'm on my way. Where are you?"

"In your house."

"Stay there. Lock the doors. You know where I keep my extra gun?"

"Yes."

"Get it."

"What's going on?" Mooner wanted to know.

"I think the crime lab tech might be Dom's fourth partner. Stay in the house. Morelli is on his way home."

I ran upstairs, got Morelli's gun, and returned to the living room. Mooner was standing guard at a window with his potato bazooka. Gary was behind him with a basket of potatoes.

"We're ready to defend the house," Mooner said.

"Okay," I said, "but don't fire anything off unless I tell you to."

Mooner and Gary saluted.

I shoved Morelli's gun into the waistband of my jeans at the small of my back, and I stood beside Mooner and looked out the window. The gun was cold and hard and uncomfortable. I popped the snap on my jeans, but it didn't help a lot. I removed the gun and shoved it under a couch cushion for safekeeping. It was a semiautomatic Glock, and I didn't actually know how to use it, anyway.

The crime lab tech stowed the ladder and was about to drive off when Dom rolled to a stop in front of Morelli's house. Dom got out and nodded at the tech. The tech got out of his van and crossed to Dom.

*Crap!*

I didn't know what to do. I had no idea what was being said. I didn't want to rush out and blunder into a perfectly benign conversation, but I also didn't want Dom to disappear, forever.

"Should we shoot them?" Mooner asked.

"No!"

The tech was talking, and Dom was nodding in agreement. Dom gave a quick glance to Morelli's house, took his phone out of his pocket, and punched a number in. Seconds later, my phone rang.

"I need the keys," Dom said.

"That's not a good idea."

"It *is* a good idea."

"At least try to stall him so I can set something up."

"For crissake," Dom said. "Just bring me the keys. He gets the van with the money and I get Loretta."

"Okay, I'll send the keys out, but I'm staying here."

"Whatever," Dom said.

If I was the partner, I'd want a hostage to ensure my escape. And I'd make a better hostage than Loretta, since the lack of toes had to slow her down. I supposed he could take Dom, but I wasn't sure anyone would care.

I retrieved the keys from my purse, opened the front door, and pitched the keys into the street. Dom scuttled over and scooped them up, and both men got into the tech's van and drove off.

I saw the van turn right at the corner, and I sprinted to my car. Mooner and Gary ran with me and jumped into the backseat. Mooner still had his bazooka and Gary had his basket of potatoes. I got to the corner and looked right. They were two blocks in front of me.

"Keep your eyes on the van," I told Mooner and Gary. "I don't want to lose them, but I can't get too close."

The van turned left, into the Burg. This was the logical place for Dom to hide the money. Dom had friends there, and there were lots of unused garages. I looked in my rearview mirror. Brenda's film crew was a car length away. Could it get any worse?

I followed the tech van as it wove through the Burg. It

turned into an alley, and I hesitated. I would be clearly visible if I followed. I took a chance and drove down a street running parallel. I waited at the cross street, but the van didn't emerge. Five minutes passed, and still no van. I parked in front of a small corner deli, and we all got out. Brenda and the film crew did the same. Mooner had his potato gun and Gary had his basket of potatoes, and Stephanie had nothing, since the Glock was still under the couch cushion.

I told everyone to stay where they were, out of sight, and not to go into the alley. There were garages on both sides. Hard to tell from where I stood, but I was guessing twelve to sixteen garages in all. The older garages, originally built with the row houses, were singles. The newer garages were two-car. I walked the alley, looking for open garage doors, listening at closed doors. Halfway down the alley, I heard an engine catch. A door to a two-car garage rolled up and a maroon Econoline with Pennsylvania plates jumped out of the garage and turned in my direction. The tech was driving. No sign of Dom. The Econoline roared at me, and I dove between garages to avoid getting hit. He missed me by inches and continued to race down the alley.

"It's him!" I yelled. "It's the fourth partner!"

"No problemo," Mooner said. "Raw russet," he told Gary.

And *phoonf!* Direct hit to the windshield. The van swerved, took out a parked car, ran into the back of the deli, and exploded. Nine million dollars in hundreds shot into the air and floated down, plus the contents of the deli's frozen-food locker.

"Sweet," Mooner said.

"Are you filming?" Brenda yelled to her cameraman. "It's raining money and popsicles!"

And in that instant, Brenda got hit with a family-size frozen pizza. Pepperoni, black olives. It whacked her in the face and knocked her to her knees.

"Ulk," she said. Her eyes rolled into the back of her head, and she went facedown.

The cameraman grabbed her feet, and the soundman grabbed her under the armpits, and they carried her back to the news truck.

The maroon Econoline was a fireball. Sirens were screaming in the distance. People were running from neighboring houses, scarfing up the money and frozen fish sticks and disappearing back into their homes. Mooner was running everywhere, stuffing hundred-dollar bills into his pants and his shirt.

I looked down the alley, and saw Dom jogging my way.

"Are you okay?" I asked him.

"I'm better than okay. I'm fucking fabulous. The sonovabitch blew himself up."

"You were in the garage a long time."

"The battery was dead," Dom said. "We had to give it a jump start."

"I thought the key disabled the bomb. Why did it explode?"

Dom was grinning. "I don't know. I'm guessing it just went off when the van rammed into the deli. The asshole should have moved the boxes of money to a different car before he took off, but he was in a rush to get away. Tell you the truth, I was practically crapping in my pants, giving the van a jump. Allen was the one who rigged the bomb, and between you and me, Allen wasn't the sharpest tack on the board."

"Did you find out about Loretta?"

"She's in the basement of the lab guy's house. He lives two blocks from Morelli. He said she's okay."

I jogged back to the deli with Dom and stuffed him into my car. Brenda was on her feet, with a big Band-Aid across her nose and tissues stuffed up her nostrils, and she was interviewing Mooner. Gary was rocked back on his heels, smiling. His prophecy had come true. The only thing left was the business about Brenda sitting on a toilet on Route 1, and I was hoping I wouldn't be around for that one.

I was moving the car so the fire trucks could get better access and saw Morelli fly in with his roof light flashing. I pulled alongside him.

"We're all okay," I said. "The fourth partner was in the van with the money. It looks like a lot of the money survived. I don't think the lab tech made it."

"What about Loretta?"

"The lab tech told Dom she's locked away in his basement."

"I've got his address," Morelli said. "Spanner fed me the information on my way over. The tech's name is Steve Fowler, and besides being a crime scene tech, he also did some moonlighting as security at the bank ten years ago."

I followed Morelli and we wound through the Burg and took a left into Morelli's neighborhood. He parked in front of a row house that looked like all the other row houses on the street. Two stories. Small front yard. Neat but unexceptional. No indication that a killer lived inside.

We all piled out of our cars and went to the door. We all looked a little grim. We weren't sure what we'd find. Amputation isn't pretty. And for that matter, we weren't convinced Loretta was still alive.

Morelli tried the door. Locked, of course. He moved to a window. Also locked. He put his elbow to it, and it shattered. He cleared some glass away, opened the window, and went in. He opened the door for us and told everyone to stay in the foyer. He drew his gun and moved to the cellar door.

Dom and I were silent, gnawing on our lower lips, barely breathing. A couple minutes passed, and there were footsteps on the cellar stairs, and next thing, Loretta was standing there in front of us. She was pale and shaking and her hair was snarled. She was crying and laughing. Borderline hysteria.

We all stared at her feet and hands. No big bandages. No sign of amputation.

"You have all your toes," I said to her.

She looked down at herself. "Yeah," she said. "What do you mean?"

"He said he chopped off two toes. I saw them."

"Not mine," Loretta said.

I looked at Morelli, and Morelli shrugged. He hadn't a clue who belonged to the toes.

———

I̶T̶ ̶W̶A̶S̶ ̶S̶I̶X̶ o'clock, and we were all in front of the television eating meatball subs, tuned in to the news. Mooner,
Gary, Zook, Loretta, Dom, Morelli, Bob, and me. Lula had
declined in favor of a night with her big Honey Pot. The
party was thrown by Mooner with money he'd collected
when the Econoline exploded. Mooner'd given twenty
thousand to Loretta and Zook, ten thousand to the animal
shelter so they could offer free cat-spaying, and he'd
bought a very used mellow yellow Corvette with the remaining money. True, the money was slightly illegal, but
hell, this was Mooner we were talking about. Almost
*everything* he did was slightly illegal.

Brenda's theme song came up, and we all sat forward.
Brenda popped onto the screen wearing a low scoop-neck
sweater and a tiny skirt. She had two black eyes and a
Band-Aid on her nose.

"Here I am with an exclusive on the nine-million-dollar-
mystery conclusion," Brenda said. "You'll have to excuse
my appearance, as I was in a freak pizza accident."

There was film of the maroon Econoline going out of control, crashing into the deli, and exploding. And then Brenda
was on film with the tissues up her nose. "And here we have
an interview with the man who took down the vicious crimi-
nal responsible for murder, mayhem, and kidnapping."

The camera panned to Mooner, and everyone in
Morelli's living room yelled and whistled.

"Tell us exactly how you did it," Brenda said, pointing the mic at Mooner.

"It was with my potato rocket," Mooner said, looking into the camera. "And my munitions man, Gary, deserves some credit for giving me exactly the right potato."

The camera returned to Brenda. "There you have it," she said. "Another exclusive from Brenda. And, sadly for you, but happily for me, this is my last piece of news on this station. I'm going national with my own reality show. And I'm cohosting the show with my very own stalker and psychic, Gary."

There was more whistling and cheering on our part, and Gary took a bow.

Dom stood and raised a bottle of beer. "Now that all this is over and Loretta's safe, I want to say, let bygones be bygones, and I still think Morelli's a piece of shit for getting Loretta pregnant and walking away, but I'm not gonna kill him like I planned."

Loretta looked up at Dom. "What the heck are you talking about? Morelli isn't Mario's father. Morelli was a jerk. I wouldn't have anything to do with him."

"Then who's the father?" Dom wanted to know.

"It was Lenny Garvis. I got pregnant the night before he died. I didn't want to make a big deal about it. Mario always knew, but I didn't tell anyone else."

Lenny Garvis! He was in Morelli's class. Two years ahead of me and mentally a few years behind. I remembered his death. The idiot choked on a peanut butter and banana sandwich. I mean, how could you possibly choke on a peanut butter sandwich?

Dom wasn't convinced. "I saw you in the garage with Morelli."

"That wasn't me," Loretta said. "That was Jenny Ragucci. She was *such* a slut."

Morelli smiled. "It could have been Jenny Ragucci. That makes much more sense. I had good luck with sluts."

I looked over at him.

"All in the past," Morelli said. "I'm a cupcake man now."

"Whoa, dude," Mooner said. "That's so, like, *cosmic*."